The Long Winter

LAURA INGALLS WILDER

The Long Winter

EGMONT

EGMONT

We bring stories to life

First published in the USA 1940
First published in Great Britain 1962
by Lutterworth Press
This edition first published in 2015 by Egmont UK Limited
The Yellow Building, 1 Nicholas Road, London W11 4AN

Text copyright © 1940 Laura Ingalls Wilder
Cover illustration © 2015 Jonathan Burton
Inside illustrations © 1953 Garth Williams

Set ISBN 978 0 6035 7168 8
Book ISBN 978 1 4052 8015 0

A CIP catalogue record for this title is available from the British Library

Printed in Great Britain by the CPI Group

63241/1

Egmont is passionate about helping to preserve the world's remaining ancient forests.
We only use paper from legal and sustainable forest sources.

This book is made from paper certified by the Forest Stewardship Council® (FSC®),
an organisation dedicated to promoting responsible management of forest resources.

For more information on the FSC, please visit www.fsc.org. To learn more about
Egmont's sustainable paper policy, please visit www.egmont.co.uk/ethical

Contents

I

Make Hay While
the Sun Shines

The mowing machine's whirring sounded cheerfully from the old buffalo wallow south of the claim shanty, where bluestem grass stood thick and tall and Pa was cutting it for hay.

The sky was high and quivering with heat over the shimmering prairie. Half-way down to sunset, the sun blazed as hotly as at noon. The wind was scorching hot. But Pa had hours of mowing yet to do before he could stop for the night.

Laura drew up a pailful of water from the well at the edge of the Big Slough. She rinsed the brown jug till it was cool to her hand. Then she filled it with the fresh, cool water, corked it tightly and started with it to the hayfield.

Swarms of little white butterflies hovered over the path. A dragon-fly with gauzy wings swiftly chased a gnat. On the stubble of cut grass the striped gophers were scampering. All at once they ran for their lives and dived into their holes. Then Laura saw a swift shadow and

1

looked up at the eyes and the claws of a hawk overhead. But all the little gophers were safe in their holes.

Pa was glad to see Laura with the water jug. He got down from the mowing machine and drank a mouthful. 'Ah! that hits the spot!' he said, and tipped up the jug again. Then he corked it, and setting it on the ground he covered it with cut grass.

'This sun almost makes a fellow want a bunch of sprouts to make a shade,' he joked. He was really glad there were no trees; he had grubbed so many sprouts from his clearing in the Big Woods, every summer. Here on the Dakota prairies there was not a single tree, not one sprout, not a bit of shade anywhere.

'A man works better when he's warmed up, anyway!' Pa said cheerfully, and chirruped to the horses. Sam and David plodded on, drawing the machine. The long, steel-toothed blade went steadily whirring against the tall grass and laid it down flat. Pa rode high on the open iron seat, watching it lie down, his hand on the lever.

Laura sat in the grass to watch him go once around. The heat there smelled as good as an oven when bread is baking. The little brown-and-yellow-striped gophers were hurrying again, all about her. Tiny birds fluttered and flew to cling to bending grass-stems, balancing lightly. A striped garter snake came flowing and curving through the forest of grass. Sitting hunched with her chin on her knees, Laura felt suddenly as big as a mountain when the snake curved up its head and stared at the high wall of her calico skirt.

Its round eyes were shining like beads, and its tongue was flickering so fast that it looked like a tiny jet of steam. The whole bright-striped snake had a gentle look. Laura knew that garter snakes will not harm anyone, and they are good to have on a farm because they eat the insects that spoil crops.

It stretched its neck low again and, making a perfectly square turn in itself because it could not climb over Laura, it went flowing around her and away in the grass.

Then the mowing machine whirred louder and the horses came nodding their heads slowly in time with their feet. David jumped when Laura spoke almost under his nose.

'Whoa!' Pa said, startled. 'Laura! I thought you'd gone. Why are you hiding in the grass like a prairie chicken?'

'Pa,' Laura said, 'why can't *I* help you make hay? Please let me, Pa. Please.'

Pa lifted his hat and ran his fingers through his sweat-damp hair, standing it all on end and letting the wind blow through it. 'You're not very big nor strong, little Half-Pint.'

'I'm going on fourteen,' Laura said. 'I can help, Pa. I know I can.'

The mowing machine had cost so much that Pa had no money left to pay for help. He could not borrow work, because there were only a few homesteaders in this new country and they were busy on their own claims. But he needed help to stack the hay.

'Well,' Pa said, 'maybe you can. We'll try it. If you can, by George! we'll get this haying done all by ourselves!'

Laura could see that the thought was a load off Pa's mind, and she hurried to the shanty to tell Ma.

'Why, I guess you can,' Ma said doubtfully. She did not like to see women working in the fields. Only foreigners

4

did that. Ma and her girls were Americans, above doing men's work. But Laura's helping in the hay would solve the problem. She decided, 'Yes, Laura, you may.'

Carrie eagerly offered to help. 'I'll carry the drinking water out to you. I'm big enough to carry the jug!' Carrie was almost ten, but small for her age.

'And I'll do your share of the housework, besides mine,' Mary offered happily. She was proud that she could wash dishes and make beds as well as Laura, though she was blind.

The sun and hot wind cured the cut grass so quickly that Pa raked it up next day. He raked it into long windrows, then he raked the windrows into big haycocks. And early the next morning, while the dawn was still cool and meadow-larks were singing, Laura rode to the field with Pa in the hayrack.

There Pa walked beside the wagon and drove the horses between the rows of haycocks. At every haycock he stopped the horses and pitched the hay up into the hayrack. It came tumbling loosely over the high edge and Laura trampled it down. Up and down and back and forth she trampled the loose hay with all the might of her legs, while the forkfuls kept coming over and falling, and she went on trampling while the wagon jolted on to the next haycock. Then Pa pitched more hay in from the other side.

Under her feet the hay climbed higher, trampled down as solid as hay can be. Up and down, fast and hard, her

5

legs kept going, the length of the hayrack and back, and across the middle. The sunshine was hotter and the smell of the hay rose up sweet and strong. Under her feet it bounced and over the edges of the hayrack it kept coming.

All the time she was rising higher on the trampled-down hay. Her head rose above the edges of the rack and she could have looked at the prairie, if she could have stopped trampling. Then the rack was full of hay and still more came flying up from Pa's pitchfork.

Laura was very high up now and the slippery hay was sloping downward around her. She went on trampling carefully. Her face and her neck were wet with sweat and sweat trickled down her back. Her sunbonnet hung by its strings and her braids had come undone. Her long brown hair blew loose in the wind.

Then Pa stepped up on the whiffletrees. He rested one foot on David's broad hip and clambered up on to the load of hay.

'You've done a good job, Laura,' he said. 'You tramped the hay down so well that we've got a big load on the wagon.'

Laura rested in the prickly warm hay while Pa drove near to the stable. Then she slid down and sat in the shade of the wagon. Pa pitched down some hay, then climbed down and spread it evenly to make the big, round bottom of a stack. He climbed on to the load and pitched more hay, then climbed down and levelled it on the stack and trampled it down.

'I could spread it, Pa,' Laura said, 'so you wouldn't have to keep climbing up and down.'

Pa pushed back his hat and leaned for a minute on the pitchfork. 'Stacking's a job for two, that's a fact,' he said. 'This way takes too much time. Being willing helps a lot, but you're not very big, little Half-Pint.' She could only get him to say, 'Well, we'll see.' But when they came back with the next load he gave her a pitchfork and let her try. The long fork was taller than she was and she did not know how to use it, so she handled it clumsily. But while Pa tossed the hay from the wagon she spread it as well as she could, walking around and around on the stack to pack it tightly. In spite of the best she could do, Pa had to level the stack for the next load.

Now the sun and the wind were hotter and Laura's legs quivered while she made them trample the hay. She was glad to rest for the little times between the field and the stack. She was thirsty, then she was thirstier, and then she was so thirsty that she could think of nothing else. It seemed for ever till ten o'clock when Carrie came lugging the jug half-full.

Pa told Laura to drink first but not too much. Nothing was ever so good as that cool wetness going down her throat. At the taste of it she stopped in surprise and Carrie clapped her hands and cried out, laughing, 'Don't tell, Laura, don't tell till Pa tastes it!'

Ma had sent them ginger-water. She had sweetened the cool well-water with sugar, flavoured it with vinegar, and put in plenty of ginger to warm their stomachs so that they could drink till they were not thirsty. Ginger-water would not make them sick, as plain cold water would when they were so hot. Such a treat made that ordinary day into a special day, the first day that Laura helped in the haying.

By noon they had hauled all the hay and finished the stack. Pa topped it himself. It takes great skill to round the top of a haystack so that it will shed rain.

Dinner was ready when they went to the shanty. Ma looked sharply at Laura and asked, 'Is the work too hard for her, Charles?'

'Oh, no! She's as stout as a little French horse. She's been a great help,' said Pa. 'It would have taken me all day to stack that hay alone, and now I have the whole afternoon for mowing.'

Laura was proud. Her arms ached and her back ached and her legs ached, and that night in bed she ached all over so badly that tears swelled out of her eyes, but she did not tell anyone.

As soon as Pa had cut and raked enough hay for another stack, he and Laura made it. Laura's arms and legs got used to the work and did not ache so badly. She liked to see the stacks that she helped to make. She helped Pa make a stack on each side of the stable door and a long stack over the whole top of the dugout stable. Besides these, they made three more big stacks.

'Now all our upland hay is cut, I want to put up a lot of slough hay,' Pa said. 'It doesn't cost anything and maybe there'll be some sale for it when new settlers come in next spring.'

So Pa mowed the coarse, tall grass in Big Slough and

Laura helped him stack that. It was so much heavier than the bluestem grass that she could not handle it with the pitchfork, but she could trample it down.

One day when Pa came clambering up to the top of the load, she told him, 'You've left a haycock, Pa.'

'I have!' said Pa, surprised. 'Where?'

'Over there, in the tall grass.'

Pa looked where she pointed. Then he said, 'That isn't a haycock, Half-Pint; that's a muskrat house.' He looked at it a moment longer. 'I'm going to have a closer look at that,' he said. 'Want to come along? The horse'll stand.'

He pushed a way through the harsh, tall grass and Laura followed close behind him. The ground underfoot was soft and marshy and water lay in pools among the grass roots. Laura could see only Pa's back and the grasses all around her, taller than she was. She stepped carefully, for the ground was growing wetter. Suddenly water spread out before her in a shimmering pool.

At the edge of the pool stood the muskrat's house. It was taller than Laura, and far larger than her arms could reach around. Its rounded sides and top were rough, hard grey. The muskrats had gnawed dry grass to bits and mixed the bits well with mud to make a good plaster for their house, and they had built it up solidly and smoothly and rounded the top carefully to shed rain.

The house had no door. No path led to it anywhere. In the grass-stubble around it and along the muddy rim of the pool, there was not one paw-print. There was nothing to tell how the muskrats went in and out of their house.

Inside those thick, still walls, Pa said, the muskrats were sleeping now, each family curled in its own little room lined softly with grass. Each room had a small round doorway that opened on to a sloping hall. The hallway curved down through the house from top to bottom and ended in dark water. That was the muskrats' front door.

After the sun had gone, the muskrats woke and went pattering down the smooth mud-floor of their hallway. They plunged into the black water and came up through the pool to the wide, wild night under the sky. All night long, in the starlight or moonlight, they swam and played along the edges of the water, feeding on roots and stems and leaves of the water-plants and grasses. When dawn was coming ghostly grey, they swam home. They dived and came up through their water-door. Dripping, they went up the slope of their hallway, each to his own grass-lined room. There they curled comfortably to sleep.

Laura put her hand on the wall of their house. The coarse plaster was hot in the hot wind and sunshine, but inside the thick mud walls, in the dark, the air must be cool. She liked to think of the muskrats sleeping there.

Pa was shaking his head. 'We're going to have a hard winter,' he said, not liking the prospect.

'Why, how do you know?' Laura asked in surprise.

'The colder the winter will be, the thicker the muskrats

11

build the walls of their houses,' Pa told her. 'I never saw a heavier-built muskrats' house than that one.'

Laura looked at it again. It was very solid and big. But the sun was blazing, burning on her shoulders through the faded, thin calico and the hot wind was blowing, and stronger than the damp-mud smell of the slough was the ripening smell of grasses parching in the heat. Laura could hardly think of ice and snow and cruel cold.

'Pa, how can the muskrats know?' she asked.

'I don't know how they know,' Pa said. 'But they do. God tells them, somehow, I suppose.'

'Then why doesn't God tell us?' Laura wanted to know.

'Because,' said Pa, 'we're not animals. We're humans, and, like it says in the Declaration of Independence, God created us free. That means we've got to take care of ourselves.'

Laura said faintly, 'I thought God takes care of us.'

'He does,' Pa said, 'so far as we do what's right. And He gives us a conscience and brains to know what's right. But He leaves it to us to do as we please. That's the difference between us and everything else in creation.'

'Can't muskrats do what they please?' Laura asked, amazed.

'No,' said Pa. 'I don't know why they can't, but you can see they can't. Look at that muskrat house. Muskrats have to build that kind of house. They always have and they always will. It's plain they can't build any other kind.

12

But folks build all kinds of houses. A man can build any kind of house he can think of. So if his house doesn't keep out the weather, that's *his* look-out; he's free and independent.'

Pa stood thinking for a minute, then he jerked his head. 'Come along, little Half-Pint. We better make hay while the sun shines.'

His eyes twinkled and Laura laughed, because the sun was shining with all its might. But all the rest of that afternoon they were rather sober.

The muskrats had a warm, thick-walled house to keep out cold and snow, but the claim shanty was built of thin boards that had shrunk in the summer heat till the narrow battens hardly covered the wide cracks in the walls. Boards and tar-paper were not very snug shelter against a hard winter.

2
An Errand to Town

O ne morning in September the grass was white with
frost. It was only a light frost that melted as soon as
sunshine touched it. It was gone when Laura looked out
at the bright morning. But at breakfast Pa said that such
an early frost was surprising.

'Will it hurt the hay?' Laura asked him, and he said,
'Oh, no. Such a light frost will only make it dry faster
when it's cut. But I'd better get a hustle on, for it won't
be long now till it's too late to make hay.'

He was hustling so fast that afternoon that he hardly
stopped to drink when Laura brought him the water-jug.
He was mowing in Big Slough.

'You cover it up, Half-Pint,' he said, handing back the
jug. 'I'm bound and determined to get this patch mowed
before sundown.' He chirruped to Sam and David and
they started again, drawing the whirring machine. Then
suddenly the machine gave a clattering kind of yelp and
Pa said, 'Whoa!'

Laura hurried to see what had happened. Pa was
looking at the cutter-bar. There was a gap in the row of

bright steel points. The cutter-bar had lost one of its teeth. Pa picked up the pieces, but they could not be mended.

'There's no help for it,' Pa said. 'It means buying another section.'

There was nothing to say to that. Pa thought a minute and said, 'Laura, I wish you'd go to town and get it. I don't want to lose the time. I can keep on mowing, after a fashion, while you're gone. Be as quick as you can. Ma will give you the five cents to pay for it. Buy it at Fuller's Hardware.'

'Yes, Pa,' Laura said. She dreaded going to town because so many people were there. She was not exactly afraid, but strange eyes looking at her made her uncomfortable.

She had a clean calico dress to wear and she had shoes. While she hurried to the house, she thought that Ma might let her wear her Sunday hair-ribbon and perhaps Mary's freshly ironed sunbonnet.

'I have to go to town, Ma,' she said, rushing in breathless.

Carrie and Mary listened while she explained, and even Grace looked up at her with big, sober blue eyes.

'I will go with you to keep you company,' Carrie volunteered.

'Oh, can she, Ma?' Laura asked.

'If she can be ready as soon as you are,' Ma gave permission.

Quickly they changed to fresh dresses and put on

their stockings and shoes. But Ma saw no reason for hair-ribbons on a weekday and she said Laura must wear her own sunbonnet.

'It would be fresher,' Ma said, 'if you took care to keep it so.' Laura's bonnet was limp from hanging down her back and the strings were limp too. But that was Laura's own fault.

Ma gave her five cents from Pa's pocketbook and with Carrie she hurried away towards town.

They followed the road made by Pa's wagon-wheels, past the well, down the dry, grassy slope into Big Slough, and on between the tall slough-grasses to the slope up on the other side. The whole shimmering prairie seemed strange then. Even the wind blowing the grasses had a wilder sound. Laura liked that and she wished they did not have to go into town where the false fronts of the buildings stood up square-topped to pretend that the stores behind them were bigger than they were.

Neither Laura nor Carrie said a word after they came to Main Street. Some men were on the store porches and two teams with wagons were tied to the hitching posts. Lonely, on the other side of Main Street, stood Pa's store building. It was rented and two men sat inside it talking.

Laura and Carrie went into the hardware store. Two men were sitting on nail kegs and one on a plough. They stopped talking and looked at Laura and Carrie. The wall behind the counter glittered with tin pans and pails and lamps.

Laura said, 'Pa wants a mowing-machine section, please.'

The man on the plough said, 'He's broken one, has he?' and Laura said, 'Yes, sir.'

She watched him wrap in paper the sharp and shining three-cornered tooth. He must be Mr Fuller. She gave him the five cents and, taking the package in her hand, she said, 'Thank you,' and walked out with Carrie.

That was over. But they did not speak until they had walked out of town. Then Carrie said, 'You did that beautifully, Laura.'

'Oh, it was just buying something,' Laura replied.

'I know, but I feel funny when people look at me. I feel . . . not scared, exactly . . .' Carrie said.

'There's nothing to be scared of,' Laura said. 'We mustn't ever be scared.' Suddenly she told Carrie, 'I feel the same way.'

'Do you, really? I didn't know that. You don't act like it. I always feel so safe when you're there,' Carrie said.

'You are safe when I'm there,' Laura answered. 'I'd take care of you. Anyway, I'd try my best.'

'I know you would,' Carrie said.

It was nice, walking together. To take care of their shoes, they did not walk in the dusty wheel-tracks. They walked on the harder strip in the middle where only horses' hoofs had discouraged the grass. They were not walking hand in hand, but they felt as if they were.

Ever since Laura could remember, Carrie had been her little sister. First she had been a tiny baby, then she had been Baby Carrie, then she had been a clutcher and tagger, always asking 'Why?' Now she was ten years old, old enough to be really a sister. And they were out together, away from even Pa and Ma. Their errand was done and off their minds, and the sun was shining, the wind was blowing, the prairie spread far all around them. They felt free and independent and comfortable together.

'It's a long way around to where Pa is,' Carrie said. 'Why don't we go this way?' and she pointed towards the part of the slough where they could see Pa and the horses.

Laura answered, 'That way's through the slough.'

'It isn't wet now, is it?' Carrie asked.

'All right, let's,' Laura answered. 'Pa didn't say to go by the road, and he did say to hurry.'

So they did not follow the road that turned to cross the slough. They went straight on into the tall slough grass.

At first it was fun. It was rather like going into the jungle-picture in Pa's big green book. Laura pushed ahead between the thick clumps of grass-stems that gave way rustling and closed again behind Carrie. The millions of coarse grass-stems and their slender long leaves were greeny-gold and golden-green in their own shade. The earth was crackled with dryness underfoot, but a faint

18

smell of damp lay under the hot smell of the grass. Just above Laura's head the grass-tops swished in the wind, but down at their roots was a stillness, broken only where Laura and Carrie went wading through it.

'Where's Pa?' Carrie asked suddenly.

Laura looked around at her. Carrie's peaked little face was pale in the shade of the grass. Her eyes were almost frightened.

'Well, we can't see him from here,' Laura said. They could see only the leaves of the thick grass waving, and the hot sky overhead. 'He's right ahead of us. We'll come to him in a minute.'

She said it confidently, but how could she know where Pa was? She could not even be sure where she was going, where she was taking Carrie. The smothering heat made sweat trickle down her throat and her backbone, but she felt cold inside. She remembered the children near Brookings, lost in the prairie grass. The slough was worse than the prairie. Ma had always been afraid that Grace would be lost in this slough.

She listened for the whirr of the mowing machine, but the sound of the grasses filled her ears. There was nothing in the flickering shadows of their thin leaves blowing and tossing higher than her eyes, to tell her where the sun was. The grasses' bending and swaying did not even tell the direction of the wind. Those clumps of grass would hold up no weight at all. There was nothing, nothing anywhere that she could climb to look out above them, to see beyond them and know where she was.

'Come along, Carrie,' she said cheerfully. She must not frighten Carrie.

Carrie followed trustfully, but Laura did not know where she was going. She could not even be sure that she was walking straight. Always a clump of grass was in her way; she must go to right or left. Even if she went to the right of one clump of grass and to the left of the next clump, that did not mean that she was not going in a circle. Lost people go in circles, and many of them never find their way home.

The slough went on for a mile or more of bending, swaying grasses, too tall to see beyond, too yielding to climb. It was wide. Unless Laura walked straight ahead they might never get out of it.

'We've gone so far, Laura,' Carrie panted. 'Why don't we come to Pa?'

'He ought to be right around here somewhere,' Laura answered. She could not follow their own trail back to the safe road. Their shoes left almost no tracks on the heat-baked mud, and the grasses, the endless swaying grasses with their low leaves hanging dried and broken, were all alike.

Carrie's mouth opened a little. Her big eyes looked up at Laura and they said, 'I know. We're lost.' Her mouth shut without a word. If they were lost, they were lost. There was nothing to say about it.

'We'd better go on,' Laura said.

'I guess so. As long as we can,' Carrie agreed.

They went on. They must surely have passed the place where Pa was mowing. But Laura could not be sure of anything. Perhaps if they thought they turned back, they would really be going farther away. They could only go on. Now and then they stopped and wiped their sweating faces. They were terribly thirsty, but there was no water. They were very tired from pushing through the grasses. Not one single push seemed hard, but going on was harder than trampling hay. Carrie's thin little face was grey-white, she was so tired.

Then Laura thought that the grasses ahead were thinner. The shade seemed lighter there and the tops of the grasses against the sky seemed fewer. And suddenly she saw sunshine, yellow beyond the dark grass stems. Perhaps there was a pond there. Oh! perhaps, perhaps there was Pa's stubble field and the mowing machine and Pa.

She saw the hay stubble in the sunshine, and she saw hay-cocks dotting it. But she heard a strange voice.

It was a man's voice, loud and hearty. It said, 'Get a move on, Manzo. Let's get this load in. It's coming night after awhile.'

Another voice drawled lazily, 'Aw-aw, Roy!'

Close together, Laura and Carrie looked out from the edge of the standing grass. The hayfield was not Pa's hayfield. A strange wagon stood there and on its rack was

21

an enormous load of hay. On the high top of that load, up against the blinding sky, a boy was lying. He lay on his stomach, his chin on his hands and his feet in the air.

The strange man lifted up a huge forkful of hay and pitched it on the boy. It buried him and he scrambled up out of it, laughing and shaking hay off his head and his shoulders. He had black hair and blue eyes, and his face and his arms were sunburned brown.

He stood up on the high load of hay against the sky and saw Laura. He said, 'Hello there!' They both stood watching Laura and Carrie come out of the tall standing grass – like rabbits, Laura thought. She wanted to turn and run back into hiding.

'I thought Pa was here,' she said, while Carrie stood small and still behind her.

The man said, 'We haven't seen anybody around here. Who is your Pa?' The boy told him, 'Mr Ingalls. Isn't he?' he asked Laura. He was still looking at her.

'Yes,' she said, and she looked at the horses hitched to the wagon. She had seen those beautiful brown horses before, their haunches gleaming in the sun and the black manes glossy on their glossy necks. They were the Wilder boys' horses. The man and the boy must be the Wilder brothers.

'I can see him from here. He's just over there,' the boy said. Laura looked up and saw him pointing. His blue eyes twinkled down at her as if he had known her a long time.

'Thank you,' Laura said primly and she and Carrie walked away, along the road that the Morgan team and the wagon had broken through the slough grass.

'Whoa!' Pa said when he saw them. 'Whew!' he said, taking off his hat and wiping the sweat from his forehead.

Laura gave him the mowing-machine section, and she and Carrie watched while he opened the tool-box, took the cutter-bar from the machine, and knocked out

the broken section. He set the new one in its place and hammered down the rivets to hold it. 'There!' he said. 'Tell your Ma I'll be late for supper. I'm going to finish cutting this piece.'

The mowing machine was humming steadily when Laura and Carrie went on towards the shanty.

'Were you much scared, Laura?' Carrie asked.

'Well, a bit, but all's well that ends well,' Laura said.

'It was my fault. I wanted to go that way,' said Carrie.

'It was my fault because I'm older,' Laura said. 'But we've learned a lesson. I guess we'll stay on the road after this.'

'Are you going to tell Ma and Pa?' Carrie timidly asked.

'We have to if they ask us,' said Laura.

3
Fall of the Year

Pa and Laura stacked the last load of slough hay on a hot September afternoon. Pa intended to mow another patch next day, but in the morning rain was falling. For three days and nights the rain fell steadily, slow, weepy rain, running down the windowpanes and pattering on the roof.

'Well, we must expect it,' Ma said. 'It's the equinoctial storm.'

'Yes,' Pa agreed, but uneasily. 'There's a weather change, all right. A fellow can feel it in his bones.'

Next morning the shanty was cold, the windowpanes were almost covered with frost, and all outdoors was white.

'My goodness,' Ma said shivering, while she laid kindling in the stove. 'And this is only the first day of October.'

Laura put on her shoes and a shawl when she went to the well for water.

The air bit her cheeks and scorched the inside of her nose with cold. The sky was coldly blue and the whole world was white. Every blade of grass was furry with frost,

25

the path was frosted, the boards of the well were streaked with thick frost, and frost had crept up the walls of the shanty, along the narrow battens that held the black tar-paper on.

Then the sun peeped over the edge of the prairie and the whole world glittered. Every tiniest thing glittered rosy towards the sun and pale blue towards the sky, and all along every blade of grass ran rainbow sparkles.

Laura loved the beautiful world. She knew that the bitter frost had killed the hay and the garden. The tangled tomato vines with their red and green tomatoes, and the pumpkin vines holding their broad leaves over the green young pumpkins, were all glittering bright in frost over the broken, frosty sod. The sod corn's stalks and long leaves were white. The frost had killed them. It would leave every living green thing dead. But the frost was beautiful.

At breakfast Pa said, 'There'll be no more haying, so we'll get in our harvest. We can't get much from a first year on sod-ground, but the sods will rot this winter. We'll do better next year.'

The ploughed ground was tumbled slabs of earth still held together by the grass-roots. From underneath these sods, Pa dug small potatoes and Laura and Carrie put them into tin pails. Laura hated the dry, dusty feeling of earth on her fingers. It sent shivers up her backbone but that couldn't be helped. Someone must pick up the potatoes.

She and Carrie trudged back and forth with their pails, till they had filled five sacks full of potatoes. That was all the potatoes there were.

'A lot of digging for a few potatoes,' said Pa. 'But five bushels are better than none, and we can piece out with the beans.'

He pulled the dead bean vines and stacked them to dry. The sun was high now, all the frost was gone, and the wind was blowing cool over the brownish and purple and fawn-coloured prairie.

Ma and Laura picked the tomatoes. The vines were wilted down, soft and blackening, so they picked even the smallest green tomatoes. There were enough ripe tomatoes to make almost a gallon of preserves.

'What are you going to do with the green ones?' Laura asked, and Ma answered, 'Wait and see.'

She washed them carefully without peeling them. She sliced them and cooked them with salt, pepper, vinegar, and spices.

'That's almost two quarts of green tomato pickle. Even if it's only our first garden on the sod and nothing could grow well, these pickles will be a treat with baked beans this winter,' Ma gloated.

'And almost a gallon of sweet preserves!' Mary added.

'Five bushels of potatoes,' said Laura, rubbing her hands on her apron because they remembered the horrid dusty feeling.

'And turnips, lots of turnips!' Carrie cried. Carrie loved to eat a raw turnip.

Pa laughed. 'When I get those beans threshed and winnowed and sacked there'll be pretty near a bushel of beans. When I get those few hills of corn cut, husked, and stored down cellar in a teacup, we'll have quite a harvest.'

Laura knew that it was a very small harvest. But the hay and corn would winter the horses and the cow through till spring, and with five bushels of potatoes and nearly a bushel of beans and Pa's hunting they could all live.

'I must cut that corn tomorrow,' Pa said.

'I see no special rush, Charles,' Ma remarked. 'The rain is over and I never saw nicer fall weather.'

'Well, that's so,' Pa admitted. The nights were cool now and the early mornings were crisp, but the days were sunny-warm.

'We could do with some fresh meat for a change,' Ma suggested.

'Soon as I get the corn in I'll go hunting,' said Pa.

Next day he cut and shocked the sod corn. The ten shocks stood like a row of little Indian tepees by the haystacks. When he had finished them, Pa brought six yellow-gold pumpkins from the field.

'The vines couldn't do much on tough sod,' he made excuse, 'and the frost caught the green ones, but we'll get a lot of seed out of these for next year.'

'Why such a hurry to get the pumpkins in?' Ma asked.

'I feel in a hurry. As if there was need to hurry,' Pa tried to explain.

'You need a good night's sleep,' said Ma.

A misty-fine rain was falling next morning. After Pa had done the chores and eaten breakfast, he put on his coat and the wide-brimmed hat that sheltered the back of his neck.

'I'll get us a brace of geese,' he said. 'I heard them flying over in the night. There'll be some in the slough.'

He took down his shotgun and sheltering it under his coat he went out into the weather.

After he had gone Ma said, 'Girls, I've thought of a surprise for Pa.'

Laura and Carrie turned round from the dishpan and Mary straightened up from the bed she was making. 'What?' they all asked her.

'Hurry and get the work done,' said Ma. 'And then, Laura, you go to the corn-patch and bring me a green pumpkin. I'm going to make a pie!'

'A pie! But how …' Mary said, and Laura said, 'A *green* pumpkin pie? I never heard of such a thing, Ma.'

'Neither did I,' said Ma. 'But we wouldn't do much if we didn't do things that nobody ever heard of before.'

Laura and Carrie did the dishes properly but in a hurry. Then Laura ran through the cool, misty rain to the corn-patch and lugged back the biggest green pumpkin.

'Stand by the oven door and dry yourself,' said Ma.

'You're not very big, Laura, but you're old enough to put on a shawl without being told.'

'I went so fast I dodged between the raindrops,' Laura said. 'I'm not much wet, Ma, honestly. Now what do I do?'

'You may cut the pumpkin in slices and peel them while I make the piecrust,' said Ma. 'Then we'll see what we'll see.'

Ma put the crust in the pie pan and covered the bottom with brown sugar and spices. Then she filled the crust with thin slices of the green pumpkin. She poured half a cup of vinegar over them, put a small piece of butter on top, and laid the top crust over all.

'There,' she said, when she had finished crimping the edges.

'I didn't know you could,' Carrie breathed, looking wide-eyed at the pie.

'Well, *I* don't know yet,' said Ma. She slipped the pie into the oven and shut the door on it. 'But the only way to find out is to try. By dinnertime we'll know.'

They all sat waiting in the tidy shanty. Mary was busily knitting to finish warm stockings for Carrie before cold weather. Laura was sewing two long breadths of muslin together to make a sheet. She pinned the edges together carefully and fastened them with a pin to her dress at the knee. Carefully holding the edges even, she whipped them together with even, tiny stitches.

The stitches must be close and small and firm and they

must be deep enough but not too deep, for the sheet must lie smooth, with not the tiniest ridge down its middle. And all the stitches must be so exactly alike that you could not tell them apart, because that was the way to sew.

Mary had liked such work, but now she was blind and could not do it. Sewing made Laura feel like flying to pieces. She wanted to scream. The back of her neck ached and the thread twisted and knotted. She had to pick out almost as many stitches as she put in.

'Blankets are wide enough to cover a bed,' she said fretfully. 'Why can't sheets be made wide enough?'

'Because sheets are muslin,' said Mary. 'And muslin isn't wide enough for a sheet.'

The eye of Laura's needle slipped through a tiny hole in her thimble and ran into her finger. She shut her mouth hard and did not say a word.

But the pie was baking beautifully. When Ma laid down the shirt that she was making for Pa and opened the oven, the rich smell of baking pie came out. Carrie and Grace stopped to look in while Ma turned the pie so that it would brown evenly.

'It's doing nicely,' Ma said.

'Oh, won't Pa be surprised!' Carrie cried.

Just before dinnertime Ma took the pie from the oven. It was a beautiful pie.

They kept dinner waiting until almost one o'clock, but Pa did not come. When he was hunting, he paid no attention to mealtimes. So at last they had dinner. The pie must wait till suppertime when Pa would come with fat geese to roast for tomorrow.

All afternoon the slow rain fell steadily. When Laura went to the well for water, the sky was low and grey. Far over the prairie the brown grasses were sodden with rain and the tall slough grass stood dripping, bent a little under the steady pressure of the falling rain.

Laura hurried back from the well. She did not like to look at the outdoors when all the grass was weeping.

Pa did not come home until suppertime. He came empty-handed except for his gun. He did not speak or smile and his eyes were wide-open and still.

'What is wrong, Charles?' Ma asked quickly.

He took off his wet coat and his dripping hat and hung them up before he answered. 'That is what I'd like to know. Something's queer. Not a goose nor a duck on the lake. None in the slough. Not one in sight. They are flying high above the clouds, flying fast. I could hear them calling. Caroline, every kind of bird is going south as fast and as high as it can fly. All of them, going south. And no other kind of game is out. Every living thing that runs or swims is hidden away somewhere. I never saw country so empty and still.'

'Never mind,' Ma said cheerfully. 'Supper's ready. You sit close by the fire, Charles, and dry yourself. I'll move the table up. Seems to me it's growing chilly.'

It was growing chilly. The cold crept under the table, crawling up from Laura's bare feet to her bare knees under her skirts. But supper was warm and good and in the lamplight all the faces were shining with the secret of the surprise for Pa.

Pa did not notice them. He ate hungrily but he did not notice what he ate. He said again, 'It's queer, not a duck nor a goose coming down to rest.'

'Likely the poor things want to get to sunshine,' Ma said. 'I'm glad we're snug, out of the rain, under this good roof.'

Pa pushed back his empty plate and Ma gave Laura a look that said, 'Now!' Smiles spread over all their faces but Pa's. Carrie wriggled in her chair and Grace bounced on Ma's lap, while Laura set down the pie.

For an instant Pa did not see it. Then he said, 'Pie!'

His surprise was even greater than they had expected. Grace and Carrie and even Laura laughed out loud.

'Caroline, however did you manage to make a pie?' Pa exclaimed. 'What kind of pie is it?'

'Taste it and see!' said Ma. She cut a piece and put it on his plate.

Pa cut off the point with his fork and put it in his mouth. 'Apple pie! Where in the world did you get apples?'

Carrie could keep quiet no longer. She almost shouted, 'It's pumpkin! Ma made it of green pumpkin!'

Pa took another small bite and tasted it carefully. 'I'd

never have guessed it,' he said. 'Ma always could beat the nation cooking.'

Ma said nothing, but a little flush came up in her cheeks and her eyes kept on smiling while they all ate that delicious pie. They ate slowly, taking small bites of the sweet spiciness to make it last as long as they could.

That was such a happy supper that Laura wanted it never to end. When she was in bed with Mary and Carrie, she stayed awake to keep on being happy. She was so sleepily comfortable and cosy. The rain on the roof was a pleasant sound.

A splash of water on her face dimly surprised her. She was sure it could not be rain, for the roof was overhead. She snuggled closer to Mary and everything slid away into dark, warm sleep.

4

October Blizzard

Laura woke up suddenly. She heard singing and a queer slapping sound.

> 'Oh, I am as happy as a big sunflower
>   (Slap! Slap)
> That nods and bends in the breezes, Oh!
>   (Slap! Slap!)
> And my heart (Slap!) is as light (Slap!) as
>   the wind that blows (Slap! Slap!)
> The leaves from off the treeses, Oh!
>   (Slap! SLAP!)'

Pa was singing his trouble song and slapping his arms on his chest.

Laura's nose was cold. Only her nose was outside the quilts that she was huddled under. She put out her whole head and then she knew why Pa was slapping himself. He was trying to warm his hands.

He had kindled the fire. It was roaring in the stove, but the air was freezing cold. Ice crackled on the quilt where leaking rain had fallen. Winds howled around the shanty and from the roof and all the walls came a sound of scouring.

Carrie sleepily asked, 'What is it?'

'It's a blizzard,' Laura told her. 'You and Mary stay under the covers.'

Careful not to let the cold get under the quilts, she crawled out of the warm bed. Her teeth chattered while she pulled on her clothes. Ma was dressing, too, beyond the curtain, but they were both too cold to say anything.

They met at the stove where the fire was blazing furiously without warming the air at all. The window was a white blur of madly swirling snow. Snow had blown under the door and across the floor and every nail in the walls was white with frost.

Pa had gone to the stable. Laura was glad that they had so many haystacks in a row between the stable and the shanty. Going from haystack to haystack, Pa would not get lost.

'A b-b-b-b-blizzard!' Ma chattered. 'In Oc-October I n-n-never heard of . . .'

She put more wood in the stove and broke the ice in the water pail to fill the teakettle.

The water pail was less than half-full. They must be sparing of water for nobody could get to the well in that storm. But the snow on the floor was clean. Laura scooped it into the wash-basin and set it on the stove to melt, for washing in.

The air by the stove was not so cold now, so she rolled Grace in quilts and brought her to the stove to dress her. Mary and Carrie shiveringly dressed themselves, close to the open oven. They all put on their stockings and shoes.

Breakfast was waiting when Pa came back. He blew in with a howl of wind and swirling snow.

'Well, those muskrats knew what was coming, didn't they, Laura?' he said as soon as he was warm enough to speak. 'And the geese too.'

'No wonder they wouldn't stop at the lake,' said Ma.

'The lake's frozen by now,' Pa said. 'Temperature's down near zero and going lower.'

He glanced at the wood box as he spoke. Laura had filled it last night, but already the wood was low. So as soon as he had eaten breakfast, Pa wrapped himself well and brought big armfuls from the woodpile.

The shanty was growing colder. The stove could not warm the air inside the thin walls. There was nothing to do but sit huddled in coats and shawls, close to the stove.

'I'm glad I put beans to soak last night,' said Ma. She lifted the lid of the bubbling kettle and quickly popped in a spoonful of soda. The boiling beans roared, foaming up, but did not quite run over.

'There's a little bit of salt pork to put in them too,' Ma said.

Now and then she spooned up a few beans and blew on them. When their skins split and curled, she drained the soda-water from the kettle and filled it again with hot water. She put in the bit of fat pork.

'There's nothing like good hot bean soup on a cold day,' said Pa. He looked down at Grace, pulling at his hand. 'Well, Blue-Eyes, what do you want?'

'A tory,' Grace said.

'Tell us the one about Grandpa and the pig on the sled,' Carrie begged. So, taking Grace and Carrie on his knees, Pa began again the stories that he used to tell Mary and Laura in the Big Woods when they were little girls. Ma and Mary knitted busily, in quilt-covered rockers drawn close to the oven, and Laura stood wrapped in her shawl, between the stove and the wall.

The cold crept in from the corners of the shanty, closer and closer to the stove. Icy-cold breezes sucked and fluttered the curtains around the beds. The little shanty quivered in the storm. But the steamy smell of boiling beans was good and it seemed to make the air warmer.

At noon Ma sliced bread and filled bowls with the hot bean broth and they all ate where they were, close to the stove. They all drank cups of strong, hot tea. Ma even gave

Grace a cup of cambric tea. Cambric tea was hot water and milk, with only a taste of tea in it, but little girls felt grown-up when their mothers let them drink cambric tea.

The hot soup and hot tea warmed them all. They ate the broth from the beans. Then Ma emptied the beans into a milk-pan, set the bit of fat pork in the middle, and laced the top with dribbles of molasses. She set the pan in the oven and shut the oven door. They would have baked beans for supper.

Then Pa had to bring in more wood. They were

thankful that the woodpile was close to the back door. Pa staggered in breathless with the first armful. When he could speak he said, 'This wind takes your breath away. If I'd thought of such a storm as this, I'd have filled this shanty with wood yesterday. Now I'm bringing in as much snow as wood.'

That was almost true. Every time Laura opened the door for him, snow swirled in. Snow fell off him and the wood was covered with snow. It was snow as hard as ice and as fine as sand, and opening the door made the shanty so cold that the snow did not melt.

'That's enough for now,' Pa said. If he let in any more cold, the wood he brought would not make enough heat to drive the cold out.

'When you get that snow swept up, Laura, bring me the fiddle,' he said. 'Soon as I can thaw out my fingers, we'll have a tune to drown the yowl of that wind.'

In a little while he was able to tune the strings and rosin the bow. Then he set the fiddle to his shoulder and sang with it:

'Oh, if I were young again,
I'd lead a different life,
Lay up some money and buy some land
And take Dinah for my wife.
But now I'm getting old and grey
I cannot work any more.

Oh carry me back
Oh, carry me back
To the old Virginia shore.
So carry me 'long and carry me 'long
And carry me till I die . . .'

'For pity's sakes!' Ma broke in. 'I'd as soon listen to the wind.' She was trying to keep Grace warm and Grace was struggling and whimpering. Ma set her down. 'There, run if you're bound to! You'll be glad enough to come back to the stove.'

'I'll tell you what!' Pa exclaimed. 'Laura and Carrie, you get out there with Grace and let's see you quickstep march! It'll warm up your blood.'

It was hard to leave the shelter of their huddled shawls, but they did as Pa said. Then his strong voice rang out with the singing fiddle:

'March! March! Ettrick and Teviotdale!
Why, my lads, dinna ye march forward in
    order?
March! March! Eskdale and Liddesdale!
All the blue bonnets are over the border!
Many a banner spread flutters above your
    head,
Many a crest that is famous in story.'

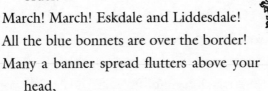

41

Round and round they marched, Laura and Carrie and Grace, singing with all their might, thumping loud thumps of their shoes on the floor.

> 'Mount, and make ready, then,
> Sons of the mountain glen,
> Fight! for your homes and the old Scottish
>   glory!'

They felt that banners were blowing above them and that they were marching to victory. They did not even hear the storm. They were warm to the tips of their toes.

Then the music ended and Pa laid the fiddle in its box. 'Well, girls, it's up to me to march out against this storm and make the stock comfortable for the night. Blamed if that old tune doesn't give me the spunk to like fighting even a blizzard!'

Ma warmed his coat and muffler by the oven while he put away the fiddle-box. They all heard the wind howling furiously.

'We'll have hot baked beans and hot tea waiting when you get back, Charles,' Ma promised him. 'And then we'll all go to bed and keep warm, and likely the storm'll be over by morning.'

But in the morning Pa sang again his sunflower song. The window was the same white blur, the winds still drove the scouring snow against the shivering little shanty.

The blizzard lasted two more long days and two more nights.

5

After the Storm

On the fourth morning, there was a queer feeling in Laura's ears. She peeped from the quilts and saw snow drifted over the bed. She heard the little crash of the stove lid and then the first crackling of the fire. Then she knew why her ears felt empty. The noise of the blizzard had stopped!

'Wake up, Mary!' she sang out, poking Mary with her elbow. 'The blizzard's over!'

She jumped out of the warm bed, into air colder than ice. The hot stove seemed to give out no heat at all. The pail of snow-water was almost solidly frozen. But the frosted windows were glowing with sunshine.

'It's as cold as ever outside,' Pa said when he came in. He bent over the stove to thaw the icicles from his moustache. They sizzled on the stove-top and went up in steam.

Pa wiped his moustaches and went on. 'The winds tore a big piece of tar-paper off the roof, tight as it was nailed

44

on. No wonder the roof leaked rain and snow.'

'Anyway, it's over,' Laura said. It was pleasant to be eating breakfast and to see the yellow-glowing windowpanes.

'We'll have Indian summer yet,' Ma was sure. 'This storm was so early, it can't be the beginning of winter.'

'I never knew a winter to set in so early,' Pa admitted. 'But I don't like the feel of things.'

'What things, Charles?' Ma wanted to know.

Pa couldn't say exactly. He said, 'There's some stray cattle by the haystacks.'

'Are they tearing down the hay?' Ma asked quickly.

'No,' said Pa.

'Then what of it, if they aren't doing any harm?' Ma said.

'I guess they're tired out by the storm,' said Pa. 'They took shelter there by the haystacks. I thought I'd let them rest and eat a little before I drove them off. I can't afford to let them tear down the stacks, but they could eat a little without doing any harm. But they aren't eating.'

'What's wrong then?' Ma asked.

'Nothing,' Pa said. 'They're just standing there.'

'That's nothing to upset a body,' said Ma.

'No,' Pa said. He drank his tea. 'Well, I might as well go drive them off.'

He put on his coat and cap and mittens again and went out.

After a moment Ma said, 'You might as well go with him, Laura. He may need some help to drive them away from the hay.'

Quickly Laura put Ma's big shawl over her head and pinned it snugly under her chin with the shawl-pin. The woollen folds covered her from head to foot. Even her hands were under the shawl. Only her face was out.

Outdoors the sun-glitter hurt her eyes. She breathed a deep breath of the tingling cold and squinted her eyes to look around her. The sky was hugely blue and all the land was blowing white. The straight, strong wind did not lift the snow, but drove it scudding across the prairie.

The cold stung Laura's cheeks. It burned in her nose and tingled in her chest and came out in steam on the air. She held a fold of the shawl across her mouth and her breath made frost on it.

When she passed the corner of the stable, she saw Pa going ahead of her and she saw the cattle. She stood and stared.

The cattle were standing in sunshine and shadow by the haystacks – red and brown and spotted cattle and one thin black one. They stood perfectly still, every head bowed down to the ground. The hairy red necks and brown necks all stretched down from bony-gaunt shoulders to monstrous, swollen white heads.

'Pa!' Laura screamed. Pa motioned to her to stay where

she was. He went on trudging, through the low-flying snow, towards those creatures.

They did not seem like real cattle. They stood so terribly still. In the whole herd there was not the least movement. Only their breathing sucked their hairy sides in between the rib bones and pushed them out again. Their hip bones and their shoulder bones stood up sharply. Their legs were braced out, stiff and still. And where their heads should be, swollen white lumps seemed fast to the ground under the blowing snow.

On Laura's head the hair prickled up and a horror went down her backbone. Tears from the sun and the wind welled out of her staring eyes and ran cold on her cheeks. Pa went on slowly against the wind. He walked up to the herd. Not one of the cattle moved.

For a moment Pa stood looking. Then he stooped and quickly did something. Laura heard a bellow and a red steer's back humped and jumped. The red steer ran staggering and bawling. It had an ordinary head with eyes and nose and open mouth bawling out steam on the wind.

Another one bellowed and ran a short, staggering run. Then another. Pa was doing the same thing to them all, one by one. Their bawling rose up to the cold sky.

At last they all drifted away together. They went silently now in the knee-deep spray of blowing snow.

Pa waved to Laura to go back to the shanty, while he inspected the haystacks.

'Whatever kept you so long, Laura?' Ma asked. 'Did the cattle get into the haystacks?'

'No, Ma,' she answered. 'Their heads were . . . I guess their heads were frozen to the ground.'

'That can't be!' Ma exclaimed.

'It must be one of Laura's queer notions,' Mary said, busily knitting in her chair by the stove. 'How could cattle's heads freeze to the ground, Laura? It's really worrying, the way you talk sometimes.'

'Well, ask Pa then!' Laura said shortly. She was not able to tell Ma and Mary what she felt. She felt that somehow, in the wild night and storm, the stillness that was underneath all sounds on the prairie had seized the cattle.

When Pa came in Ma asked him, 'What was wrong with the cattle, Charles?'

'Their heads were frozen over with ice and snow,' Pa said. 'Their breath frozen over their eyes and their noses till they couldn't see nor breathe.'

Laura stopped sweeping. 'Pa! Their own breath! Smothering them,' she said in horror.

Pa understood how she felt. He said, 'They're all right now, Laura. I broke the ice off their heads. They're breathing now and I guess they'll make it to shelter somewhere.'

Carrie and Mary were wide-eyed and even Ma looked horrified. She said briskly, 'Get your sweeping done, Laura, and Charles, for pity's sake, why don't you take off your wraps and warm yourself?'

48

'I got something to show you,' Pa said. He took his hand carefully out of his pocket. 'Look here, girls, look at what I found hidden in a haystack.'

Slowly he opened his hand. In the hollow of his mitten sat a little bird. He put it gently in Mary's hands.

'Why, it's standing straight up!' Mary exclaimed, touching it lightly with her finger-tips.

They had never seen a bird like it. It was small, but it looked exactly like the picture of the great auk in Pa's big green book, *The Wonders of The Animal World*.

It had the same white breast and black back and wings, the same short legs placed far back, and the same large, webbed feet. It stood straight up on its short legs, like a tiny man with black coat and trousers and white shirt

49

front, and its little black wings were like arms.

'What is it, Pa? Oh, what is it?' Carrie cried in delight and she held Grace's eager hands. 'Mustn't touch, Grace.'

'I never saw anything like it,' said Pa. 'It must have tired out in the storm winds and dropped down and struck against the haystack. It had crawled into the hay for shelter.'

'It's a great auk,' Laura declared. 'Only it's a little one.'

'It's full-grown, it isn't a nestling,' said Ma. 'Look at its feathers.'

'Yes, it's full-grown, whatever it is,' Pa agreed.

The little bird stood up straight on Mary's soft palm and looked at them all with its bright black eyes.

'It's never seen humans before,' said Pa.

'How do you know, Pa?' Mary asked.

'Because it isn't afraid of us,' Pa said.

'Oh, can we keep it, Pa? Can't we, Ma?' Carrie begged.

'Well, that depends,' Pa said.

Mary's finger-tips touched the little bird all over, while Laura told her how white its smooth breast was and how very black its back and tail and little wings. Then they let Grace carefully touch it. The little auk sat still and looked at them.

They set it on the floor and it walked a little way. Then it pushed its webbed feet tiptoe against the boards and flapped its little wings.

'It can't get going,' said Pa. 'It's a water-bird. It must

start from the water where it can use those webbed feet to get up speed.'

Finally they put it in a box in the corner. It stood there looking at them, with its round, bright black eyes, and they wondered what it ate.

'That was a queer storm all around,' said Pa. 'I don't like it.'

'Why, Charles, it was only a blizzard,' Ma said. 'We'll likely have nice warm weather now. It's beginning to warm up a little already.'

Mary took up her knitting again and Laura went on sweeping. Pa stood by the window and after awhile Carrie led Grace away from the little auk and they looked out too.

'Oh, look! Jackrabbits!' Carrie exclaimed. All around the stable, dozens of jackrabbits were hopping.

'The rascals have been living on our hay, all through the storm,' Pa said. 'I ought to take my gun and get us a rabbit stew.'

But he had been standing at the window looking at them without making a move towards his gun.

'Please let them go, Pa, this one time,' Laura pleaded. 'When they came because they had to, they had to find shelter.'

Pa looked at Ma, and Ma smiled. 'We aren't hungry, Charles, and I'm thankful we all got through that storm.'

'Well, I guess I can spare the jackrabbits a little hay!'

said Pa. He took the water pail and went to the well.

The air that came in when he opened the door was very cold, but the sun was already beginning to melt the snow on the south side of the shanty.

6

Indian Summer

There were only slivers of ice on the water pail next morning and the day was sunny and warm. Pa took his traps to set them for muskrats in Big Slough, and Carrie and Grace played outdoors.

The little auk would not eat. It did not utter a sound, but Carrie and Laura thought that it looked up at them desperately. It would die without food, but it did not seem to know how to eat anything that they offered it.

At dinnertime Pa said that the ice was melting on Silver Lake; he thought that the strange little bird could take care of itself on the open water. So after dinner Laura and Mary put on their coats and hoods and they went with Pa to set the little auk free.

Silver Lake was ruffling pale blue and silver under the warm, pale sky. Ice was around its edges and flat grey cakes of ice floated on the ripples. Pa took the little auk from his pocket. In its smooth black coat and neat white shirt-front of tiny feathers, it stood up on his palm. It saw the land and the sky and the water, and eagerly it rose up on its toes and stretched out its little wings.

But it could not go, it could not fly. Its wings were too small to lift it.

'It does not belong on land,' said Pa. 'It's a water-bird.'

He squatted down by the thin white ice at the lake's edge and reaching far out he tipped the little bird from his hand into the blue water. For the briefest instant, there it was, and then it wasn't there. Out among the ice cakes it went streaking, a black speck.

'It gets up speed, with those webbed feet,' said Pa, 'to lift it from the . . . There it goes!'

Laura barely had time to see it, rising tiny in the great blue-sparkling sky. Then, in all that glittering of sunlight, it was gone. Her eyes were too dazzled to see it any more. But Pa stood looking, still seeing it going towards the south.

They never knew what became of that strange little bird that came in the dark with the storm from the far north and went southward in the sunshine. They never saw nor heard of another bird like it. They never found out what kind of bird it was.

Pa still stood looking far away across the land. All the prairie curves were softly coloured, pale browns and tan and fawn-grey and very faint greens and purples, and far away they were grey-blue. The sunshine was warm and the air hazy. Only a little cold was around Laura's feet, near the thin, dry ice at the lake's edge.

Everything was still. No wind stirred the grey-bleached grass and no birds were on the water or in the sky. The lake faintly lapped at the rim of that stillness.

Laura looked at Pa and she knew he was listening too. The silence was as terrible as cold is. It was stronger than any sound. It could stop the water's lapping and the thin, faint ringing in Laura's ears. The silence was no sound, no movement, no thing; that was its terror. Laura's heart jumped and jumped, trying to get away from it.

'I don't like it,' Pa said, slowly shaking his head. 'I don't like the feel of the weather. There's something . . .' He could not say what he meant and he said again, 'I don't like it. I don't like it at all.'

Nobody could say, exactly, that anything was wrong with that weather. It was beautiful Indian summer. Frosts came every night and sometimes a light freeze, but all the days were sunny. Every afternoon Laura and Mary took long walks in the warm sunshine, while Carrie played with Grace near the house.

'Get yourselves full of sunshine while you can,' Ma said. 'It will soon be winter and you'll have to stay indoors.'

Out in the bright soft weather they were storing up sunshine and fresh air, in themselves, for the winter when they could not have any.

But often, while they were walking, Laura quickly looked at the north. She did not know why. Nothing was there. Sometimes in the warm sunshine she stood still and listened and she was uneasy. There was no reason why.

'It's going to be a hard winter,' Pa said. 'The hardest we ever saw.'

'Why, Charles,' Ma protested. 'We're having fine weather now. That one early storm is no reason why the whole winter will be bad.'

'I've trapped muskrats a good many years,' said Pa, 'and I never saw them build their walls so thick.'

'Muskrats!' said Ma.

'The wild things know, somehow,' Pa said. 'Every wild creature's got ready for a hard winter.'

'Maybe they just made ready for that bad storm,' Ma suggested.

But Pa was not persuaded. 'I don't like the feel of things, myself,' he said. 'This weather seems to be holding back something that it might let loose any minute. If I were a wild animal, I'd hunt my hole and dig it plenty deep. If I were a wild goose, I'd spread my wings and get out of here.'

Ma laughed at him. 'You *are* a goose, Charles! I don't know when I've seen a more beautiful Indian summer.'

7
Indian Warning

One afternoon a little crowd of men gathered in Harthorn's store in town. The trains, which had been stopped by the blizzard, were running again, and men had come in to town from their claims to buy some groceries and hear the news.

Royal and Almanzo Wilder had come from their homesteads, Almanzo driving his own fine team of matched Morgans, the best team in all that country. Mr Boast was there, standing in the middle of the little crowd and setting it laughing when he laughed. Pa had walked in with his gun on his arm, but he had not seen so much as a jackrabbit, and now he was waiting while Mr Harthorn weighed the piece of salt pork that he had had to buy instead.

No one heard a footstep, but Pa felt that someone was behind him and he turned to see who it was. Then suddenly Mr Boast stopped talking. All the others looked to see what Mr Boast saw, and they stood up quickly from the cracker boxes and the plough. Almanzo slid down from the counter. Nobody said anything.

It was only an Indian, but somehow the sight of him kept them all quiet. He stood there and looked at them, at Pa, at Mr Boast, at Royal Wilder and each of the other men, and finally at Almanzo.

He was a very old Indian. His brown face was carved in deep wrinkles and shrivelled on the bones, but he

stood tall and straight. His arms were folded under a grey blanket, holding it wrapped around him. His head was shaved to a scalp-block and an eagle's feather stood up from it. His eyes were bright and sharp. Behind him the sun was shining on the dusty street and an Indian pony stood there waiting.

'Heap big snow come,' this Indian said.

The blanket slid on his shoulder and one naked brown arm came out. It moved in a wide sweep, to north, to west, to east, and gathered them all together and swirled.

'Heap big snow, big wind,' he said.

'How long?' Pa asked him.

'Many moons,' the Indian said. He held up four fingers, then three fingers. Seven fingers, seven months; blizzards for seven months.

They all looked at him and did not say anything.

'You white men,' he said. 'I tell-um you.'

He showed seven fingers again. 'Big snow.' Again, seven fingers. 'Big snow.' Again seven fingers. '*Heap* big snow, many moons.'

Then he tapped his breast with his forefinger. 'Old! Old! I have seen!' he said proudly.

He walked out of the store to his waiting pony and rode away towards the west.

'Well, I'll be jiggered,' Mr Boast said.

'What was that about seven big snows?' Almanzo asked. Pa told him. The Indian meant that every seventh winter was a hard winter and that at the end of three times seven years came the hardest of all. He had come to tell the white men that this coming winter was a twenty-first winter, that there would be seven months of blizzards.

'You suppose the old geezer knows what he's talking about?' Royal wanted to know. No one could answer that.

'Just on the chance,' Royal said, 'I say we move in to town for the winter. My feed store beats a claim shanty all hollow for wintering in. We can stay back there till spring. How'd it suit you, Manzo?'

'Suits me,' said Almanzo.

'How do you feel about moving in to town, Boast?' Pa asked.

Mr Boast slowly shook his head. 'Don't see how we could. We've got too much stock, cattle and horses, and chickens. There's no place in town to keep them even if I could afford to pay rent. We're fixed pretty well for the winter on the claim. I guess Ellie and I better stay with it.'

Everyone was sober. Pa paid for his groceries and set out, walking quickly towards home. Now and then he looked back at the northwest sky. It was clear and the sun was shining.

Ma was taking bread from the oven when Pa came in. Carrie and Grace had run to meet him; then came in with him. Mary went on quietly sewing but Laura jumped up.

'Is anything wrong, Charles?' Ma asked, tipping the

61

good-smelling loaves from the pan on to a clean white cloth. 'You're home early.'

'Nothing's wrong,' Pa answered. 'Here are your sugar and tea and a bit of salt pork. I didn't get a rabbit. Not a thing's wrong,' he repeated, 'but we're moving to town as quick as we can. I've got to haul in hay, first, for the stock. I can haul one load before dark if I hustle.'

'Goodness, Charles!' Ma gasped, but Pa was on his way to the stable. Carrie and little Grace stared at Ma and at Laura and at Ma again. Laura looked at Ma and Ma looked helplessly at her.

'Your Pa never did such a thing before,' Ma said.

'Nothing's wrong, Ma. Pa said so,' Laura answered. 'I must run and help him with the hay.'

Ma came out to the stable, too, and Pa talked to her while he slapped the harness on the horses.

'It's going to be a hard winter,' Pa said. 'If you must have the truth, I'm afraid of it. This house is nothing but a claim shanty. It doesn't keep out the cold, and look what happened to the tar-paper in the first blizzard. Our store building in town is boarded and papered, sided on the outside and ceiled on the inside. It's good and tight and warm, and the stable there is built warm too.'

'But what's the need to hurry so?' Ma asked.

'I feel like hurrying,' Pa said. 'I'm like the muskrat, something tells me to get you and the girls inside thick walls. I've been feeling this way for some time, and now that Indian . . .'

He stopped.

'What Indian?' Ma asked him. She looked as if she were smelling the smell of an Indian whenever she said the word. Ma despised Indians. She was afraid of them, too.

'There's some good Indians,' Pa always insisted. Now he added, 'And they know some things that we don't. I'll tell you all about it at supper, Caroline.'

They could not talk while Pa pitched hay from the stack and Laura trampled it down in the rack. The hay rose higher under her fast-moving legs until the load was tall above the horses' backs.

'I'll handle it myself in town, Pa said. 'Town's no place for a girl to be doing a boy's work.'

So Laura slid down from the high top of the load into what was left of the haystack, and Pa drove away. The Indian summer afternoon was warm and sweet-smelling and still. The low ripples of softly coloured land stretched far away and the sky was gentle over them. But under the softness and gentleness there was something waiting. Laura knew what Pa meant.

' "Oh, that I had the wings of a bird!" ' Laura thought of those words in the Bible. If she had had the wings of a bird, she, too, would have spread them and flown, fast, fast, and far away.

She went soberly to the house to help Ma. None of

63

them had wings; they were only moving to town for the winter. Ma and Mary did not mind, but Laura knew she would not like to live among so many people.

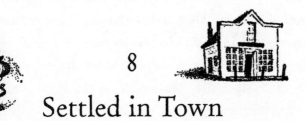

8
Settled in Town

Pa's store building was one of the best in town. It stood by itself on the east side of Main Street. Its false front was tall and square-cornered, with one upstairs window in it. Downstairs there were two windows with the front door between them.

Pa did not stop the loaded wagon there. He turned the corner to Second Street, that was only a road, and drove in behind the store to its lean-to door. There was a good wooden stable with one haystack already beside it, and beyond them, in Second Street, Laura saw a house newly built of fresh boards. Pa's stable and store building had already weathered grey, like the other stores in Main Street.

'Well, here we are!' said Pa. 'It won't take us long to get settled in.'

He untied Ellen, the cow, and her big calf from behind the wagon, and Laura led them to their stalls in the stable, while Pa unloaded the wagon. Then he drove it on to the stable and began to unhitch the horses.

The lean-to's inside door opened under the stairs that

went up from the back room. The narrow, back room would be the kitchen, of course, and it had a window, in its other end, looking out across the road that was Second Street and on across vacant lots to the side of a little vacant store. Farther over the prairie to the north-east, Laura could see the two-storey railway depot.

Ma stood in the bare front room, looking at it and thinking where to put all their things.

In the big, empty room stood a coal heater and a shiny boughten desk and boughten chair.

'Why, where did that desk and chair come from?' Laura exclaimed.

'They're Pa's,' said Ma. 'Judge Carroll's new partner has a desk so Judge Carroll let Pa have his old desk and chair and the coal heater for part of the rent.'

The desk had drawers and a top with pigeonholes under a marvellous flexible cover made of narrow slats of wood that could be pulled, curving down or pushed up again. When it was pushed up it disappeared.

'We'll put the rocking chairs by the other window,' Ma went on. 'Then Mary'll have the sunshine all afternoon and I can see to read to us until sundown. We'll do that first thing, Mary, so you can settle down and keep Grace out of our way.'

Ma and Laura set the rocking chairs by the window. Then they edged the table through the doorways and put it between the coal heater and the door to the kitchen.

'That will be the warm place to eat,' said Ma.

'Can we put up the curtains now?' Laura asked. The two windows were like strange eyes looking in. Strangers went by in the street, and across the street stood the staring store buildings. Fuller's Hardware was there, with the drugstore beside it, and Power's Tailor Shop, and Loftus' Groceries, Dry Goods and General Merchandise.

'Yes, the sooner the better,' said Ma. She unpacked the muslin curtains and she and Laura put them up. A wagon went by while they did it and suddenly five or six boys came down Second Street and after a moment as many girls.

'School's out for the day,' said Ma. 'You and Carrie'll be going to school tomorrow.' Her voice was glad.

Laura did not say anything. No one knew how she dreaded meeting strangers. No one knew of the fluttering in her breast and the gone feeling in her stomach when she had to meet them. She didn't like town; she didn't want to go to school.

It was so unfair that *she* had to go! Mary wanted to be a schoolteacher, but she couldn't be because she was blind. Laura didn't want to teach, but she must do it to please Ma. Probably all her life she must go among strange people and teach strange children; she would always be scared and she must never show it.

No! Pa had said she must never be afraid and she would not be. She would be brave if it killed her. But even if she could get over being afraid, she could not like strange people. She knew how animals would act, she understood what animals thought, but you could never be sure about people.

Anyway, the curtains at the windows kept strangers from looking in. Carrie had set the plain chairs around the table. The floor was bright, clean pine boards, and the large room looked very pleasant when Laura and Ma had laid a braided-rag rug before each door.

Pa was setting up the cookstove in the kitchen. When he had put the stovepipe together, straight and solid, he brought in the dry-goods-box cupboard and set it against the wall on the other side of the doorway.

'There!' he said. 'The stove and the cupboard'll both be handy to the table in the other room.'

'Yes, Charles, that's well thought out,' Ma praised him. 'Now, when we get the beds upstairs, we'll soon be through.'

Pa handed up the pieces of the bedsteads while Ma and Laura drew them through the trap-door at the top of the stairs. He crowded the fat featherbeds through, and the blankets, quilts, and pillows, and then he and Carrie went to fill the strawticks from the haystack. They must fill the strawticks with hay, because there was no straw in this new country where no grain had yet been raised.

Under the attic roof, a building-paper partition made two rooms. One had a window to the west and one to the east. From the eastern window at the top of the stairs, Ma and Laura could see the far sky line and the prairie, the new house and the stable, and Pa and Carrie busily stuffing hay into the strawticks.

'Pa and I will have this room at the head of the stairs,' Ma decided. 'You girls can have the front one.'

They set up the bedsteads and laid in the slats. Then Pa pushed the fat, crackling strawticks up to them and Laura and Carrie made the beds while Ma went down to get supper.

The sunset was shining on the western window and flooding the whole room with golden light while they levelled the sweet-smelling, crackling hay in the strawticks and laid the feather-beds on top and stroked them softly smooth. Then, one on each side of a bed, they spread the sheets and the blankets and quilts, drawing them even and folding and tucking them in square at the corners. Then each plumped up a pillow and set it in place and the bed was made.

When the three beds were done, there was nothing more to do.

Laura and Carrie stood in the warm-coloured, chilly sunset light, looking out of the window. Pa and Ma were talking in the kitchen downstairs and two strange men were talking in the street. Farther away, but not very far, someone was whistling a tune and there were many little sounds besides that, all together, made the sound of a town.

Smoke was coming up from behind the store fronts. Past Fuller's Hardware, Second Street went west on the prairie to a lonely building standing in the dead grasses. It had four windows and the sunset was shining through them, so there must be even more windows on the other side. It had a boarded-in entry, like a nose, in its front-gable end and a stovepipe that was not smoking. Laura said, 'I guess that's the schoolhouse.'

'I wish we didn't have to go,' Carrie almost whispered.

'Well, we do have to,' said Laura.

Carrie looked at her wonderingly. 'Aren't you . . . scared?'

'There's nothing to be *scared* of!' Laura answered boldly. 'And if there was, we wouldn't be scared.'

Downstairs was warm from the fire in the cookstove, and Ma was saying that this place was so well-built that it took hardly any fire to heat it. She was getting supper, and Mary was setting the table.

'I don't need any help,' Mary said happily. 'The cupboard is in a different place, but Ma put all the dishes in the same places in the cupboard, so I find them just as easily as ever.'

The front room was spacious in the lamplight when Ma set the lamp on the supper-table. The creamy curtains, the varnished yellow desk and chair, the cushions in the rocking chairs, the rag rugs and the red tablecloth, and the pine colour of the floor and walls and ceiling were gay. The floor and the walls were so solid that not the smallest cold draught came in.

'I wish we had a place like this out on the claim,' Laura said.

'I'm glad we have it in town where you girls can go

71

to school this winter,' said Ma. 'You couldn't walk in from the claim every day, if the weather was bad.'

'It's a satisfaction to me to be where we're sure of getting coal and supplies,' Pa declared. 'Coal beats brushwood all hollow for giving steady heat. We'll keep enough coal in the lean-to to outlast any blizzard, and I can always get more from the lumberyard. Living in town, we're in no danger of running short of any kind of supplies.'

'How many people are there in town now?' Ma asked him.

Pa counted up. 'Fourteen business buildings and the depot; and then Sherwood's and Garland's and Owen's houses – that's eighteen families, not counting three or four shacks in the back streets. Then the Wilder boys are baching in the feed store, and there's a man named Foster moved in with his ox team and staying at Sherwood's. Count them all, there must be as many as seventy-five or eighty people living here in town.'

'And to think there wasn't a soul here this time last fall,' said Ma. Then she smiled at Pa. 'I'm glad you see some good at last, Charles, in staying in a settled place.'

Pa had to admit that he did. But he said, 'On the other hand, all this costs money and that's scarcer than hen's teeth. The railroad's the only place a man can get a dollar for a day's work and it's not hiring anybody. And the only hunting left around here is jackrabbits. Oregon's the place to be nowadays. The country out there'll be settled up, too, pretty soon.'

'Yes, but now is the time for the girls to be getting some schooling,' Ma said firmly.

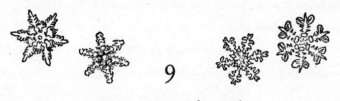

9

Cap Garland

Laura did not sleep very well. All night, it seemed, she knew that the town was close around her and that she must go to school in the morning. She was heavy with dread when she woke and heard steps going by in the street below and strange men speaking. The town was waking up too; the storekeepers were opening their stores.

The walls of the house kept strangers outside. But Laura and Carrie were heavyhearted because they must go out of the house and meet strangers. And Mary was sad because she could not go to school.

'Now Laura and Carrie, there's no cause to worry,' Ma said. 'I'm sure you can keep up with your classes.'

They looked at Ma in surprise. She had taught them so well at home that they knew they could keep up with their classes. They were not worried about that. But they only said, 'Yes, Ma.'

They hurried to wash the dishes and make their bed and hurriedly Laura swept their bedroom floor. Then they dressed carefully in their woollen winter dresses and nervously combed their hair and braided it. They tied on their Sunday hair-ribbons. With the steel buttonhook they buttoned their shoes.

'Hurry up, girls!' Ma called. 'It's past eight o'clock.'

At that moment, Carrie nervously jerked one of her shoe-buttons off. It fell and rolled and vanished down a crack of the floor.

'Oh, it's gone!' Carrie gasped. She was desperate. She could not go where strangers would see that gap in the row of black buttons that buttoned up her shoe.

'We must take a button off one of Mary's shoes,' Laura said.

But Ma had heard the button fall, downstairs. She found it and sewed it on again, and buttoned the shoe for Carrie.

At last they were ready. 'You look very nice,' Ma said, smiling. They put on their coats and hoods and took their schoolbooks. They said good-bye to Ma and Mary and they went out into Main Street.

The stores were all open. Mr Fuller and Mr Bradley had finished sweeping out; they stood holding their brooms and looking at the morning. Carrie took hold of Laura's hand. It helped Laura, to know that Carrie was even more scared than she was.

Bravely they crossed wide Main Street and walked steadily on along Second Street. The sun was shining brightly. A tangle of dead weeds and grasses made shadows beside the wheel-tracks. Their own long shadows went

before them, over many footprints in the paths. It seemed a long, long way to the schoolhouse that stood on the open prairie with no other buildings near.

In front of the schoolhouse strange boys were playing ball, and two strange girls stood on the platform before the entry door.

Laura and Carrie came nearer and nearer. Laura's throat was so choked that she could hardly breathe. One of the strange girls was tall and dark. Her smooth, black hair was twisted into a heavy knot at the back of her head. Her dress of indigo blue wool was longer than Laura's brown one.

Then suddenly Laura saw one of the boys spring into the air and catch the ball. He was tall and quick and he moved as beautifully as a cat. His yellow hair was sun-bleached almost white and his eyes were blue. They saw Laura and opened wide. Then a flashing grin lighted up his whole face and he threw the ball to her.

She saw the ball curving down through the air, coming swiftly. Before she could think, she had made a running leap and caught it.

A great shout went up from the other boys. 'Hey, Cap!' they shouted. 'Girls don't play ball!'

'I didn't think she'd catch it,' Cap answered.

'I don't want to play,' Laura said. She threw back the ball.

'She's as good as any of us!' Cap shouted. 'Come on and play,' he said to Laura, and then to the other girls, 'Come on, Mary Power and Minnie! You play with us, too!'

But Laura picked up the books she had dropped and took Carrie's hand again. They went on to the other girls at the schoolhouse door. Those girls would not play with boys, of course. She did not know why she had done such a thing and she was ashamed, fearful of what these girls must be thinking of her.

'I'm Mary Power,' the dark girl said, 'and this is Minnie Johnson.' Minnie Johnson was thin and fair and pale, with freckles.

'I'm Laura Ingalls,' Laura said, 'and this is my little sister, Carrie.'

Mary Power's eyes smiled. They were dark blue eyes, fringed with long, black lashes. Laura smiled back and she made up her mind that she would twist up her own hair tomorrow and ask Ma to make her next dress as long as Mary's.

'That was Cap Garland that threw you the ball,' Mary Power said.

There was no time to say anything more, for the teacher came to the door with the hand-bell, and they all went in to school.

They hung their coats and hoods on a row of nails in the entry, where the broom stood in a corner by the water-pail on its bench. Then they went into the schoolroom.

It was so new and shining that Laura felt timid again, and Carrie stood close to her. All the desks were patent desks, made of wood varnished as smooth as glass. They had black iron feet and the seats were curved a little, with curving backs that were part of the desks behind them. The desk-tops had grooves to hold pencils and shelves underneath them for slates and books.

There were twelve of these desks in a row up each side of the big room. A large heating stove stood in the middle of the room, with four more desks in front of it and four more behind it. Almost all those seats were empty. On the girls' side of the room, Mary Power and Minnie Johnson sat together in one of the back seats. Cap Garland and three other big boys sat in back seats on the boys' side – a few little boys and girls sat in front seats. They had all been coming to school, for a week now, and knew where to sit, but Laura and Carrie did not.

The teacher said to them, 'You're new, aren't you?' She was a smiling young lady, with curled bangs. The bodice of her black dress was buttoned down the front with twinkling jet buttons. Laura told her their names and she said, 'And I'm Florence Garland. We live back of your father's place, in the next street.'

So Cap Garland was Teacher's brother and they lived in the new house out on the prairie beyond the stable.

'Do you know the Fourth Reader?' Teacher asked.

'Oh, yes, ma'am!' Laura said. She did indeed know every word of it.

'Then I think we'll see what you can do with the Fifth,' Teacher decided. And she told Laura to take the back seat in the middle row, across the aisle from Mary Power. Carrie she put in front, near the little girls, and then she went up to her desk and rapped on it with her ruler.

'The school will come to attention,' she said. She

79

opened her Bible. 'This morning I will read the twenty-third Psalm.'

Laura knew the Psalms by heart, of course, but she loved to hear again every word of the twenty-third, from ' "The Lord is my shepherd: I shall not want," ' to, ' "Surely goodness and mercy shall follow me all the days of my life: and I will dwell in the house of the Lord forever." '

Then Teacher closed the Bible and on all the desks the pupils opened their textbooks. School work had begun.

Every day Laura liked the school more. She had no seatmate, but at recess and noontimes she was with Mary Power and Minnie Johnson. After school they walked to Main Street together, and by the end of that week they were meeting in the mornings and walking together to school. Twice Cap Garland urged them to play ball with the boys at recess, but they stayed inside the schoolhouse and watched the game through the window.

The brown-eyed, dark-haired boy was Ben Woodworth who lived at the depot. His father was the sick man that Pa had sent out with the last teamster the year before. The 'prairie cure' had truly almost cured his consumption of the lungs and he had come West again for more for it. He was the depot agent now.

The other boy was Arthur Johnson. He was thin and fair like his sister Minnie. Cap Garland was strongest and quickest. Inside the window, Laura and Mary and Minnie all watched him throwing the ball and leaping to catch it. He was not as handsome as black-haired Ben, but there was something about him. He was always good-natured and his grin was like a flash of light. It was like the sun coming up at dawn; it changed everything.

Mary Power and Minnie had gone to schools in the East, but Laura found it easy to keep up with them in their lessons. Cap Garland was from the East, too, but even in arithmetic he could not beat Laura.

Every night after supper she put her books and her slate on the red-checkered tablecloth in the lamplight, and she studied next day's lessons with Mary. She read the arithmetic problems aloud, and Mary did them in her head while she worked them on the slate. She read the history lesson and the geography to Mary until both of them could answer every question. If ever Pa could get money enough to send Mary to the college for the blind, Mary must be ready to go.

'And even if I never can go to college,' Mary said, 'I am learning as much as I can.'

Mary and Laura and Carrie were all enjoying school so much that they were sorry when Saturday and Sunday interrupted it. They looked forward to Monday. But when Monday came Laura was cross because her red flannel underwear was so hot and scratchy.

It made her back itch, and her neck, and her wrists, and where it was folded around her ankles, under her stockings and shoe-tops, that red flannel almost drove her crazy.

At noon she begged Ma to let her change to cooler underthings. 'It's too hot for my red flannels, Ma!' she protested.

'I know the weather's turned warm,' Ma answered gently. 'But this is the time of year to wear flannels, and you would catch cold if you took them off.'

Laura went crossly back to school and sat squirming because she must not scratch. She held the flat geography open before her, but she wasn't studying. She was trying to bear the itching flannels and wanting to get home where she could scratch. The sunshine from the western windows had never crawled so slowly.

Suddenly there was no sunshine. It went out, as if someone had blown out the sun like a lamp. The outdoors was grey, the windowpanes were grey, and at the same moment a wind crashed against the schoolhouse, rattling windows and doors and shaking the walls.

Miss Garland started up from her chair. One of the little Beardsley girls screamed and Carrie turned white.

Laura thought, 'It happened this way on Plum Creek, the Christmas when Pa was lost.' Her whole heart hoped and prayed that Pa was safe at home now.

Teacher and all the others were staring at the windows, where nothing but greyness could be seen. They all looked frightened. Then Miss Garland said, 'It is only a storm, children. Go on with your lessons.'

82

The blizzard was scouring against the walls, and the winds squealed and moaned in the stovepipe.

All the heads bent over the books as Teacher had told them to do. But Laura was trying to think how to get home. The schoolhouse was a long way from Main Street, and there was nothing to guide them.

All the others had come from the East that summer. They had never seen a prairie blizzard. But Laura and Carrie knew what it was. Carrie's head was bowed limply above her book, and the back of it, with the white parting between the braids of fine, soft hair, looked small and helpless and frightened.

There was only a little fuel at the schoolhouse. The school board was buying coal, but only one load had been delivered. Laura thought they might outlive the storm in the schoolhouse, but they could not do it without burning all the costly patent desks.

Without lifting her head Laura looked up at Teacher. Miss Garland was thinking and biting her lip. She could not decide to dismiss school because of a storm, but this storm frightened her.

'I ought to tell her what to do,' Laura thought. But she could not think what to do. It was not safe to leave the schoolhouse and it was not safe to stay there. Even the twelve patent desks might not last long enough to keep them warm until the blizzard ended. She thought of her wraps and Carrie's, in the entry. Whatever happened she must somehow keep Carrie warm. Already the cold was coming in.

There was a loud thumping in the entry. Every pupil started and looked at the door.

It opened and a man stumbled in. He was bundled in overcoat, cap, and muffler, all solid white with snow driven into the woollen cloth. They could not see who he was until he pulled down the stiffened muffler.

'I came out to get you,' he told Teacher.

He was Mr Foster, the man who owned the ox team and had come in from his claim to stay in town for the winter at Sherwood's, across the street from Teacher's house.

Miss Garland thanked him. She rapped her ruler on the desk and said, 'Attention! School is dismissed. You may bring your wraps from the entry and put them on by the stove.'

Laura said to Carrie, 'You stay here. I'll bring your wraps.'

The entry was freezing cold; snow was blowing in between the rough boards of the walls. Laura was chilled before she could snatch her coat and hood from their nail. She found Carrie's and carried the armful into the schoolhouse.

Crowded around the stove, they all put on their wraps and fastened them snugly. Cap Garland did not smile. His blue eyes narrowed and his mouth set straight while Mr Foster talked.

Laura wrapped the muffler snugly over Carrie's white face and took firm hold of her mittened hand. She told Carrie, 'Don't worry, we'll be all right.'

'Now, just follow me,' said Mr Foster, taking Teacher's arm. 'And keep close together.'

He opened the door, led the way with Miss Garland. Mary Power and Minnie each took one of the little Beardsley girls. Ben and Arthur followed them closely, then Laura went out with Carrie into blinding snow. Cap shut the door behind them.

They could hardly walk in the beating, whirling wind. The schoolhouse had disappeared. They could see nothing but swirling whiteness and snow and then a glimpse of each other, disappearing like shadows.

Laura felt that she was smothering. The icy particles of snow whirled scratching into her eyes and smothered her breathing. Her skirts whipped around her, now wrapped so tightly that she could not step, then whirled and lifted to her knees. Suddenly tightening, they made her stumble. She held tightly to Carrie, and Carrie, struggling and staggering, was pulled away by the wind and then flung back against her.

'We can't go on this way,' Laura thought. But they had to.

She was alone in the confusion of whirling winds and snow except for Carrie's hand that she must never let go. The winds struck her this way and that. She could not see nor breathe, she stumbled and was falling, then suddenly she seemed to be lifted and Carrie bumped against her. She tried to think. The others must be somewhere ahead. She must walk faster and keep up with them or she and Carrie would be lost. If they were lost on the prairie they would freeze to death.

But perhaps they were all lost. Main Street was only two blocks long. If they were going only a little way to north or south they would miss the block of stores and beyond was empty prairie for miles.

Laura thought they must have gone far enough to reach Main Street, but she could see nothing.

The storm thinned a little. She saw shadowy figures ahead. They were darker grey in the whirling grey-whiteness. She went on as fast as she could, with Carrie, until she touched Miss Garland's coat.

They had all stopped. Huddled in their wraps, they stood like bundles close together in the swirling mist. Teacher and Mr Foster were trying to talk, but the winds confused their shouts so that no one could hear what they said. Then Laura began to know how cold she was.

Her mittened hand was so numb that it hardly felt Carrie's hand. She was shaking all over and deep inside her there was a shaking that she could not stop. Only in her very middle there was a solid knot that ached, and her shaking pulled this knot tighter so that the ache grew worse.

She was frightened about Carrie. The cold hurt too much, Carrie could not stand it. Carrie was so little and thin, she had always been delicate, she could not stand such cold much longer. They must reach shelter soon.

Mr Foster and Teacher were moving again, going a little to the left. All the others stirred and hurried to follow them. Laura took hold of Carrie with her other hand, that had been in her coat pocket and was not quite so numb, and then suddenly she saw a shadow go by them. She knew it was Cap Garland.

He was not following the others to the left. With hands in his pockets and head bent, he went trudging straight ahead into the storm. A fury of winds thickened the air with snow and he vanished.

Laura did not dare follow him. She must take care of Carrie and Teacher had told them to follow her. She was sure that Cap was going towards Main Street, but perhaps she was mistaken and she could not take Carrie away from the others.

She kept tight hold of Carrie and hurried to follow Mr Foster and Teacher as fast as she could. Her chest sobbed for air and her eyes strained open in the icy snow-particles that hurt them like sand. Carrie struggled bravely, stumbling and flopping, doing her best to stay on her feet and keep on going. Only for instants when the snow-whirl was thinner could they glimpse the shadows moving ahead of them.

Laura felt that they were going in the wrong direction. She did not know why she felt so. No one could see anything. There was nothing to go by – no sun, no sky, no direction in the winds blowing fiercely from all directions. There was nothing but the dizzy whirling and the cold.

It seemed that the cold and the winds, the noise of the winds and the blinding, smothering, scratching snow, and the effort and the aching, were forever. Pa had lived through three days of a blizzard under the bank of Plum Creek. But there were no creek banks here. Here there was nothing but bare prairie. Pa had told about sheep caught in a blizzard, huddled together under the snow. Some of them had lived. Perhaps people could do that, too. Carrie was too tired to go much farther, but she was too heavy for Laura to carry. They must go on as long as they could, and then . . .

Then, out of the whirling whiteness, something hit her. The hard blow crashed against her shoulder and all through her. She rocked on her feet and stumbled against something solid. It was high, it was hard, it was the corner of two walls. Her hands felt it, her eyes saw it. She had walked against some building.

With all her might she yelled, 'Here! Come here! Here's a house!'

All around the house the winds were howling so that at first no one heard her. She pulled the icy stiff muffler from her mouth and screamed into the blinding storm. At last she saw a shadow in it, two tall shadows thinner than the shadowy wall she clung to – Mr Foster and Teacher. Then other shadows pressed close around her.

No one tried to say anything. They crowded together and they were all there – Mary Power and Minnie, each with a little Beardsley girl, and Arthur Johnson and Ben Woodworth with the small Wilmarth boys. Only Cap Garland was missing.

They followed along the side of that building till they came to the front of it, and it was Mead's Hotel, at the very north end of Main Street.

Beyond it was nothing but the railroad track covered with snow, the lonely depot and the wide, open prairie. If Laura had been only a few steps nearer the others, they would all have been lost on the endless prairie north of town.

For a moment they stood by the hotel's lamplit windows. Warmth and rest were inside the hotel, but the blizzard was growing worse and they must all reach home.

Main Street would guide all of them except Ben Woodworth. No other buildings stood between the hotel and the depot where he lived. So Ben went into the hotel to stay till the blizzard was over. He could afford to do that because his father had a regular job.

Minnie and Arthur Johnson, taking the little Wilmarth boys, had only to cross Main Street to Wilmarth's grocery store and their home was beside it. The others went on down Main Street, keeping close to the buildings. They passed the saloon, they passed Royal Wilder's feed store and then they passed Barker's grocery. The Beardsley Hotel was next and there the little Beardsley girls went in.

The journey was almost ended now. They passed Couse's Hardware store and they crossed Second Street to Fuller's Hardware. Mary Power had only to pass the drugstore now. Her father's tailor shop stood next to it.

Laura and Carrie and Teacher and Mr Foster had to cross Main street now. It was a wide street. But if they missed Pa's house, the haystacks and the stable were still between them and the open prairie.

They did not miss the house. One of its lighted windows made a glow that Mr Foster saw before he ran into it. He went on around the house corner with Teacher to go by the clothes-line, the haystacks and the stable to the Garland house.

Laura and Carrie were safe at their own front door. Laura's hands fumbled at the doorknob, too stiff to turn it. Pa opened the door and helped them in.

He was wearing overcoat and cap and muffler. He had set down the lighted lantern and dropped a coil of rope. 'I was just starting out after you,' he said.

In the still house Laura and Carrie stood taking deep breaths. It was so quiet there where the winds did not push and pull at them. They were still blinded, but the whirling icy snow had stopped hurting their eyes.

Laura felt Ma's hands breaking away the icy muffler, and she said, 'Is Carrie all right?'

'Yes, Carrie's all right,' said Pa.

Ma took off Laura's hood and unbuttoned her coat and helped her pull out of its sleeves. 'These wraps are driven full of ice,' Ma said. They crackled when she shook them and little drifts of whiteness sifted to the floor.

'Well,' Ma said, ' "All's well that ends well." You're not frostbitten. You can go to the fire and get warm.'

Laura could hardly move but she stooped and with her fingers dug out the caked snow that the wind had driven in between her woollen stockings and the tops of her shoes. Then she staggered towards the stove.

'Take my place,' Mary said, getting up from her rocking chair. 'It's the warmest.'

Laura sat stiffly down. She felt numb and stupid. She rubbed her eyes and saw a pink smear on her hand. Her eyelids were bleeding where the snow had scratched them. The sides of the coal heater glowed red-hot and she could feel the heat on her skin, but she was cold inside. The heat from the fire couldn't reach that cold.

Pa sat close to the stove holding Carrie on his knee. He had taken off her shoes to make sure that her feet were not frozen and he held her wrapped in a shawl. The shawl shivered with Carrie's shivering. 'I can't get warm, Pa,' she said.

'You girls are chilled through. I'll have you a hot drink in a minute,' said Ma, hurrying into the kitchen.

She brought them each a steaming cup of ginger tea.

'My, that smells good!' said Mary and Grace leaned on Laura's knee looking longingly at the cup till Laura gave her a sip and Pa said, 'I don't know why there's not enough of that to go around.'

'Maybe there is,' said Ma, going into the kitchen again.

It was so wonderful to be there, safe at home, sheltered from the winds and the cold. Laura thought that this must be a little bit like Heaven, where the weary are at rest. She could not imagine that Heaven was better than being where she was, slowly growing warm and comfortable, sipping the hot, sweet, ginger tea, seeing Ma, and Grace, and Pa and Carrie, and Mary all enjoying their own cups of it and hearing the storm that could not touch them here.

'I'm glad you didn't have to come for us, Pa,' Laura said drowsily. 'I was hoping you were safe.'

'So was I,' Carrie told Pa, snuggling against him. 'I remembered that Christmas, on Plum Creek, when you didn't get home.'

'I did, too,' Pa said grimly. 'When Cap Garland came into Fuller's and said you were all heading out to the open prairie, you can bet I made tracks for a rope and lantern.'

'I'm glad we got in all right,' Laura woke up to say.

'Yes, we'd have had a posse out looking for you,

92

though we'd have been hunting for a needle in a haystack,' said Pa.

'Best forget about it,' said Ma.

'Well, he did the best he could,' Pa went on. 'Cap Garland's a smart boy.'

'And now, Laura and Carrie, you're going to bed and get some rest,' said Ma. 'A good long sleep is what you need.'

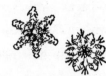

IO

Three Days' Blizzard

When Laura's eyes opened in the morning she saw that every clinched nail in the roof overhead was furry-white with frost. Thick frost covered every windowpane to its very top. The daylight was still and dim inside the stout walls that kept out the howling blizzard.

Carrie was awake too. She peeked anxiously at Laura from under the quilts on the bed by the stovepipe where she and Grace slept. She blew out a breath to see how cold it was. Even close to the stovepipe her breath froze white in the air. But that house was so well-built that not one bit of snow had been driven through the walls or the roof.

Laura was stiff and sore and so was Carrie. But morning had come and they must get up. Sliding out of bed into the cold that took her breath away, Laura snatched up her dress and shoes and hurried to the top of the stairs. 'Ma, can we dress down there?' she called, thankful for the warm, long red flannels under her flannel nightgown.

'Yes, Pa's at the stable,' Ma answered.

The cookstove was warming the kitchen and the lamplight made it seem even warmer. Laura put on her petticoats and dress and shoes. Then she brought down her sisters' clothes and warmed them and carried Grace downstairs wrapped in quilts. They were all dressed and washed when Pa came in with the milk half frozen in the pail.

After he had got his breath and melted the frost and snow from his moustaches, he said, 'Well, the hard winter's begun.'

'Why, Charles,' Ma said. 'It isn't like you to worry about winter weather.'

'I'm not worrying,' Pa replied. 'But it's going to be a hard winter.'

'Well, if it is,' said Ma, 'here we are in town where we can get what we need from the stores even in a storm.'

There would be no more school till the blizzard was over. So, after the housework was done, Laura and Carrie and Mary studied their lessons and then settled down to sew while Ma read to them.

Once she looked up and listened and said, 'It sounds like a regular three days' blizzard.'

'Then there won't be any more school this week,' said Laura. She wondered what Mary and Minnie were doing. The front room was so warm that the frost on the windows had melted a little and turned to ice. When she breathed on it to clear a peephole she could see against the glass the blank white swirling snow. She could not even see Fuller's Hardware store, across the street, where Pa had gone to sit by the stove and talk with the other men.

Up the street, past Couse's Hardware store and the Beardsley Hotel and Barker's grocery, Royal Wilder's feed store was dark and cold. No one would come to buy feed in that storm, so Royal did not keep up the fire in the heater. But the back room, where he and Almanzo were baching, was warm and cosy and Almanzo was frying pancakes.

Royal had to agree that not even Mother could beat Almanzo at making pancakes. Back in York state when they were boys and later on Father's big farm in Minnesota they had never thought of cooking; that was woman's work. But since they had come West to take up homestead claims they had to cook or starve; and Almanzo had to do the cooking because he was handy at almost anything and also because he was younger than Royal who still thought that he was the boss.

The fact was that Almanzo was nineteen years old. But that was a secret because he had taken a homestead claim, and according to law a man must be twenty-one years old to do that. Almanzo did not consider that he was breaking the law and he knew he was not cheating the Government. Still, anyone who knew that he was nineteen years old could take his claim away from him.

Almanzo looked at it this way: the Government wanted this land settled; Uncle Sam would give a farm to any man who had the nerve and muscle to come out here and break the sod and stick to the job till it was done. But the politicians far away in Washington could not know the settlers so they must make rules to regulate them and one rule was that a homesteader must be twenty-one years old.

None of the rules worked as they were intended to. Almanzo knew that men were making good wages by filing claims that fitted all the legal rules and then handing over the land to the rich men who paid their wages. Everywhere, men were stealing the land and doing it according to all the rules. But of all the homestead laws Almanzo thought that the most foolish was the law about a settler's age.

Anybody knew that no two men were alike. You could measure cloth with a yardstick, or distance by miles, but you could not lump men together and measure them by any rule. Brains and character did not depend on anything but the man himself. Some men did not have the sense at sixty that some had at sixteen. And Almanzo considered that he was as good, any day, as any man twenty-one years old.

Almanzo's father thought so too. A man had the right to keep his sons at work for him until they were twenty-one years old. But Almanzo's father had put his boys to work early and trained them well. Almanzo had learned to save money before he was ten and he had been doing a man's work on the farm since he was nine. When he was seventeen, his father had judged that he was a man and

had given him his own free time. Almanzo had worked for fifty cents a day and saved money to buy seed and tools. He had raised wheat on shores in western Minnesota and made a good crop.

He considered that he was as good a settler as the Government could want and that his age had nothing to do with it. So he had said to the land agent, 'You can put me down as twenty-one,' and the agent had winked at him and done it. Almanzo had his own homestead claim now and the seed wheat for next year that he had brought from Minnesota, and if he could stick it out on these prairies and raise crops for four years more he would have his own farm. .

He was making pancakes, not because Royal could boss him any more but because Royal could not make good pancakes and Almanzo loved light, fluffy, buckwheat pancakes with plenty of molasses.

'Whew! listen to that!' Royal said. They had never heard anything like that blizzard.

'That old Indian knew what he was talking about,' said Almanzo. 'If we're in for seven months of this . . .' The three pancakes on the griddle were holding their bubbles in tiny holes near their crisping edges. He flipped them over neatly and watched their brown-patterned sides rise in the middle.

The good smell of them mixed with the good smells of fried salt pork and boiling coffee. The room was warm and the lamp with its tin reflector, hung on a nail, lighted it strongly. Saddles and bits of harness hung on the rough board walls. The bed was in one corner, and the table was drawn up to the stove hearth so that Almanzo could put the pancakes on the white ironstone plates without moving one step.

'This can't last seven months. That's ridiculous,' said Royal. 'We're bound to have some spells of good weather.'

Almanzo replied airily, 'Anything can happen and most usually does.' He slid his knife under the edges of the pancakes. They were done and he flipped them on to Royal's plate and greased the griddle again with the pork rind.

Royal poured molasses over the cakes. 'One thing can't happen,' he said. 'We can't stick it out here till spring unless they keep the trains running.'

Almanzo poured three more rounds of batter from the batter pitcher on to the sizzling griddle. He lounged against the warm partition, by the stovepipe, waiting for the cakes to rise.

'We figured on hauling in more hay,' he said. 'We've got plenty of dry feed for the team.'

'Oh, they'll get the trains through,' Royal said, eating. 'But if they didn't we'd be up against it. How about coal and kerosene and flour and sugar? For that matter, how long would my stock of feed last, if the whole town came piling in here to buy it?'

Almanzo straightened up. 'Say!' he exclaimed. 'Nobody's going to get my seed wheat! No matter what happens.'

'Nothing's going to happen,' Royal said. 'Whoever heard of storms lasting seven months? They'll get the trains running again.'

'They better,' said Almanzo, turning the pancakes. He thought of the old Indian, and he looked at his sacks of seed wheat. They were stacked along the end of the room and some were under the bed. The seed wheat did not belong to Royal; it belonged to him. He had raised it in Minnesota. He had ploughed and harrowed the ground and sowed the grain. He had cut it and bound it, threshed and sacked it, and hauled it a hundred miles in his wagon.

If storms like this storm delayed the trains so that no more seed came from the East until after sowing time, his crop for next year, his homestead would depend on his having that seed wheat to sow. He would not sell it for any money. It was seed that made crops. You could not sow silver dollars.

'I'm not going to sell so much as a peck of my seed wheat,' he said.

'All right, all right, nobody's bothering your wheat,' Royal answered. 'How about some pancakes?'

'This makes twenty-one,' Almanzo said, putting them on Royal's plate.

'How many did you eat while I was doing the chores?' Royal asked him.

'I didn't count 'em,' Almanzo grinned. 'But gosh, I'm working up an appetite, feeding you.'

'So long as we keep on eating, we don't have to wash the dishes,' said Royal.

II

Pa Goes to Volga

At noon on Tuesday the blizzard ended. Then the wind died down and in the clear sky the sun shone brightly.

'Well, that's over,' Pa said cheerfully. 'Now maybe we'll have a spell of good weather.'

Ma sighed comfortably. 'It's good to see the sun again.'

'And to hear the stillness,' Mary added.

They could hear again the small sounds of the town. Now and then a store door slammed. Ben and Arthur went by, talking, and Cap Garland came whistling down Second Street. The only usual sound that they did not hear was the train's whistle.

At supper Pa said that the train was stopped by the snow-filled big cut near Tracy. 'But they'll shovel through it in a couple of days,' he said. 'In weather like this, who cares about trains?'

Early next morning he went across the street to Fuller's store, hurrying back. He told Ma that some of the men were going to take the handcar from the depot and go meet the train at Volga, clearing the track as they went. Mr Foster had agreed to do Pa's chores if Pa went along.

'I have been in one place so long, I would like to travel a little,' Pa said.

'Go along, Charles, you might as well,' Ma agreed. 'But can you clear the track so far in one day?'

'We think so,' said Pa. 'The cuts are small from here to Volga and it's only about fifty miles. The worst stretch is east of Volga and the train crews are working at that. If we clear the rest of the way for them, we ought to come back with the regular train day after tomorrow.'

He was putting on an extra pair of woollen socks while he talked. He wound the wide muffler around his neck, crossed it on his chest, and buttoned his overcoat snugly over it. He fastened his ear muffs, put on his warmest mittens, and then with his shovel on his shoulder he went to the depot.

It was almost schooltime but, instead of hurrying to school, Laura and Carrie stood in Second Street watching Pa set out on his trip.

The handcar was standing on the track by the depot and men were climbing on to it as Pa came up.

'All ready, Ingalls! All aboard!' they called. The north wind blowing over the dazzling snow brought every word to Laura and Carrie.

Pa was on the car in a moment. 'Let's go, boys!' he gave the word as he gripped a handbar.

Mr Fuller and Mr Mead and Mr Hinz took their places in a row, facing Pa and Mr Wilmarth and Royal Wilder. All their mittened hands were on the two long wooden handlebars that crossed the handcar, with the pump between them.

'All ready, boys! Let 'er go gallagher!' Mr Fuller sang out and he and Mr Mead and Mr Hinz bent low, pushing down their handlebar. Then as their heads and their handlebar came up, Pa and the other two bent down, pushing their handlebar. Down and up, down and up, the rows of men bent and straightened as if they were bowing low to each other in turn, and the handcar's wheels began slowly to turn and then to roll rapidly along the track towards Volga. And as they pumped, Pa began to sing and all the others joined in:

> 'We'll *ROLL* the O-old *CHAR*iot a*LONG*,
> We'll *ROLL* the O-old *CHAR*iot a*LONG*,
> We'll *ROLL* the O-old *CHAR*iot a*LONG*.
> And we *WON'T* drag *ON* be*HIND!*'

Up and down, up and down, all the backs moved evenly with the song and smoothly rolled the wheels, faster and faster.

> 'If the sinner's in the way,
> We will stop and take him in,
> And we *WON'T* drag *ON* be*HIND!*

We'll *ROLL* the O-old *CHAR*iot a*LONG*,
We'll *ROLL* the O-old *CHAR* –'

Bump! and the handcar was stuck fast in a snowbank.

'All off!' Mr Fuller sang out. 'Not this time, we don't roll it over!'

Picking up their shovels, all the men stepped down from the handcar. Bright snow dust flew in the wind from chunks of snow flung away by their busy shovels.

'We ought to be getting to school,' Laura said to Carrie.

'Oh please, let's wait just a minute more and see . . .' Carrie said, gazing with squinting eyes across the glittering snow at Pa hard at work in front of the handcar.

In a moment or two all the men stepped on to it again, laying down their shovels and bending to the handlebars.

> 'If the Devil's in the way,
> We will roll it over him,
> And we *WON'T* drag ON be*HIND!*'

Smaller and smaller grew the dark handcar and the two rows of men bowing in turn to each other, and fainter and fainter the song came back over the glittering snowfields.

> 'We'll roll – the o-old – chariot along,
> We'll roll – the o-old – chariot along,
> We'll roll – the o-old – chariot along,
> And we won't drag on behind . . .'

Singing and pumping, rolling the car along, shovelling its way through snowbanks and cuts, Pa went away to Volga.

All the rest of the day and all the next day there was an emptiness in the house. Morning and evening Mr Foster did the chores and, after he had left the stable, Ma sent Laura to make sure that he had done them properly. 'Surely Pa will be home tomorrow,' Ma said on Thursday night.

At noon the next day the long, clear train whistle sounded over the snow-covered prairie, and from the kitchen window Laura and Carrie saw the black smoke billowing on the sky and the roaring train coming beneath it. It was the work-train, crowded with singing, cheering men.

'Help me get the dinner on, Laura,' Ma said. 'Pa will be hungry.'

Laura was taking up the biscuits when the front door opened and Pa called, 'Look, Caroline! See who's come home with me?'

Grace stopped her headlong rush towards Pa and backed, staring, her fingers in her mouth. Ma put her gently aside as she stepped to the doorway with the dish of mashed potatoes in her hand.

'Why, Mr Edwards!' Ma said.

'I told you we'd see him again, after he saved our homestead for us,' said Pa.

Ma set the potatoes on the table. 'I have wanted so much to thank you for helping Mr Ingalls file on his claim,' she said to Mr Edwards.

Laura would have known him anywhere. He was the same tall, lean, lounging wildcat from Tennessee. The laughing lines in his leather-brown face were deeper, a knife scar was on his cheek that had not been there before, but his eyes were as laughing and lazy and keen as she remembered them. 'Oh, Mr Edwards!' she cried out.

'You brought our presents from Santa Claus,' Mary remembered.

'You swam the creek,' Laura said. 'And you went away down the Verdigris river . . .'

Mr Edwards scraped his foot on the floor and bowed low. 'Mrs Ingalls and girls, I surely am glad to see you all again.'

He looked into Mary's eyes that did not see him and his voice was gentle when he said, 'Are these two handsome young ladies your small little girls that I dandled on my knee, Ingalls, down on the Verdigris?'

Mary and Laura said that they were and that Carrie had been the baby then.

'Grace is our baby now,' Ma said, but Grace would not go to meet Mr Edwards. She would only stare at him and hang on to Ma's skirts.

'You're just in time, Mr Edwards,' Ma said hospitably. 'I'll have dinner on the table in one minute,' and Pa urged, 'Sit right up, Edwards, and don't be bashful! There's plenty of it, such as it is!'

Mr Edwards admired the well-built, pleasant house and heartily enjoyed the good dinner. But he said he was going on West with the train when it pulled out. Pa could not persuade him to stay longer.

'I'm aiming to go far West in the spring,' he said. 'This here country, it's too settled-up for me. The politicians are a-swarming in already, and ma'am if'n there's any worst pest than grasshoppers it surely is politicians. Why, they'll tax the lining out'n a man's pockets to keep up these here county-seat towns! I don't see nary use for a county, nohow. We all got along happy and content without 'em.

'Feller come along and taxed me last summer. Told me I got to put in every last least thing I had. So I put in Tom and Jerry, my horses, at fifty dollars apiece, and my oxen yoke, Buck and Bright, I put in at fifty, and my cow at thirty-five.

' "Is that all you got?" he says. Well, I told him I'd put in five children I reckoned was worth a dollar apiece.

' "Is that all?" he says. "How about your wife?" he says.

' "By Mighty!" I says to him. "She says I don't own her and I don't aim to pay no taxes on her," I says. And I didn't.'

'Why, Mr Edwards, it is news to us that you have a family,' said Ma. 'Mr Ingalls said nothing of it.'

'I didn't know it myself,' Pa explained. 'Anyway, Edwards, you don't have to pay taxes on your wife and children.'

'He wanted a big tax list,' said Mr Edwards. 'Politicians, they take pleasure a-prying into a man's affairs and I aimed to please 'em. It makes no matter. I don't aim to pay taxes. I sold the relinquishment on my claim and in the spring when the collector comes around I'll be gone from there. Got no children and no wife, nohow.'

Before Pa or Ma could speak, the train whistle blew

loud and long. 'There's the call,' said Mr Edwards, and got up from the table.

'Change your mind and stay awhile, Edwards,' Pa urged him. 'You always brought us luck.'

But Mr Edwards shook hands all around and last with Mary who sat beside him.

'Good-bye all!' he said, and going quickly out of the door he ran towards the depot.

Grace had looked and listened wide-eyed all the time without trying to say a word. Now that Mr Edwards had vanished so suddenly, she took a deep breath and asked, 'Mary, was that the man who saw Santa Claus?'

'Yes,' Mary said. 'That was the man who walked to Independence, forty miles, in the rain and saw Santa Claus there and brought back the Christmas presents for Laura and me when we were little girls.'

'He has a heart of gold,' said Ma.

'He brought us each a tin cup and a stick of candy,' Laura remembered. She got up slowly and began to help Ma and Carrie clear the table. Pa went to his big chair by the stove.

Mary lifted her handkerchief from her lap, as she started to leave the table, and something fluttered to the floor. Ma stooped to pick it up. She stood holding it, speechless, and Laura cried, 'Mary! A twenty dollar – you dropped a *twenty dollar bill*!'

'I couldn't!' Mary exclaimed.

'That Edwards,' said Pa.

'We can't keep it,' Ma said. But clear and long came the last farewell whistle of the train.

'What will you do with it, then?' Pa asked. 'Edwards is gone and we likely won't see him again for years, if ever. He is going to Oregon in the spring.'

'But, Charles . . . Oh, why did he do it?' Ma softly cried out in distress.

'He gave it to Mary,' said Pa. 'Let Mary keep it. It will help her go to college.'

Ma thought for a moment, then said, 'Very well,' and she gave the bill to Mary.

Mary held it carefully, touching it with her finger-tips, and her face shone. 'Oh, I do *thank* Mr Edwards.'

'I hope he never has need of it himself, wherever he goes,' said Ma.

'Trust Edwards to look out for himself,' Pa assured her.

Mary's face was dreamy with the look it had when she was thinking of the college for the blind. 'Ma,' she said, 'with the money you made keeping boarders last year, this makes thirty-five dollars and twenty-five cents.'

12

Alone

On Saturday the sun was shining and the wind was blowing softly from the south. Pa was hauling hay from the homestead, for the cow and the horses must eat a great deal of hay to keep themselves warm in cold weather.

In the sunshine from the western windows Mary rocked gently, and Laura's steel knitting needles flashed. Laura was knitting lace, of fine white thread, to trim a petticoat. She sat close to the window and watched the street, for she was expecting Mary Power and Minnie Johnson. They were coming to spend the afternoon, bringing their crocheting.

Mary was talking about the college that perhaps someday she could go to.

'I am keeping up with you in your lessons, Laura,' she said. 'I do wish, if I do go to college, that you could go, too.'

'I suppose I'll be teaching school,' Laura said, 'so I couldn't go anyway. And I guess you care more about it than I do.'

'Oh, I do care about it!' Mary softly exclaimed. 'I want

it more than *anything*. There's so much to learn, I always wanted to go studying on and on. And to think that I can, if we can save the money, even now that I'm blind. Isn't it wonderful?'

'Yes, it is,' Laura agreed soberly. She did hope that somehow Mary could go. 'Oh, bother! I've miscounted the stitches!' she exclaimed. She unravelled the row and began to pick the tiny stitches up again on the fine needle.

'Well,' she said, '"The Lord helps them that help themselves" and you surely will go to college, Mary, if . . .' She forgot what she was saying. The little loops of thread were dimming before her eyes as if she were going blind. She could not see them. The spool of thread dropped from her lap and rolled away on the floor as she jumped up.

113

'What's the matter?' Mary cried out.

'The light's gone!' Laura said. There was no sunshine. The air was grey and the note of the wind was rising. Ma came hurrying in from the kitchen.

'It's storming, girls!' she had time to say, then the house shook as the storm struck it. The darkening store fronts across the street disappeared in a whirl of snow. 'Oh, I wish Charles had got home!' Ma said.

Laura turned from the window. She drew Mary's chair over to the heater, and from the coal hod she shovelled more coal on the fire. Suddenly the storm wind howled into the kitchen. The back door slammed hard and Pa came in, snowy and laughing.

'I beat the blizzard to the stable by the width of a gnat's eyebrow!' he laughed. 'Sam and David stretched out and came lickety-split! We made it just in the nick of time! This is one blizzard that got fooled!'

Ma took his coat and folded it to carry the snow out to the lean-to. 'Just so you're here, Charles,' she murmured.

Pa sat down and leaned to the heater, holding out his hands to warm them. But he was uneasily listening to the wind. Before long he started up from his chair.

'I'm going to do the chores before this gets any worse,' he said. 'It may take me some time but don't worry, Caroline. Your clothesline'll hold and get me back all right.'

He was gone till dark and longer. Supper was waiting

when he came in, stamping his feet and rubbing his ears.

'Gosh all hemlock! but it's growing cold fast!' he exclaimed. 'The snow strikes like buckshot. And listen to that wind howl!'

'I suppose this is blocking the trains?' Ma said.

'Well, we've lived without a railroad,' Pa answered cheerfully, but he gave Ma the look that warned her to say no more about it while the girls were listening. 'We're snug and warm, as we've been before without even the people and the stores,' he went on. 'Now let's have that hot supper!'

'And after supper, Pa, you'll play the fiddle, won't you?' Laura said. 'Please.'

So after supper Pa called for his fiddle and Laura brought it to him. But when he had tuned the strings and rosined the bow he played a strange melody. The fiddle moaned a deep, rushing undertone and wild notes flickered high above it, rising until they thinned away in nothingness, only to come wailing back, the same notes but not quite the same, as if they had been changed while out of hearing.

Queer shivers tingled up Laura's backbone and prickled over her scalp, and still the wild, changing melody came from the fiddle till she couldn't bear it and cried, 'What is it, Pa? Oh, what is that tune?'

'Listen.' Pa stopped playing and held his bow still, above the strings. 'The tune is outdoors. I was only following it.'

They all listened to the winds playing that tune until Ma said, 'We will likely hear enough of that without your playing it, Charles.'

'We'll have something different, then,' Pa agreed. 'What'll it be?'

'Something to warm us up,' Laura asked, and the fiddle, gay and bright, began to warm them up. Pa played and sang, 'Little Annie Rooney is My Sweetheart!' and 'The Old Grey Mare, She Ain't what She Used to Be', till even Ma's toes were keeping time to it. He played the Highland Fling, and Irish jigs, and out on the clickety-clattering floor Laura and Carrie danced till their breath was gone.

When Pa laid the fiddle in the box he meant that now was bedtime.

It was hard to leave the warm room and go upstairs. Laura knew that in the cold up there every nail-point that came through the roof was fuzzy with frost. The downstairs windows were thickly covered with it, but somehow those frosty nails made her feel much colder.

She wrapped the two hot flatirons in their flannels and led the way. Mary and Carrie followed. Upstairs the air was so cold that it shrivelled the insides of their noses, while they unbuttoned and dropped their shoes and shivered out of their dresses.

'God will hear us if we say our prayers under the covers,' Mary chattered, and she crawled between the cold blankets.

There had not been time for the hot irons to warm the beds. In the still cold under the frosty-nailed roof, Laura could feel the quivering of the bedsteads that Mary and Carrie were shaking in. The deep roar and the shrill wild cries of the winds were all around that little space of stillness.

'What in the world are you doing, Laura?' Mary called. 'Hurry and come help warm the bed!'

Laura could not answer without unclenching her teeth to rattle. She stood at the window in her nightdress and stocking-feet. She had scraped away the frost from a place on the glass and she was trying to look through it. She cupped her hands beside her eyes to shield them from the glimmer of lamplight that came up from the stairway. But still she could see nothing. In the roaring night outside, there was not one speck of light.

At last she crawled in beside Mary and curled up tightly, pressing her feet against the warm flatiron.

'I was trying to see a light,' she explained. 'There must be a light in some house.'

'Didn't you?' Mary asked.

'No,' Laura said. She had not been able even to see the light from the window downstairs where she knew the lamp was shining.

Carrie was quiet in her bed by the stovepipe that came up from the hot stove below. It helped to warm her and she had a hot flatiron too. She was fast asleep when Ma came up to tuck Grace in beside her.

'Are you warm enough, girls?' Ma whispered, bending over the bed and snuggling the covers more closely around them.

'We're getting warm, Ma,' Laura answered.

'Then good-night and sweet dreams.'

But even after Laura was warm she lay awake listening to the wind's wild tune and thinking of each little house, in town, alone in the whirling snow with not even a light from the next house shining through. And the little town was alone on the wide prairie. Town and prairie were lost in the wild storm which was neither earth nor sky, nothing but fierce winds and a blank whiteness.

For the storm was white. In the night, long after the sun had gone and the last daylight could not possibly be there, the blizzard was whirling white.

A lamp could shine out through the blackest darkness and a shout could be heard a long way, but no light and no cry could reach through a storm that had wild voices and an unnatural light of its own.

The blankets were warm and Laura was no longer cold but she shivered.

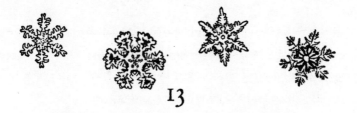

13

We'll Weather the Blast

Mixed with those wild voices, Laura heard the clatter of stove lids and Pa's singing, 'Oh, I am as happy as a big sunflower that nods and bends in the breezes, Oh!'

'Caroline!' Pa called up the stairs, 'the fires will be going well by the time you get down here. I'm going to the stable.'

Laura heard Ma stirring. 'Lie still, girls,' she said. 'No need for you to get up till the house is warmer.'

It was terribly cold outside the bedcovers. But the roaring and shrilling of the storm would not let Laura sleep again. The frosted nails in the roof above her were like white teeth. She lay under them only a few minutes before she followed Ma downstairs.

The fire was burning brightly in the cookstove, and in the front room the heater's side was red-hot, but still the rooms were cold and so dark that it did not seem to be daytime.

Laura broke the ice on the water in the water pail. She filled the washbasin and set it on the stove. Then she and Ma waited, shivering, for the water to warm so that they could wash their faces. Laura had begun to like living in town but this was the same old wintertime.

When Pa came in, his whiskers were blown full of snow and his nose and ears were cherry-red.

'Jerusalem crickets! This is a humdinger!' he exclaimed. 'Good thing the stable is tight. I had to dig my way into it. Snow was packed as high as the door. Lucky I put your clothesline where I did, Caroline. I had to come back to the lean-to to get the shovel, but there was the clothesline to hang on to. Hot pancakes and fried pork look good to me! I'm hungry as a wolf.'

The water was warm in the washbasin for him, and while he washed and combed his hair at the bench by the door, Laura set the chairs to the table and Ma poured the fragrant tea.

The hot cakes were good, with crisped slices of fat pork and the brown-and-amber grease from the pan, and dried-apple sauce and sugar syrup besides. There was no butter, for Ellen was nearly dry, and Ma divided last night's milk between Grace's cup and Carrie's.

'Let's be thankful for the little milk we have,' she said, 'because there'll be less before there's more.'

They were chilly at the table so, after breakfast, they all gathered around the heater. In silence they listened to the winds and the sound of snow driven against the walls and the windows. Ma roused herself with a little shake.

'Come, Laura. Let's get the work done. Then we

can sit by the fire with an easy conscience.'

In that well-built house it was strange that the fire did not warm the kitchen. While Ma put the beans to parboil and Laura washed the dishes, they wondered how cold it was now in the claim shanty. Ma put more coal on the fire and took the broom and Laura shivered at the foot of the stairs. She must go up to make the beds, but the cold came down the stairs and went through her woollen dress and petticoats and red flannels as if she were standing there in her bare skin.

'We'll leave the beds open to air, Laura,' said Ma. 'They're upstairs out of sight and you can do them when the house warms up.'

She finished sweeping and the kitchen work was done. They went back to the front room and sitting down they put their cold feet on the footrest of the heater to warm.

Pa went into the kitchen and came back in his big coat and muffler, his cap in his hand.

'I'm going across the street to Fuller's to hear the news,' he said.

'Must you, Charles?' Ma asked him.

'Somebody may be lost,' he answered. Putting on his cap he went to the door, but paused to say, 'Don't worry about me! I know how many steps it takes to cross the street, and if I don't strike a building then, I'll go no farther away till I do find one.' He shut the door behind him.

Laura stood at the window. She had cleared a peephole through the frost but she saw only blank whiteness. She could not see Pa at the door nor tell when he left it. She went slowly back to the heater. Mary sat silently rocking Grace. Laura and Carrie just sat.

'Now, girls!' Ma said. 'A storm outdoors is no reason for gloom in the house.'

'What good is it to be in town?' Laura said. 'We're just as much by ourselves as if there wasn't any town.'

'I hope you don't expect to depend on anybody else, Laura.' Ma was shocked. 'A body can't do that.'

'But if we weren't in town Pa wouldn't have to go out in this blizzard to find out if somebody else is lost.'

'Be that as it may be,' Ma said firmly, 'it is time for our Sunday school lessons. We will each say the verse we learned this week and then we'll see how many of the old lessons we remember.'

First Grace, then Carrie, then Laura and Mary, and Ma repeated their verses.

'Now Mary,' Ma said, 'you tell us a verse, then Laura will do the same, and then Carrie. See which one can keep on longest.'

'Oh, Mary will win,' Carrie said, discouraged before she began.

'Come on! I'll help you,' Laura urged.

'Two against one isn't fair,' Mary objected.

'It is too fair!' Laura contradicted. 'Isn't it, Ma? When

Mary's been learning Bible verses so much longer than Carrie has.'

'Yes,' Ma decided. 'I think it is fair enough but Laura must only prompt Carrie.'

So they began, went on and on until Carrie could remember no more even when Laura prompted her. Then Mary and Laura went on, against each other, until at last Laura had to give up.

She hated to admit that she was beaten, but she had to. 'You beat me, Mary. I can't remember another one.'

'Mary won! Mary won!' Grace cried, clapping her hands and Ma said, smiling, to Mary, 'That's my bright girl.'

They all looked at Mary who was looking at nothing with her large, beautiful blue eyes that had no sight in them. She smiled with joy when Ma praised her and then her face changed as the light does when a blizzard comes. For a minute she looked as she used to look when she could see, and she and Laura were quarrelling. She never would give up to Laura because she was the older and the boss.

Then her whole face blushed pink and in a low voice she said, 'I didn't beat you, Laura. We're even. I can't remember another verse, either.'

Laura was ashamed. She had tried so hard to beat Mary at a game, but no matter how hard she tried she could never be as good as Mary was. Mary was truly good. Then for the first time Laura wanted to be a schoolteacher so that she could make the money to send Mary to college. She thought, 'Mary is going to college, no matter how hard I have to work to send her.'

At that moment the clock struck eleven times.

'My goodness, the dinner!' Ma exclaimed. She hurried into the kitchen to stir up the fire and season the bean soup. 'Better put more coal in the heater, Laura,' she called. 'Seems like the house hasn't warmed up like it should have.'

It was noon when Pa came in. He came in quietly and went to the heater where he took off his coat and cap. 'Hang these up for me, will you, Laura? I'm pretty cold.'

'I'm sorry, Charles,' Ma said from the kitchen. 'I can't seem to get the house warm.'

'No wonder,' Pa answered. 'It's forty degrees below zero and this wind is driving the cold in. This is the worst storm yet, but luckily everyone is accounted for. Nobody's lost from town.'

After dinner Pa played hymn tunes on his fiddle, and all the afternoon they sang. They sang:

> 'There's a land that is fairer than day,
> And by faith we can see it afar . . .'

And:

> 'Jesus is a rock in a weary land,
> A weary land, a weary land,
> Jesus is a rock in a weary land,
> A shelter in the time of storm.'

They sang Ma's favourite, 'There is a Happy Land, Far, Far Away'. And just before Pa laid the fiddle in its box because the time had come when he must get to the stable and take care of the stock, he played a gallant, challenging tune that brought them all to their feet, and they all sang lustily,

> 'Then let the hurricane roar!
> It will the sooner be o'er.
> We'll weather the blast
> And land at last
> On Canaan's happy shore!'

The hurricane was roaring, the icy snow as hard as buckshot and fine as sand was whirling, swirling, beating upon the house.

14

One Bright Day

That blizzard lasted two days. On Tuesday morning Laura woke up suddenly. She lay with her eyes wide open, listening to hear again what had awakened her. There was no sound at all. Then she knew. The stillness had startled her awake. There was no noise of winds, no swish! swish! of icy snow scouring the walls and roof and window.

The sun was glowing bright through the frost on the window at the top of the stairs, and downstairs Ma's smile was like sunshine.

'The blizzard's over,' she said. 'It was only a two days' blizzard.'

'You never can tell what a blizzard will do,' Pa agreed.

'It may be that your hard winter won't prove to be so hard after all,' Ma said happily. 'Now the sun is shining, they should have the trains running again in no time, and, Laura, I'm sure there will be school today. Better get yourself ready for it while I get breakfast.'

126

Laura went upstairs to tell Carrie and to put on her school dress. In the warm kitchen again she scrubbed her face and neck well with soap and pinned up her braids. Pa breezed in gaily from doing the chores.

'Old Sol's bright and shining this morning!' he told them. 'Looks like his face was well washed in snow.'

Hashed brown potatoes were on the table and Ma's wild ground-cherry preserves shone golden in a glass bowl. Ma stacked a platter with toast browned in the oven, and then took from the oven a small dish of butter.

'I had to warm the butter,' she said. 'It was frozen as hard as a rock. I could not cut it. I hope Mr Boast brings us some more soon. This is what the cobbler threw at his wife.'

Grace and Carrie were puzzled, while all the others laughed. It showed how happy Ma was that she would make jokes.

'That was his awl,' Mary said. And Laura exclaimed, 'Oh, no! It was the last. That was all he had.'

'Girls, girls,' Ma said gently because they were laughing too much at the table. Then Laura said, 'But I thought we were out of butter when we didn't have any yesterday.'

'Pancakes were good with salt pork,' said Ma. 'I saved the butter for toast.' There was just enough butter for a scraping on every slice.

Breakfast was so merry in the warmth and stillness and light that the clock was striking half past eight before they finished, and Ma said, 'Run along, girls. This one time I'll do your housework.'

The whole outdoors was dazzling, sparkling brightly in bright sunshine. All the length of Main Street was a high drift of snow, a ridge taller than Laura. She and Carrie had to climb to its top and get carefully down its other side. The snow was packed so hard that their shoes made no marks on it and their heels could dig no dents to keep them from slipping.

In the schoolyard was another glittering drift almost as high as the schoolhouse. Cap Garland and Ben and Arthur and the little Wilmarth boys were skating down it on their shoes, as Laura used to slide on Silver Lake, and Mary Power and Minnie were standing out in the cold sunshine by the door watching the fun the boys were having.

'Hello, Laura!' Mary Power said gladly, and she tucked her mittened hand under Laura's arm and squeezed it. They were pleased to see each other again. It seemed a long time since Friday, and even since the Saturday afternoon that they had meant to spend together. But there was no time to talk, for Teacher came to the door and girls and boys must go in to their lessons.

At recess Mary Power and Laura and Minnie stood at the window and watched the boys sliding down the snowdrift. Laura wished she could go outdoors to play too.

'I wish we weren't too big now,' she said. 'I don't think it's any fun being a young lady.'

'Well, we can't help growing up,' Mary Power said.

'What would you do if you were caught in a blizzard, Mary?' Minnie Johnson was asking.

'I guess I would just keep on walking. You wouldn't freeze if you kept on walking,' Mary answered.

'But you'd tire yourself out. You'd get so tired you'd die,' said Minnie.

'Well, what would you do?' Mary Power asked her.

'I'd dig into a snowbank and let the snow cover me up. I don't think you'd freeze to death in a snow bank. Would you Laura?'

'I don't know,' Laura said.

'Well, what would you do, Laura, if you got caught in a blizzard?' Minnie insisted.

'I wouldn't get caught,' Laura answered. She did not like to think about it. She would rather talk with Mary Power about other things. But Miss Garland rang the bell and the boys came trooping in, red with the cold and grinning.

That whole day long everyone was as cheerful as the sunshine. At noon Laura and Mary Power and Carrie, with the Beardsley girls, raced in the shouting crowd over the big snowdrifts home to dinner. On top of the high drift that was Main Street, some went north and some went south and Laura and Carrie slid down its east side to their own front door.

Pa was already in his place at the table, Mary was lifting Grace on to the pile of books in her chair, and Ma was setting a dish of steaming baked potatoes before Pa. 'I do wish we had some butter for them,' she said.

'Salt brings out the flavour,' Pa was saying, when a loud knocking sounded on the kitchen door. Carrie ran to open it and, big and furry as a bear in his buffalo coat, Mr Boast came in.

'Come in, Boast! Come in, come in!' Pa kept saying. They were so glad to see him. 'Come in and put your feet under the table. You're just in time!'

'Where is Mrs Boast?' Mary inquired.

'Yes, indeed! Didn't she come with you?' Ma said eagerly.

Mr Boast was getting out of his wraps. 'Well, no. You see, Ellie thought she must do the washing while the sun shone. I told her we'll have more good days but she said then she'd come to town on one of *them*. She sent you some butter. It's from our last churning. My cows are going dry. The weather we've been having, I couldn't take care of them.'

Mr Boast sat up to the table and they all began on the good baked potatoes, with butter, after all.

'Glad to know you came through the storm all right,' Pa said.

'Yes, we were lucky. I was watering the stock at the well when the cloud came up. I hurried them in, had them all snug in the stable and got half-way to the house before the storm struck,' Mr Boast told them.

The baked potatoes and hot biscuits with butter were delicious, and to finish the dinner there were more biscuits with some of Ma's rich tomato preserves.

'There's no more salt pork in town,' Pa said. 'Getting all our supplies from the East, this way, we run a little short when the trains don't get through.'

'What do you hear about the train?' Mr Boast asked him.

'They've put extra gangs to work on the Tracy cut, Woodworth says,' Pa replied. 'And they're bringing out snowploughs. We can look for a train before the end of the week.'

'Ellie's counting on my getting some tea and sugar and flour,' said Mr Boast. 'The storekeepers raising price any?'

'Not that I know of,' Pa reassured him. 'Nothing's running short but meat.'

Dinner was eaten and Mr Boast said he must be getting along to reach home before night. He promised to bring Mrs Boast in to see them all one day soon. Then he and Pa went up Main Street to Harthorn's grocery and Laura and Carrie, hand in hand, went joyously climbing up the drifts and sliding down them, back to school.

All that happy afternoon they were full of the clear, cold air and as bright as the sunshine. They knew their lessons perfectly, they enjoyed reciting them. Every face in school was smiling, and Cap Garland's flashing grin included them all.

It was good to see the town alive again and to know that again all the weekdays would be school days.

But in the night Laura dreamed that Pa was playing the wild storm-tune on his fiddle and when she screamed to him to stop, the tune was a blinding blizzard swirling around her and it had frozen her to solid ice.

Then she was staring at the dark, but for a long time that nightmare held her stiff and cold. It was not Pa's fiddle she heard, but the stormwind itself and the swish! swish! of icy snow on the walls and the roof. At last she was able to move. So cold that the dream still seemed half real, she snuggled close to Mary and pulled the quilts over their heads.

'What is it?' Mary murmured in her sleep.

'A blizzard,' Laura answered.

15

No Trains

It was not worth while to get up in the morning. The daylight was dim, the windows were white and so were the nails in the roof. Another blizzard was roaring, screaming, and swishing around the house. There would be no school.

Laura lay sluggish and half awake. She would rather sleep than wake up to such a day. But Ma called, 'Good morning, girls! Time to get up!'

Quickly, because of the cold, Laura put on her dress and her shoes and went downstairs.

'Why, what is the trouble, Laura?' Ma asked, looking up from the stove.

Laura almost wailed, 'Oh Ma! How can I ever teach school and help send Mary to college? How can I ever amount to anything when I can get only one day of school at a time?'

'Now Laura,' Ma said kindly. 'You must not be so

easily discouraged. A few blizzards more or less can make no great difference. We will hurry and get the work done, then you can study. There is enough figuring in your arithmetic to keep you busy for a good many days, and you can do as much of it as you want to. Nothing keeps you from learning.'

Laura asked, 'Why is the table here in the kitchen?' The table left hardly room to move about.

'Pa didn't build the fire in the heater this morning,' Ma answered.

They heard Pa stamping in the lean-to and Laura opened the door for him. He looked sober. The little milk in the pail was frozen solid.

'This is the worst yet, I do believe,' Pa said while he held his stiff hands over the stove. 'I didn't start a fire in the heater, Caroline. Our coal is running low, and this storm will likely block the trains for some time.'

'I thought as much when I saw you hadn't built the fire.' Ma answered. 'So I moved the table in here. We'll keep the middle door shut and the cookstove warms this room nicely.'

'I'll go over to Fuller's right after breakfast,' said Pa. He ate quickly and while he was putting on his wraps again Ma went upstairs. She brought down her little red Morocco pocketbook, with the shining, smooth mother-of-pearl sides and the steel clasps, in which she kept Mary's college money.

Pa slowly put out his hand and took it. Then he cleared his throat and said, 'Mary, it may be the town's running short of supplies. If the lumberyard and the stores are putting up prices too high . . .'

He did not go on and Mary said, 'Ma has my college money put away. You could spend that.'

'If I do have to, Mary, you can depend on my paying it back,' Pa promised.

After he had gone, Laura brought Mary's rocking chair from the cold front room and set it to warm before the open oven. As soon as Mary sat in it Grace climbed into her lap.

'I'll be warm, too,' Grace said.

'You're a big girl now and too heavy,' Ma objected, but Mary said quickly, 'Oh no, Grace! I like to hold you, even if you are a big three-year-old girl.'

The room was so crowded that Laura could hardly wash the dishes without bumping into some sharp edge. While Ma was making the beds in the upstairs cold, Laura polished the stove and cleaned the lamp chimney. Then she unscrewed the brass chimney holder and filled the lamp carefully with kerosene. The last clear drop poured out from the spout of the kerosene can.

'Oh! we didn't tell Pa to get kerosene!' Laura exclaimed before she thought.

'Don't we have kerosene?' Carrie gasped, turning around quickly from the cupboard where she was putting away the dishes. Her eyes were frightened.

'My goodness, yes, I've filled the lamp brimful,' Laura answered. 'Now I'll sweep the floor and you dust.'

All the work was done when Ma came downstairs. 'The wind is fairly rocking the house up there,' she told them, shivering by the stove. 'How nicely you have done everything, Laura and Carrie,' she smiled.

Pa had not come back, but surely he could not be lost, in town.

Laura brought her books and slate to the table, close to Mary in her rocking chair. The light was poor but Ma did not light a lamp. Laura read the arithmetic problems one by one to Mary, and did them on the slate while Mary solved them in her head. They worked each problem backward to make sure that they had the correct answer. Slowly they worked lesson after lesson and as Ma had said, there were many more to come.

At last they heard Pa coming through the front room. His overcoat and cap were frozen white with snow and he carried a snowy package. He thawed by the stove and when he could speak, he said, 'I didn't use your college money, Mary.

'There's no coal at the lumberyard,' he went on. 'People burned so much in this cold weather and Ely didn't have much on hand. He's selling lumber to burn now, but we can't afford to burn lumber at fifty dollars a thousand.'

'People are foolish to pay it,' Ma said gently. 'Trains are bound to get through before long.'

'There is no more kerosene in town,' Pa said. 'And no meat. The stores are sold out of pretty nearly everything. I got two pounds of tea, Caroline, before they ran out of that. So we'll have our bit of tea till the trains come through.'

'There's nothing like a good cup of tea in cold weather,' said Ma. 'And the lamp is full. That's enough kerosene to last quite awhile if we go to bed early to save coal. I am so glad you thought to get the tea. We would miss that!'

Slowly Pa grew warm and without saying anything more he sat down by the window to read the *Chicago Inter-Ocean* that had come in the last mail.

'By the way,' he said, looking up, 'school is closed until coal comes.'

'We can study by ourselves,' Laura said stoutly. She and Mary murmured to each other over the arithmetic problems, Carrie studied the speller, while Ma worked at her mending and Pa silently read the paper. The blizzard grew worse. It was by far the most violent blizzard that they had ever heard.

The room grew colder. There was no heat from the front room to help the cookstove. The cold had crept into the front room and was sneaking in under the door. Beneath the lean-to door it was crawling in too. Ma brought the braided rugs from the front room and laid them, folded, tightly against the bottoms of the doors.

At noon Pa went to the stable. The stock did not need feeding at noon, but he went to see that the horses and the cow and the big calf were still safely sheltered.

He went out again in mid-afternoon. 'Animals need a lot of feed to keep them warm in such cold,' he explained to Ma. 'The blizzard is worse than it was, and I had a hard tussle this morning to get hay into the stable in these winds. I couldn't do it if the haystack wasn't right at the door. Another good thing, the snowdrifts are gone. They've been scoured away, down to the bare ground.'

The storm howled even louder when he went out into it, and a blast of cold came through the lean-to though Ma had pushed the folded rug against the inner door as soon as Pa shut it.

Mary was braiding a new rug. She had cut worn-out woollen clothes in strips, and Ma had put each colour in a separate box. Mary kept the boxes in order and remembered where each colour was. She was braiding the rag-strips together in a long braid that coiled down in a pile beside her chair. When she came to the end of a strip, she chose the colour she wanted and sewed it on. Now and then she felt the growing pile.

'I do believe I have nearly enough done,' she said. 'I'll be ready for you to sew the rug tomorrow, Laura.'

'I wanted to finish this lace first,' Laura objected. 'And

these storms keep making it so dark I can hardly see to count the stitches.'

'The dark doesn't bother me,' Mary answered cheerfully. 'I can see with my fingers.'

Laura was ashamed of being impatient. 'I'll sew your rug whenever you're ready,' she said willingly.

Pa was gone a long time. Ma set the supper back to keep warm. She did not light the lamp, and they all sat thinking that the clothesline would guide Pa through the blinding blizzard.

'Come, come girls!' Ma said, rousing herself. 'Mary, you start a song. We'll sing away the time until Pa comes.' So they sang together in the dark until Pa came.

There was lamplight at supper, but Ma told Laura to leave the dishes unwashed. They must all go to bed quickly, to save the kerosene and the coal.

Only Pa and Ma got up next morning at chore time. 'You girls stay in bed and keep warm as long as you like,' Ma said, and Laura did not get up until nine o'clock. The cold was pressing on the house and seeping in, rising higher and higher, and the ceaseless noise and the dusk seemed to hold time still.

Laura and Mary and Carrie studied their lessons. Laura sewed the rag braid into a round rug and laid it heavy over Mary's lap so that Mary could see it with her fingers. The rug made this day different from the day before, but Laura felt that it was the same day over again when they sang again in the dark until Pa came and ate the same supper of potatoes and bread with dried-apple sauce and tea and left the dishes unwashed and went to bed at once to save kerosene and coal.

Another day was the same. The blizzard winds did not stop roaring and shrieking, the swishing snow did not stop swishing, the noise and the dark and the cold would never end.

Suddenly they ended. The blizzard winds stopped. It was late in the third afternoon. Laura blew and scraped at the frost on a windowpane till through the peephole she

could see snow scudding down Main Street low to the ground before a straight wind. A reddish light shone on the blowing snow from the setting sun. The sky was clear and cold. Then the rosy light faded, the snow was blowing grey-white, and the steady wind blew harder. Pa came in from doing the chores.

'Tomorrow I must haul some hay,' he said. 'But now I'm going across to Fuller's to find out if anybody but us is alive in this blame town. Here for three whole days we haven't been able to see a light, nor smoke, nor any sign of a living soul. What's the good of a town if a fellow can't get any good of it?'

'Supper's almost ready, Charles,' Ma said.

'I'll be back in a jiffy!' Pa told her.

He came back in a few minutes asking, 'Supper ready?' Ma was dishing it up and Laura setting the chairs to the table.

'Everything's all right in town,' Pa said, 'and word from the depot is that they'll start work tomorrow morning on that big cut this side of Tracy.'

'How long will it take to get a train through?' Ma asked.

'Can't tell,' Pa replied. 'That one clear day we had, they cleaned it out, ready to come through next day. But they shovelled the snow up, both sides of the cut, and now it's packed full, clear to the top of the banks. Something like thirty feet deep of snow, frozen solid, they've got to dig out now.'

'That won't take very long in pleasant weather,' Ma said. 'Surely we're bound to have that. We've already had more, and worse, storms than we had all last winter.'

16

Fair Weather

Morning was bright and clear but there was no school. There would be no more school until the train came bringing coal.

Outdoors the sun was shining but frost was still on the window and the kitchen seemed stale and dull. Carrie gazed out through the peephole in the frost while she wiped the breakfast dishes, and drearily Laura sloshed the cooling water in the dishpan.

'I want to go somewhere!' Carrie said fretfully. 'I'm tired of staying in this old kitchen!'

'We were thankful enough for this warm kitchen yesterday,' Mary gently reminded her. 'And now we may be thankful the blizzard's over.'

'You wouldn't go to school, anyway,' Laura said crossly. She was ashamed as soon as she heard the words, but when Ma said reproachfully, 'Laura,' she felt more cross than before.

'When you girls have finished your work,' Ma went on,

covering the well-kneaded bread and setting it before the oven to rise, 'you may put on your wraps, and Mary may, too, and all go out in the yard for a breath of fresh air.'

That cheered them. Laura and Carrie worked quickly now, and in a little while they were hurrying into their coats and shawls and hoods, mufflers and mittens. Laura guided Mary through the lean-to, and they all burst out into the glittering cold. The sun glare blinded them and the cold took their breath away.

'Throw back your arms and breathe deep, deep!' Laura cried. She knew that cold is not so cold if you are not afraid of it. They threw back their arms and breathed the cold in, and through their cringing noses it rushed deep into their chests and warmed them all over. Even Mary laughed aloud.

'I can smell the snow!' she said. 'So fresh and clean!'

'The sky is bright blue and the whole world is sparkling white,' Laura told her. 'Only the houses stick up out of the snow and spoil it. I wish we were where there aren't any houses.'

'What a dreadful idea,' said Mary. 'We'd freeze to death.'

'I'd build us an igloo,' Laura declared, 'and we'd live like Eskimos.'

'Ugh, on raw fish,' Mary shuddered. 'I wouldn't.'

The snow crunched and creaked under their feet. It was packed so hard that Laura could not scoop up a handful to make a snowball. She was telling Carrie how soft the snow used to be in the Big Woods of Wisconsin when Mary said, 'Who's that coming? It sounds like our horses.'

Pa came riding up to the stable. He was standing on a queer kind of sled. It was a low platform made of new boards and it was as long as a wagon and twice as wide. It had no tongue, but a long loop of chain was fastened to the wide-apart runners and the whiffletrees were fastened to the chain.

'Where did you get that funny sled, Pa?' Laura asked.

'I made it,' Pa said. 'At the lumberyard.' He got his pitchfork from the stable. 'It does look funny,' he admitted. 'But it would hold a whole haystack if the horses could pull it. I don't want to lose any time getting some hay here to feed the stock.'

Laura wanted to ask him if he had any news of the train, but the question would remind Carrie that there was no more coal or kerosene and no meat until a train could come. She did not want to worry Carrie. They were all so brisk and cheery in this bright weather, and if sunny weather lasted for a while the train would come and there would be nothing to worry about.

While she was thinking this, Pa stepped on to the low, big sled.

'Tell your Ma they've brought a snowplough and a full work train out from the East and put them to work at the Tracy cut, Laura,' he said. 'A few days of this fine weather and they'll have the train running all right.'

'Yes, Pa, I'll tell her,' Laura said thankfully, and Pa drove away, around the street corner and out along Main Street towards the homestead.

Carrie sighed a long sigh and cried, 'Let's tell her right away!' From the way she said it, Laura knew that Carrie had been wanting to ask Pa about the train too.

'My, what rosy cheeks!' Ma said when they went into the dusky, warm kitchen. The cold, fresh air shook out of their wraps while they took them off. The heat above the stove made their cold fingers tingle pleasantly, and Ma was glad to hear about the work train and the snowplough.

'This good weather will likely last for some time now, we have had so many storms,' Ma said.

The frost was melting on the window and freezing into thin sheets of ice over the cold glass. With little trouble Laura pried it off and wiped the panes dry. She settled herself in the bright daylight and knitted her lace, looking out now and then at the sunshine on the snow. There was not a cloud in the sky and no reason to worry about Pa though he did not come back as soon as should be expected.

At ten o'clock he had not come. At eleven there was still no sign of him. It was only two miles to the homestead and back, and half an hour should load the shed with hay.

'I wonder what's keeping Pa?' Mary said finally.

'Likely he's found something to do at the claim,' Ma said. She came to the window then and looked at the north-western sky. There was no cloud in it.

'There's no cause to worry,' Ma went on. 'It may be the storms have done some damage to the shanty, but that's soon mended.'

At noon the Saturday baking of bread was out of the oven, three crusty golden hot loaves, and the boiled potatoes were steaming dry and the tea was brewed, and still Pa had not returned.

They were all sure that something had happened to him, though no one said so and no one could think what it might be. The steady old horses would surely not run away. Laura thought of claim jumpers. Pa had no gun if claim jumpers were in the deserted shanty. But claim jumpers could not have come through the blizzards. There were no bears or panthers or wolves or Indians. There was no river to ford.

What could happen to hinder or hurt a man driving gentle horses, in good weather, only a mile in a sled over the snow to the homestead and the same way back again with a load of hay?

Then Pa came driving around the corner of Second Street and by the window. Laura saw him going by, snowy on the mound of snowy hay that hid the sled and seemed to be dragging on the snow. He stopped by the stable, unhitched the horses and put them in their stalls and then came stamping into the lean-to. Laura and Ma had put the dinner on the table.

'By George! that dinner looks good!' said Pa. 'I could eat a raw bear without salt!'

Laura poured hot water from the teakettle into the washbasin for him. Ma said gently, 'Whatever kept you so long, Charles?'

'Grass,' said Pa. He buried his face in his hands full of soapy water and Laura and Ma looked at each other amazed. What did Pa mean? In a minute he reached for the roller towel and went on, 'That confounded grass under the snow.

'You can't follow the road,' Pa went on, wiping his hands. 'There's nothing to go by, no fences or trees. As soon as you get out of town there's nothing but snow-drifts in all directions. Even the lake's covered up. The drifts are packed hard by the wind, and frozen, so the sled slides right along over them and you'd think you could make a beeline to wherever you wanted to go.

'Well, first thing I knew, the team went down to their chins in that hard snow. I'd hit the slough, and the snow looks as hard there as anywhere, but underneath it there's grass. The slough grass holds up that crust of snow on nothing but grass stems and air. As soon as the horses get on to it, down they go.

'I've spent this whole morning rassling with that dumb horse, Sam . . .'

'Charles,' Ma said.

'Caroline,' Pa answered, 'it's enough to make a saint

149

swear. David was all right, he's got horse sense, but Sam went plumb crazy. There those two horses are, down to their backs in snow, and every try they make to get out only makes the hole bigger. If they drag the sled down into it, I never will get it out. So I unhitch the sled. Then I try to get the team up on to hard going again, and there's Sam gone crazy-wild, plunging and snorting and jumping and wallowing all the time deeper into that confounded snow.

'It must have been a job,' Ma agreed.

'He was threshing around so, I was afraid he'd hurt David,' said Pa. 'So I got down into it and unhitched them from each other. I held on to Sam and I tramped the snow down as well as I could, trying to make a hard enough path for him to walk on, up on to the top of the drifts. But he'd rear and plunge and break it down till I tell you it'd wear out any man's patience.'

'Whatever did you do, Charles?' Ma said.

'Oh, I got him out finally,' said Pa. 'David followed me as gentle as a lamb, stepping carefully and coming right on up. So I hitched him on to the sled and he dragged it around the hole. But I had to hang on to Sam all the time. There was nothing to tie him to. Then I hitched them both up together again and started on. We went about a hundred feet and down they went again.'

'Mercy!' Ma exclaimed.

'So that's the way it was,' said Pa. 'The whole morning.

Took me the whole half a day to go a couple of miles and get back with one load of hay, and I'm tireder than if I'd done a hard day's work. I'm going to drive David single this afternoon. He can't haul so big a load but it'll be easier on both of us.'

He ate dinner in a hurry and hurried out to hitch David to the sled alone. Now they knew what Pa was doing and they were not worried, but they were sorry for David, falling through the deceitful snowdrifts, and for Pa, unhitching and helping the horse out and hitching him to the sled again.

Still, the whole afternoon was sunny, without a cloud in the sky, and before dark Pa had hauled two small loads of hay.

'David follows me like a dog,' Pa told them all at supper. 'When he breaks through the snow he stands still until I trample a solid path up. Then he follows me up out of the hole as carefully as if he understood all about it and I bet he does. Tomorrow I'm going to hitch him on to the sled by a long rope, so I won't have to unhitch him when he falls in. I'll only have to help him out and then, on the long rope, he can haul the sled around the hole.'

After supper Pa went to Fuller's Hardware to buy the rope. He came back soon with news. The work train with the snowplough had got half-way through the Tracy cut that day.

'It takes longer this time to get through,' he said,

'because every time they cleared the track they threw the snow up on both sides, making the cut that much deeper. But Woodworth at the depot says they'll likely get a train through by the day after tomorrow.'

'That's good news,' said Ma. 'I'll be thankful to have some meat again.'

'That's not all,' Pa went on. 'We're going to get the mail, train or no train. They're sending it through by team, and Gilbert, the mail carrier, is leaving here for Preston in the morning. He's making a sled now. So if you want to send a letter, you can.'

'There is that letter I've been writing to the folks in Wisconsin,' said Ma. 'I wasn't intending to finish it so soon, but perhaps I may as well.'

So she brought the letter to the tablecloth under the lamp, and after she had thawed the ink bottle they all sat around the table thinking of last things to say while Ma wrote them down with her little red pen that had a mother-of-pearl handle shaped like a feather. When her neat, clear writing filled the paper she turned it and filled it again crosswise. On the other side of the paper she did the same so that every inch of paper held all the words that it possibly could.

Carrie had been only a baby in Wisconsin. She did not remember the aunts and uncles and the cousins Alice and Ella and Peter, and Grace had never seen them. But Laura and Mary remembered them perfectly.

'Tell them I still have my doll, Charlotte,' said Laura, 'and I wish we had one of black Susan's great-great-great-grand kittens.'

' "Descendants" takes less space,' said Ma. 'I'm afraid this letter will be overweight.'

'Tell them there isn't a cat in this whole country,' said Pa.

'I wish to goodness there was,' said Ma. 'We need one for the mice.'

'Tell them we wish they could spend Christmas with us this year like they did in the Big Woods,' said Mary.

' "*As* they did," Mary,' said Ma.

'My goodness!' Laura exclaimed, 'When *is* Christmas? I'd forgotten all about it. It's almost here.'

Grace bounced on Mary's lap and cried. 'When is Christmas coming? When is Santa Claus?'

Mary and Carrie had told her all about Santa Claus. Now Mary did not know what to say to her and neither did Laura. But Carrie spoke up.

'Maybe Santa Claus can't get here this winter, Grace, on account of the storms and the snow,' Carrie said. 'You see, even the train can't.'

'Santa Claus comes on a sled,' Grace said anxiously, looking at them with wide blue eyes. 'He can come, can't he, Pa? Can't he, Ma?'

'Of course he can, Grace,' said Ma. Then Laura said stoutly, 'Santa Claus can come anywhere.'

'Maybe he'll bring us the train,' said Pa.

In the morning he took the letter to the post office and there he saw Mr Gilbert put the mailbag into the sled and drive away, well wrapped in buffalo robes. He had twelve miles to go to Preston.

'He'll meet another team there with mail from the East and bring it back,' Pa explained to Ma. 'He ought to get back tonight, if he doesn't have too much trouble crossing the sloughs.'

'He has good weather for the trip,' Ma said.

'I'd better be taking advantage of it myself,' said Pa.

He went out to harness David to the sled by the long rope. He hauled one load of hay that morning. At noon, while they sat at table, the light darkened and the wind began to howl.

'Here she comes!' Pa said. 'I hope Gilbert has made it safe to Preston.'

17
Seed Wheat

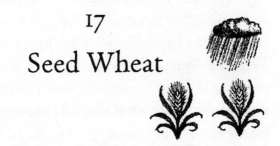

The cold and the dark had come again. The nails in the roof were white with frost, the windowpanes were grey. Scraping a peephole only showed the blank, whirling whiteness against the other side of the glass. The stout house quivered and shook; the wind roared and howled. Ma kept the rag rugs tightly against the bottom of the doors, and the cold came crawling in.

It was hard to be cheerful. Morning and afternoon, holding the clothesline, Pa went to the stable to feed the horses, the cow, and the heifer. He had to be sparing of the hay. He came in so cold that he could hardly get warm. Sitting before the oven, he took Grace on his knee and hugged Carrie close to him, and he told them the stories of bears and panthers that he used to tell Mary and Laura. Then in the evening he took his fiddle and played the merry tunes.

When it was bedtime, and the cold upstairs must be faced, Pa played them up to bed.

'Ready now, all together!' he said. 'Right, left, right, left – March!'

Laura went first, carrying the wrapped hot flatiron, Mary came behind with her hand on Laura's shoulder. Last marched Carrie with the other flatiron and the music went with them up the stairs:

> 'March! March! Eskdale and Liddesdale!
> All the blue bonnets are over the border!
> Many a banner spread flutters about your
>   head
> Many a crest that is famous in story.
> Mount, and make ready then,
> Sons of the mountain glen!
> Fight for your homes and the old Scottish
>   glory!'

It helped a bit. Laura hoped that she seemed cheerful enough to encourage the others. But all the time she knew that this storm had blocked the train again. She knew that almost all the coal was gone from the pile in the lean-to. There was no more coal in town. The kerosene was low in the lamp though Ma lighted it only while they ate supper. There would be no meat until the train came. There was no butter and only a little fat-meat dripping was left to spread on bread. There were still potatoes, but no more than flour enough for one more bread baking.

When Laura had thought all this, she thought that surely a train must come before the last bread was gone. Then she began to think again about the coal, the kerosene, the little bit of dripping left, and the flour in the bottom of the flour sack. But surely, surely, the train must come.

A day and all night, the house trembled, the winds roared and screamed, the snow scoured against the walls and over the roof where the frosty nails came through. In the other houses there were people, there must be lights, but they were too far away to seem real.

In the back room behind the feed store, Almanzo was busy. He had taken saddles, harness, and clothes from the end wall and piled them on the bed. He had pushed the table against the cupboard and in the cleared space he had set a chair for a sawhorse.

He had set a frame of two-by-fours a foot from the end wall. Now he was sawing boards one by one and nailing them on the frame. The rasping of the saw and the hammering were hardly louder than the blizzard's noise.

When he had built the inner wall up halfway, he took out his jackknife and ripped open a sack of his seed wheat. He lifted up the hundred-and-twenty-five-pound sack and carefully let the wheat pour into the space between the new wall and the old one.

'I figure she'll hold it all,' he said to Royal who sat whittling by the stove. 'When I build all the way up so the bin won't show.'

'It's your funeral,' said Royal. 'It's your wheat.'

'You bet your life it's my wheat!' Almanzo replied. 'And it's going into my ground, come spring.'

'What makes you think I'd sell your wheat?' Royal demanded.

'You're pretty near sold out of grain already,' Almanzo answered. 'This blizzard'll let up sometime, or it'll be the first one that didn't, and soon as it does the whole town'll come piling in here to buy wheat. Harthorn and Loftus have got just three sacks of flour left between 'em, and this storm'll hold up the train till after Christmas at best.'

'All that don't mean I'd sell your wheat,' Royal insisted.

'Maybe not, but I know you, Roy. You're not a farmer, you're a storekeeper. A fellow comes in here and looks around and says, "What's the price of your wheat?" You say, "I'm sold out of wheat." He says, "What's that in those sacks?" You tell him, "That's not my wheat, it's Manzo's." So the fellow says, "What'll you boys sell it for?" And don't try to tell me you'll say, "We won't sell it," No, siree, Roy, you're a storekeeper. You'll say to him, "What'll you give?" '

'Well, maybe I would,' Royal admitted. 'What's the harm in that?'

'The harm is that they'll bid up prices sky-high before a train gets through. I'll be out hauling hay or somewhere and you'll figure that I wouldn't refuse such a price, or you'll think you know better than I do what's for my best

interests. You never would believe I mean what I say when I say it, Royal Wilder.'

'Well, well, keep your shirt on, Manzo,' said Royal. 'I am considerable older than you be and maybe I do know best.'

'Maybe you do and maybe you don't. Be that as it may

be, I'm going to run my own business my own way. I'm nailing up my seed wheat so nobody'll see it and nobody'll bring up any question about it and it'll be right here when seedtime comes.'

'All right, all right,' Royal said. He went on carefully whittling a linked chain out of a stick of pine and Almanzo, bracing his legs, lifted the sacks one by one to his shoulder and let the wheat pour into its hiding place. Now and then a heavier blow of the winds shook the walls and now and then the red-hot stove puffed out smoke. A louder roar of the storm made them both listen and Almanzo said, 'Golly, this one's a daisy!'

'Roy,' he said after a while, 'whittle me a plug to fit this knothole, will you? I want to get this job done before chore time.'

Royal came to look at the knothole. He rounded it with his knife and chose a piece of wood that would make a plug to fit.

'If prices go up like you say, you're a fool not to sell your wheat,' he remarked. 'They'll have the train running before spring. You can buy your seed back and make a profit like I'm figuring on doing.'

'You said that before,' Almanzo reminded him. 'I'd rather be sure than sorry. You don't know when the train'll be running and you don't know they'll ship in seed wheat before April.'

'Nothing's sure but death and taxes,' said Royal.

'Seedtime's pretty sure to come around,' Almanzo said. 'And good seed makes a good crop.'

'You talk like Father,' Royal mentioned. He tried the plug against the knothole and set to whittling it again. 'If the train don't get through in a couple of weeks or so, I wonder how this town'll hold out. There's not much left in the grocery stores.'

'Folks manage to get along when they've got to,' said Almanzo. 'Pretty near everybody brought out supplies last summer like we did. And we can make ours stretch till warm weather if we must.'

18

Merry Christmas

The blizzard stopped at last. After three days of its ceaseless noise, the stillness rang in Laura's ears.

Pa hurried away to get a load of hay and when he came back he put David in the stable. The sun was still glittering on the snow, there was no cloud in the north-west, and Laura wondered why he stopped hauling hay.

'What's wrong, Charles?' Ma asked quietly when Pa came in.

Pa answered, 'Gilbert made it to Preston and back. He's brought the mail!'

It was as if Christmas had happened unexpectedly. Ma hoped for the church paper. Laura and Mary and Carrie hoped that Reverend Alden had sent them something to read; sometimes he did. Grace was excited because they were excited. It was hard to wait for Pa to come back from the post office.

He was gone a long time. As Ma said, it did no good to be impatient. Every man in town was at the post office and Pa must wait his turn.

When at last he came, his hands were full. Ma reached

eagerly for the church papers and Laura and Carrie both tried to take the bundle of *Youth's Companions*. There were newspapers too.

'Here! Here!' Pa laughed. 'Don't mob a fellow! And that's not the whole of it. Guess what I got!'

'A letter? Oh Pa, did you get a letter?' Laura cried.

'Who is it from?' Ma asked.

'You've got the *Advances*, Caroline,' Pa replied. 'And Laura and Carrie've got the *Youth's Companions*. I've got the *Inter-Ocean* and the *Pioneer Press*. Mary gets the letter.'

Mary's face shone. She felt the letter's size and thickness. 'A big, fat letter! Please read it, Ma.'

So Ma opened the letter and read it aloud.

The letter was from Reverend Alden. He was sorry that he had not been able to come back and help organize a church last spring, but he had been sent farther north. He hoped to be with them when spring came again. The children of the Sunday School in Minnesota were sending a bundle of *Youth's Companions* to the girls, and would send another bundle next year. His church had shipped them a Christmas barrel and he hoped the clothing would fit. As his own Christmas gift and some slight return for their hospitality to him and to Reverend Stuart last winter at Silver Lake, he had put in a Christmas turkey. He wished them all a Merry Christmas and a Happy New Year.

There was a little silence when Ma had finished reading. Then she said, 'We have this good letter, anyway.'

'Gilbert brought word that they're putting on a double work crew and two snowploughs at the Tracy cut,' Pa told them. 'We may get the barrel by Christmas.'

'It's only a few days,' Ma said.

'A lot can be done in a few days,' said Pa. 'If this spell of clear weather holds out, no reason they can't get the train through.'

'Oh, I hope the Christmas barrel comes,' Carrie said.

'The hotels have shut down,' Pa told Ma the news. 'They've been burning lumber and now Banker Ruth has bought out the lumberyard, down to the last shingle.'

'We couldn't afford to burn lumber anyway,' said Ma. 'But Charles, we are almost out of coal.'

'We'll burn hay,' Pa answered cheerfully.

'Hay?' Ma said, and Laura asked, 'How can we burn hay, Pa?'

She thought of how quickly the prairie fires swept through dry grass. Flame licks through the light, thin stems and is gone before the frail ashes can fall. How could a room be kept warm by a fire so quickly burning out, when even the steady glow of hard coal could not keep out the cold?

'We will have to contrive,' Pa told her. 'We'll manage it! Needs must, when the devil drives.'

'Likely the train will get through in time,' Ma said.

Pa put on his cap again and asked Ma to make dinner a little late. He had time to haul another load of hay if he hustled. He went out and Ma said, 'Come, girls, put the bundle of *Youth's Companions* away. We must get out the washing while the weather's clear.'

All that day Laura and Carrie and Mary looked forward to the *Youth's Companions* and often they spoke of them.

But the bright day was short. They stirred and punched the clothes boiling on the stove; they lifted them on the broom handle into the tub where Ma soaped and rubbed them. Laura rinsed them, Carrie stirred the blueing bag in the second rinse-water until it was blue enough. Laura made the boiled starch. And when for the last time Ma went out into the cold to hang the freezing wash on the line, Pa had come for dinner.

Then they washed the dishes, they scrubbed the floor and blacked the stove, and washed the inside of the windowpanes. Ma brought in the frozen-dry clothes and they sorted them and sprinkled them and rolled them tightly, ready for ironing. Twilight had come. It was too late to read that day and after supper there was no lamplight because they must save the last of the kerosene.

'Work comes before pleasure,' Ma always said. She smiled her gentle smile for Laura and Carrie and said now, 'My girls have helped me do a good day's work,' and they were rewarded.

'Tomorrow we'll read a story,' Carrie said happily.

'Tomorrow we have to do the ironing,' Laura reminded her.

'Yes, and we should air the bedding and give the upstairs a thorough cleaning, in this good weather,' said Ma.

Pa came in and heard them. 'Tomorrow I'm going to work on the railroad,' he said.

Mr Woodworth had word to put at work on the tracks all the men he could get. The superintendent at the Tracy cut was driving the work there and shovel gangs were shovelling eastward from Huron.

'If muscle and will-power can do it, we'll have a train through by Christmas!' Pa declared.

That night he came back from work with a broad smile on his sun-red face. 'Good news!' he called out. 'The work train will come through sometime tomorrow! The regular train'll come next, day after tomorrow probably.'

'Oh, good! Good! Goody!' Laura and Carrie exclaimed together, and Ma said, 'That is good news, indeed. What is wrong with your eyes, Charles?'

His eyes were red and puffed. He answered cheerfully, 'Shovelling snow in the sunshine is hard on eyes. Some of the men are snow-blind. Fix me up a little weak salt-water, will you, Caroline? And I'll bathe them after I do the chores.'

When he had gone to the stable, Ma dropped into a chair near Mary. 'I'm afraid, girls, this will be a poor Christmas,' she said. 'What with these awful storms and trying to keep warm, we've had no time to plan for it.'

'Maybe the Christmas barrel . . .' Carrie began.

'We mustn't count on it,' said Mary.

'We could wait for Christmas till it comes,' Laura suggested. 'All but . . .' and she picked up Grace who was listening wide-eyed.

'Can't Santa Claus come?' Grace asked, and her lower lip began to tremble.

Laura hugged her and looked over her golden head at Ma.

Ma said firmly, 'Santa Claus always comes to good little girls, Grace. But girls,' she went on, 'I have an idea. What do you think of saving my church papers and your bundle of *Youth's Companions* to open on Christmas Day?'

After a moment Mary said, 'I think it is a good idea. It will help us to learn self-denial.'

'I don't want to,' Laura said.

'Nobody does,' said Mary. 'But it's good for us.'

Sometimes Laura did not even want to be good. But after another silent moment she said, 'Well, if you and Mary want to, Ma, I will. It will give us something to look forward to for Christmas.'

'What do you say about it, Carrie?' Ma asked, and in a small voice Carrie said, 'I will, too, Ma.'

'That's my good girls,' Ma approved them. She went on, 'We can find a little something in the stores for . . .' and she glanced at Grace. 'But you older girls know, Pa hasn't been able to get any work for wages this year. We can't spare money for presents, but we can have a happy Christmas just the same. I'll try to contrive something extra for dinner and then we'll all open our papers and read them, and when it's too dark to read Pa will play the fiddle.'

'We haven't much flour left, Ma,' Laura said.

'The storekeepers are asking twenty-five cents a pound for flour so Pa's waiting for the train,' Ma replied. 'There's nothing to make a pie, anyway, and no butter or eggs for a cake and no more sugar in town. But we'll think of something for Christmas dinner.'

Laura sat thinking. She was making a little picture frame of cross-stitch in wools on thin, silver-coloured cardboard. Up the sides and across the top she had made a pattern of small blue flowers and green leaves. Now she was outlining the picture-opening in blue. While she put the tiny needle through the perforations in the cardboard and drew the fine, coloured wool carefully after it, she was thinking how wistfully Carrie had looked at the beautiful thing. She decided to give it to Carrie for Christmas. Someday, perhaps, she could make another for herself.

How fortunate it was that she had finished knitting the lace for her petticoat. She would give that to Mary. And to Ma she would give the cardboard hair receiver that she had already embroidered to match the picture frame. Ma could hang it on the corner of her looking glass, and when she combed her hair she would put the combings in it to use later in the hair-switch she was making.

'But what can we do for Pa?' she asked.

'I declare I don't know,' Ma worried. 'I can't think of a thing.'

'I've got some pennies,' Carrie said.

'There's my college money,' Mary began, but Ma said, 'No, Mary, we won't touch that.'

'I have ten cents,' Laura said thoughtfully. 'How many pennies have you, Carrie?'

'I have five,' Carrie told her.

'We'd need twenty-five to get Pa a pair of braces,' Laura said. 'He needs a new pair.'

'I have a dime,' said Ma. 'So that is settled. Laura, you and Carrie had better go and buy them as soon as Pa has gone to work tomorrow morning.'

Next day, when their morning work was done, Laura and Carrie crossed the snowy street to Mr Harthorn's store. Mr Harthorn was there alone and the shelves were bare. On both long walls there were only a few pairs of men's boots and women's shoes and some bolts of calico.

The bean barrel was empty. The cracker barrel was empty. The little brine in the bottom of the pork barrel had no pork in it. The long, flat codfish box held only a little salt scattered on its bottom. The dried-apple box and the dried-blackberry box were empty.

'I'm sold out of groceries till the train gets here,' Mr Harthorn said. 'I was expecting a bill of groceries when the train stopped.'

Some pretty handkerchiefs, combs, and hairpins, and two pairs of braces were in the showcase. Laura and Carrie looked at the braces. They were plain, dull grey.

'Shall I do them up for you?' Mr Harthorn asked.

Laura did not like to say no, but she looked at Carrie and saw that Carrie hoped she would.

'No, thank you, Mr Harthorn,' Laura said. 'We will not take them now.'

Out in the glittering cold again, she said to Carrie, 'Let's go to Loftus' store and see if we can't find prettier ones.'

They bent their heads against the strong, cold wind and struggled along the icy path on the store porches till they reached the other Dry Goods and Groceries.

The store was bare and echoing, too. Every barrel and box was empty, and where the canned goods had been there were only two flat cans of oysters.

'I'm expecting a stock of groceries when the train comes tomorrow,' Mr Loftus told them. 'It won't get here any too soon either.'

In his showcase was a pair of blue braces, with small red flowers beautifully machine-woven along them, and bright brass buckles. Laura had never seen such pretty ones. They were just right for Pa.

'How much are they?' she asked, almost sure that they would cost too much. But the price was twenty-five cents. Laura gave Mr Loftus her own two five-cent pieces, Carrie's five pennies, and Ma's thin silver ten-cent piece. She took the slim package and the wind blew her and Carrie breathlessly home.

At bedtime that night no one spoke of hanging up stockings. Grace was too young to know about hanging stockings on Christmas Eve and no one else expected a present. But they had never been so eager for Christmas Day, because the tracks were clear now and the train would come tomorrow.

Laura's first thought in the morning was, 'The train is coming today!' The window was not frosted, the sky was clear, the snowy prairie was turning rosy in early sunshine. The train would surely come and joyfully Laura thought about her Christmas surprises.

She slid out of bed without waking Mary and quickly pulled on her dress in the cold. She opened the box where she kept her own things. She took out the roll of knitted lace, already wrapped carefully in tissue paper. Then she found the prettiest card she had ever been given in Sunday school and she took the little embroidered picture frame and the cardboard hair receiver. With these in her hands, she hurried tiptoe downstairs.

Ma looked up in surprise. The table was set and Ma was putting on each plate a little package wrapped in red-and-white striped paper.

'Merry Christmas, Ma!' Laura whispered. 'Oh, what are they?'

'Christmas presents,' Ma whispered. 'Whatever have you got there?'

Laura only smiled. She put her packages at Ma's plate

172

and Mary's. Then she slipped the Sunday school card into the embroidered frame. 'For Carrie,' she whispered. She and Ma looked at it; it was beautiful. Then Ma found a piece of tissue paper to wrap it in.

Carrie and Grace and Mary were already clambering down the stairs, calling, 'Merry Christmas! Merry Christmas!'

'Oo-oo!' Carrie squealed. 'I thought we were waiting for Christmas till the Christmas barrel came on the train! Oo-oo, look! look!'

'What is it?' Mary asked.

'There are presents at every plate on the table!' Carrie told her.

'No, no, Grace, mustn't touch,' Ma said. 'We will all wait for Pa.' So Grace ran around the table, looking but not touching.

Pa came with the milk and Ma strained it. Then Pa stepped into the lean-to and came back grinning broadly. He handed Ma the two cans of oysters from Loftus' store.

'Charles!' Ma said.

'Make us an oyster soup for Christmas dinner, Caroline!' Pa told her. 'I got some milk from Ellen, not much, and it's the last, she's as good as dry. But maybe you can make it do.'

'I'll thin it out with water,' said Ma. 'We'll have oyster soup for Christmas dinner!'

Then Pa saw the table. Laura and Carrie laughed aloud,

shouting, 'Merry Christmas, Merry Christmas, Pa!' and Laura told Mary, 'Pa's surprised!'

'Hurrah for Santa Claus!' Pa sang out. 'The old fellow made it in, if the train didn't!'

They all sat down at their places and Ma gently held back Grace's hands. 'Pa opens his first, Grace,' she said.

Pa picked up his package. 'Now what can this be, and who gave it to me?' He untied the string, unfolded the paper, and held up the new red-flowered braces.

'Whew!' he exclaimed. 'Now how am I ever going to wear my coat? These are too fine to cover up.' He looked around at all the faces. 'All of you did this,' he said. 'Well, I'll be proud to wear them!'

'Not yet, Grace,' Ma said. 'Mary is next.'

Mary unwrapped the yards of fine knitted lace. She fingered it lovingly and her face was shining with delight. 'I'll save it to wear when I go to college,' she said. 'It's another thing to help me to go. It will be so pretty on a white petticoat.'

Carrie was looking at her present. The picture was of the Good Shepherd in His blue and white robes, holding in His arms a snow-white lamb. The silvery cardboard embroidered in blue flowers made a perfect frame for it.

'Oh, how lovely. How lovely,' Carrie whispered.

Ma said the hair-receiver was just what she had been needing.

Then Grace tore the paper from her gift and gave a gurgle of joy. Two little, flat wooden men stood on a platform between two flat red posts. Their hands held on to two strings twisted tightly together above their heads. They wore peaked red caps and blue coats with gold buttons. Their trousers were red-and-green stripes. Their boots were black with turned-up toes.

Ma gently pressed the bottoms of the posts inward. One of the men somersaulted up and the other swung in to his place. Then the first came down while the second went up and they nodded their heads and jerked their arms and swung their legs, dancing and somersaulting.

'Oh, look! Oh, look!' Grace shouted. She could never have enough of watching the funny little men dancing.

The small striped packages at each place held Christmas candy.

'Wherever did you get candy, Pa?' Laura wondered.

'I got it some time ago. It was the last bit of sugar in town,' said Pa. 'Some folks said they'd use it for sugar, but I made sure of our Christmas candy.'

'Oh, what a lovely Christmas,' Carrie sighed. Laura thought so too. Whatever happened, they could always have a merry Christmas. And the sun was shining, the sky was blue, the railroad tracks were clear, and the train was coming. The train had come through the Tracy cut that morning. Sometime that day they would hear its whistle and see it stopping by the depot.

At noon Ma was making the oyster soup. Laura was setting the table, Carrie and Grace were playing with the jumping-jack. Ma tasted the soup and set the kettle back on the stove. 'The oysters are ready,' she said, and stooping she looked at the slices of bread toasting in the oven. 'And the bread is toasted. Whatever is Pa doing?'

'He's bringing in hay,' said Laura.

Pa opened the door. Behind him the lean-to was almost full of slough hay. He asked, 'Is the oyster soup ready?'

'I'm taking it up,' Ma replied. 'I'm glad the train is coming, this is the last of the coal.' Then she looked at Pa and asked, 'What is wrong, Charles?'

Pa said slowly, 'There is a cloud in the north-west.'

'Oh, not another blizzard!' Ma cried.

'I'm afraid so,' Pa answered. 'But it needn't spoil our dinner.' He drew his chair up to the table. 'I've packed plenty of hay into the stable and filled the lean-to. Now for our oyster soup!'

The sun kept on shining while they ate. The hot soup was good, even though the milk was mostly water. Pa crumbled the toast into his soup plate. 'This toasted bread is every bit as good as crackers,' he told Ma. 'I don't know but better.'

Laura enjoyed the good soup, but she could not stop thinking of that dark cloud coming up. She could not stop listening for the wind that she knew would soon come.

It came with a shriek. The windows rattled and the house shook.

'She must be a daisy!' Pa said. He went to the window but he could not see out. Snow came on the wind from the sky. Snow rose from the hard drifts as the wind cut them away. It all met in the whirling air and swirled madly. The sky, the sunshine, the town, were gone, lost in that blinding dance of snow. The house was alone again.

Laura thought, 'The train can't come now.'

'Come, girls,' Ma said. 'We'll get these dishes out of the way, and then we'll open our papers and have a cosy afternoon.'

'Is there coal enough, Ma?' Laura asked.

Pa looked at the fire. 'It will last till suppertime,' he said. 'And then we'll burn hay.'

Frost was freezing up the windowpanes and the room was cold near the walls. Near the stove, the light was too dim for reading. When the dishes were washed and put away, Ma set the lamp on the red-checked tablecloth and lighted it. There was only a little kerosene in the bowl where the wick coiled, but it gave a warm and cheery light. Laura opened the bundle of *Youth's Companions* and she and Carrie looked eagerly at the wealth of stories printed on the smooth, white paper.

'You girls choose a story,' Ma said, 'and I will read it out loud, so we can all enjoy it together.'

So, close together between the stove and the bright

177

table, they listened to Ma's reading the story in her soft, clear voice. The story took them all far away from the stormy cold and dark. When she had finished that one, Ma read a second and a third. That was enough for one day; they must save some for another time.

'Aren't you glad we saved those wonderful stories for Christmas day?' Mary sighed happily. And they were. The whole afternoon had gone so quickly. Already it was chore time.

When Pa came back from the stable, he stayed some time in the lean-to and came in at last with his arms full of sticks.

'Here is your breakfast fuel, Caroline,' he said, laying his armful down by the stove. 'Good hard sticks of hay. I guess they will burn all right.'

'Sticks of hay?' Laura exclaimed.

'That's right, Laura,' Pa spread his hands in the warmth above the stove. 'I'm glad that hay's in the lean-to. I couldn't carry it in through the wind that's blowing now, unless I brought it one blade at a time, in my teeth.'

The hay *was* in sticks. Pa had somehow twisted and knotted it tightly till each stick was almost as hard as wood.

'Sticks of hay!' Ma laughed. 'What won't you think of next? Trust you, Charles, to find a way.'

'You are good at that yourself,' Pa smiled at her.

For supper there were hot boiled potatoes and a slice

of bread apiece, with salt. That was the last baking of bread, but there were still beans in the sack and a few turnips. There was still hot tea with sugar, and Grace had her cup of cambric tea made with hot water because there was no more milk. While they were eating, the lamp began to flicker. With all its might the flame pulled itself up, drawing the last drops of kerosene up the wick. Then it fainted down and desperately tried again. Ma leaned over and blew it out. The dark came in, loud with the roar and the shrieking of the storm.

'The fire is dying, anyway, so we may as well go to bed,' Ma said gently. Christmas Day was over.

Laura lay in bed and listened to the winds blowing, louder and louder. They sounded like the pack of wolves howling around the little house on the prairie long ago, when she was small and Pa had carried her in his arms. And there was the deeper howl of the great buffalo wolf that she and Carrie had met on the bank of Silver Lake.

She started trembling, when she heard the scream of the panther in the creek bed, in Indian territory. But she knew it was only the wind. Now she heard the Indian war whoops when the Indians were dancing their war dances all through the horrible nights by the Verdigris river.

The war whoops died away and she heard crowds of people muttering, then shrieking and fleeing screaming away from fierce yells chasing them. But she knew she heard only the voices of the blizzard winds. She pulled the bedcovers over her head and covered her ears tightly to shut out the sounds, but still she heard them.

19

Where There's a Will

The hay made a quick, hot fire, but it burned away more swiftly than kindling. Ma kept the stove's draughts closed and all day long she was feeding the fire. All day long, except when he went through the storm to do the chores, Pa was twisting more sticks of hay in the lean-to. The storm grew fiercer and the cold more cruel.

Often Pa came to the stove to warm his hands. 'My fingers get so numb,' he said, 'I can't make a good twist.'

'Let me help you, Pa,' Laura begged.

He did not want to let her. 'Your hands are too small for such work,' he told her. Then he admitted, 'But somebody's got to help. It is going to be more than one person can do, to keep this stove going and haul hay for it.' Finally he decided, 'Come along, I'll show you how.'

Laura put on Pa's old coat and her hood and muffler and went into the lean-to with Pa.

The lean-to was not ceiled inside. The wind was blowing snow through all the cracks of the board walls. Snow travelled in little drifts across the floor and sifted over the hay.

Pa picked up a double handful of hay and shook the snow from it.

'Shake off all the snow,' he told Laura. 'If you leave it on, it will melt when you take the sticks in and make them too wet to burn.'

Laura picked up all the hay her hands could hold and shook the snow from it. Then, watching Pa, she followed his motions in twisting the hay. First he twisted the long strand as far as his two hands could do it. Then he put the right-hand end of it under his left elbow and held it there, tight against his side, so that it could not untwist. Then his right hand took the other end from his left hand. His left hand slid down as near as it could get to the end under his left elbow and took hold of it. Pa twisted the strand again. This time he put its other end under his left elbow. He repeated these motions, again and again and again, till the whole strand of hay was twisted tight and kinking in the middle. Each time he twisted and tucked the end under his left arm, the tight twist coiled around itself.

When the whole length of the twist had wound itself tight, Pa bent the ends of hay together and tucked them into the last kink. He dropped the hard stick of hay on the floor and looked at Laura.

She was trying to tuck in the ends as Pa had done. The hay was twisted so tightly that she couldn't push them in.

'Bend your twist a little to loosen it,' said Pa. 'Then slip

the ends in between the kinks and let it twist itself back tight. That's the way!'

Laura's stick of hay was uneven and raggedy, not smooth and hard like Pa's. But Pa told her that it was well done for the first one; she would do better next time.

She made six sticks of hay, each better than the one before; the sixth one was as it should be. But now she was so cold that her hands could not feel the hay.

'That's enough!' Pa told her. 'Gather them up, and we'll go warm ourselves.'

They carried the sticks of hay into the kitchen. Laura's feet were numb from cold; they felt like wooden feet. Her hands were red and when she held them in the warm air above the stove they tingled and stung and smarted where the sharp blades of the grass had cut them. But she had helped Pa. The sticks of hay that she had made gave him time enough to get thoroughly warm before they must go into the cold to twist more hay.

All that day and all the next day, Laura helped Pa twist hay while Ma kept the fire going and Carrie helped her take care of Grace and do the housework. For dinner they had baked potatoes and mashed turnips with pepper and salt, and for supper Ma chopped the potatoes and heated them in the oven because there was no fat to fry them in. But the food was hot and good, and there was plenty of tea and still some sugar.

'This is the last loaf of bread,' Ma said, the second night at supper. 'We really must have some flour, Charles.'

'I'll buy some as soon as this storm lets up,' Pa said. 'No matter what it costs.'

'Use my college money, Pa,' Mary said. 'Thirty-five dollars and twenty-five cents will buy all the flour we could want.'

'That's our good girl, Mary,' said Ma. 'But I hope we won't have to spend your college money. I suppose prices depend on when they can get the train through?' she said to Pa.

'Yes,' Pa said. 'That's what they depend on.'

Ma got up and put another stick of hay on the fire. When she lifted the stove lid, a reddish-yellow smoky light flared up and drove back the dark for a moment. Then the dark came back again. The wild screaming of the storm seemed louder and nearer in the dark.

'If only I had some grease I could fix some kind of a light,' Ma considered. 'We didn't lack for light when I was a girl, before this newfangled kerosene was ever heard of.'

'That's so,' said Pa. 'These times are too progressive. Everything has changed too fast. Railroads and telegraph and kerosene and coal stoves – they're good things to have but the trouble is, folks get to depend on em'.'

In the morning the winds were still howling and outside the thick-frosted windows the snow was still whirling. But by mid-morning a straight, strong wind was blowing from the south and the sun was shining. It was very cold, so cold that the snow squeaked under Laura's feet in the lean-to.

Pa went across the street to get the flour. He was gone some time, and when he came back he was carrying a grain sack on his shoulder. He let it slide to the floor with a thump.

'Here's your flour, Caroline, or what will have to take the place of it,' he said. 'It is wheat, the last that's left of the Wilder boys' stock. There is no flour in the stores. Banker Ruth bought the last sack this morning. He paid fifty dollars for it, a dollar a pound.'

'My goodness, Charles,' Ma gasped.

'Yes. We couldn't buy much flour at that price, so I guess it's just as well Ruth got it. We may as well learn now how to cook wheat. How will it be, boiled?'

'I don't know, Charles. It isn't as if we had anything to eat on it,' said Ma.

'It's a pity there isn't a grist mill in town,' Pa said.

'We have a mill,' Ma replied. She reached to the top of the cupboard and took down the coffee mill.

'So we have,' said Pa. 'Let's see how it works.'

Ma set the little brown wooden box on the table. She turned the handle for a moment, to loosen every last grain of coffee from the grinders. Then she pulled out the little drawer, emptied it, and wiped it carefully. Pa opened the sack of wheat.

The black iron hopper in the top of the mill held half a cupful of the grain. Ma shut its top. Then she sat down, placed the square box between her knees to hold it firmly, and began turning the handle around and around. The mill gave out its grinding noise.

'Wheat will grind just like coffee,' Ma said. She looked into the little drawer. The broken bits of wheat were crushed out flat. 'Not like coffee, either,' Ma said. 'The wheat hasn't been roasted and has more moisture in it.'

'Can you make bread of that?' Pa asked.

'Of course I can,' Ma replied. 'But we must keep the mill grinding if I'm to have enough to make a loaf for dinner.'

'And I must go haul some hay to bake it with,' said Pa. He took a round, flat wooden box from his pocket and handed it to Ma. 'Here's something you can maybe use to make a light.'

'Is there any word of the train, Charles?' Ma asked him.

'They're working again at that. Tracy cut,' said Pa. 'It's packed full of snow again, to the top of the snow-banks they threw up on both sides when they cleared it last time.'

He went to the stable to hitch David to the sled. Ma looked into the box. It was full of yellow axle grease. But there was no time then to think about making a light. The fire was dying and Ma put the last stick of hay on it. Laura hurried into the lean-to to twist more hay.

In a few minutes Ma came to help her. 'Mary is grinding the wheat,' Ma said. 'We must twist a lot of hay to keep the fire going. We must have a good warm fire when Pa comes back. He will be almost frozen.'

It was late afternoon before Pa came back. He unhitched the sled near the back door and put David in the stable. Then he pitched the hay into the lean-to until there was hardly space to squeeze through from door to door. When that was done, he came in to the stove. He was so cold that it was some time before he was warm enough to speak.

'I'm sorry to be so late, Caroline,' he made excuse. 'The snow is much deeper than it was. I had a hard time digging the hay out of the drift.'

'I think we may as well have dinner at this time every day,' Ma answered. 'What with saving fire and light, the days are so short that there's hardly time for three meals. A late dinner will serve for supper as well.'

The brown bread that Ma had made from the ground wheat was very good. It had a fresh, nutty flavour that seemed almost to take the place of butter.

'I see you've got your sourdough working again,' Pa remarked.

'Yes,' Ma answered. 'We don't need yeast or milk to make good bread.'

'"Where there's a will there's a way,"' said Pa. He helped himself to another potato and sprinkled it with salt. 'Potatoes and salt aren't to be sneezed at either. Salt brings out the full flavour of a potato; it's not all hidden with butter and gravy.'

'Don't put sugar in your tea, Pa, and you'll get the full flavour of the tea,' Laura said naughtily.

Pa's eyes twinkled at her. 'A good hot cup of tea brings out the flavour of the sugar, Half-Pint,' he answered. Then he asked Ma, 'How did you make out with the axle grease, for a light?'

'I haven't had time yet,' Ma told him. 'But as soon as we finish eating I'm going to make a button lamp.'

'What's a button lamp?' Pa asked.

'Wait and see,' said Ma.

When he had gone to do the chores for the night Ma told Carrie to bring her the rag bag. She took some of the axle grease from the box and spread it in an old saucer.

Then she cut a small square of calico. 'Now find me a button in the button bag, Carrie.'

'What kind of button, Ma?' Carrie asked, bringing the button bag from the cold front room.

'Oh, one of Pa's old overcoat buttons,' said Ma.

She put the button in the centre of the square of calico. She drew the cloth together over the button and wound a thread tightly around it and twisted the corners of calico straight upward in a tapering bunch. Then she rubbed a little axle grease up the calico and set the button into the axle grease in the saucer.

'Now we'll wait till Pa comes,' she said.

Laura and Carrie hurried to finish washing the dishes in the gathering dusk. It was dark when Pa came in.

'Give me a match, Charles, please,' Ma said. She lighted the taper tip of the button lamp. A tiny flame flickered and grew stronger. It burned steadily, melting the axle grease and drawing it up through the cloth into itself, keeping itself alight by burning. The little flame was like the flame of a candle in the dark.

'You're a wonder, Caroline,' said Pa. 'It's only a little light, but it makes all the difference.'

Warming his hands above the stove, he looked down at the little pile of twisted hay. 'But I don't need a light to twist hay,' he said. 'And we must have more now. There's not enough here for morning.'

He went out to twist hay and Laura took the coffee mill

from Mary. Turning the little handle around and around made the arm and shoulder ache so badly that they must take turns at the grinding. The little mill ground wheat so slowly that they had to keep it grinding all the time to make flour enough to bake for each meal.

Ma took off Grace's shoes and warmed her feet by the oven door while she slipped off her little dress, pulled on her nightgown, and wrapped her in the shawl that was warming over a chair by the stove.

'Come, Carrie, if you're good and warm,' she said. 'I'll put Grace in bed with you now.'

When Grace and Carrie were tucked in bed with the warm shawl and the hot flatiron Ma came downstairs.

'I'll grind wheat now, Laura,' she said. 'You and Mary go to bed. As soon as Pa comes in we'll go to bed, too, to save this hay that is so hard to get and to twist.'

20

Antelope!

There came a sunny day when the loose snow was rolling like drifts of smoke across the frozen white prairie.

Pa came hurrying into the house. 'There's a herd of antelope west of town!' he said, as he took his shotgun down from its hooks and filled his pockets with cartridges.

Laura threw Ma's shawl around her and ran into the cold front room. She scratched a peephole through the frost on the window and she saw a crowd of men gathering in the street. Several were on horseback. Mr Foster and Almanzo Wilder were riding the beautiful Morgan horses. Cap Garland came running and joined the men on foot who were listening to Pa. They all carried guns. They looked excited and their voices sounded excited and loud.

'Come back where it's warm, Laura,' Ma called.

'Think of venison!' Laura said, hanging up the shawl. 'I hope Pa gets *two* antelopes!'

'I will be glad to have some meat to go with the brown bread,' Ma said. 'But we must not count chickens before they are hatched.'

'Why, Ma, Pa will get an antelope, if there are any antelopes,' said Laura.

Carrie brought a dish of wheat to fill the hopper of the coffee mill that Mary was grinding. 'Roast venison,' Carrie said. 'With gravy, gravy on the potatoes and the brown bread!'

'Wait a minute, Mary!' Laura exclaimed. 'Listen. There they go!'

The steady wind rushed by the house and whistled shrill along the eaves, but they could dimly hear the voices and the feet of men and horses moving away along Main Street.

At the end of the street they paused. They could see, a mile away across the snowdrifts and the blowing snow, the grey herd of antelope drifting southward.

'Slow and easy does it,' said Pa. 'Give us time to work around 'em to the north before you boys close in from the south. Come in slow and herd 'em towards us without scaring 'em, if you can, till they're in gunshot. There's no hurry, we've got the day before us and if we work it right we ought to get us one apiece.'

'Maybe we'd better ride to the north and you fellows on foot surround 'em from the south,' Mr Foster said.

'No, let it go as Ingalls said,' Mr Harthorn told him. 'Come on, boys!'

'String out,' Pa called. 'And go slow and easy. Don't scare 'em!'

On the Morgans, Almanzo and Mr Foster took the lead. The cold wind made the horses eager to go. They pricked their ears forward and back and tossed their heads, jingling the bits and pretending to shy a little at their own shadows. They stretched their noses forward, pulling on the bits and prancing to go faster.

'Hold her steady,' Almanzo said to Mr Foster. 'Don't saw on the bits, she's tender-mouthed.'

Mr Foster did not know how to ride. He was as nervous as Lady and he was making her more nervous. He bounced in the saddle and did not hold the reins steadily. Almanzo was sorry he had let him ride Lady.

'Careful, Foster,' Almanzo said. 'That mare will jump out from under you.'

'What's the matter with her? What's the matter with her?' Mr Foster chattered in the cold wind. 'Oh, there they are!'

In the clear air the antelope seemed nearer than they were. Beyond the drifting herd the men on foot were working westward. Almanzo saw Mr Ingalls at the head of the line. In a few more minutes they would have the herd surrounded.

He turned to speak to Mr Foster and he saw Lady's saddle empty. At that instant a shot deafened him and both horses jumped high and far. Almanzo reined Prince down, as Lady streaked away.

Mr Foster was jumping up and down, waving his gun

and yelling. Crazy with excitement, he had jumped off Lady, let go her reins, and fired at the antelope that were too far away to hit.

Heads and tails up, the antelope were skimming away as if the wind were blowing them above the snowdrifts. Brown Lady overtook the grey herd and reached its middle, running with them.

'Don't shoot! Don't shoot!' Almanzo yelled, though he knew that his yells were useless against the wind. The antelope were already passing through the line of men on foot, but no one fired at them for fear of hitting the mare. The glossy brown Morgan, head up and black mane and tail flying, went over a prairie swell in the midst of the grey, low cloud of antelope and vanished. In a moment the horse and the herd passed over another white curve, then, growing smaller, they appeared again and again the prairie swallowed them.

'Looks like you've lost her, Wilder,' Mr Harthorn said. 'Too bad.'

The other riders had come up. They sat still, on their horses, watching the distant prairie. The antelope herd, with Lady small and dark in it, appeared once more as a flying grey smudge that quickly vanished.

Mr Ingalls came and the other men on foot. Cap Garland said, 'Tough luck, Wilder. Guess we might as well have risked a shot.'

'You're a mighty hunter before the Lord, Foster,' Gerald Fuller said.

'He's the only man that got a shot,' said Cap Garland. 'And what a shot!'

'I'm sorry. I must have let the mare go,' Mr Foster said. 'I was so excited, I didn't think. I thought the horse would stand. I never saw an antelope before.'

'Next time you take a shot at one, Foster, wait till

you're within range,' Gerald Fuller told him.

No one else said anything. Almanzo sat in the saddle while Prince fought the bit, trying to get free to follow his mate. Frightened as Lady was, and racing with the herd, the danger was that she would run herself to death. Trying to catch her would do no good; chasing the herd would only make it run faster.

Judging by the landmarks, the antelope were five or six miles to the west when they turned northward.

'They're making for Spirit Lake,' Mr Ingalls said. 'They'll shelter there in the brush and then they'll range back into the bluffs of the river. We'll not see them again.'

'What about Wilder's horse, Mr Ingalls?' Cap Garland asked.

Pa looked at Almanzo and then he looked again at the north-west. There was no cloud there but the wind blew strongly and bitter cold.

'That's the only horse in this country that can race an antelope, unless it's her mate here, and you'll kill him trying to catch them,' Pa said. 'It's a day's journey to Spirit Lake at best, and no one knows when a blizzard'll hit. I wouldn't risk it myself, not this winter.'

'I don't intend to,' said Almanzo. 'But I'll just circle around and come into town from the north. Maybe I'll catch sight of the mare. If not, maybe she'll find her own way back. So long! See you in town!'

He let Prince go into a canter and set off towards the north, while the others shouldered their guns and turned straight towards town.

He rode with his head bowed against the wind but on each prairie swell or high snowbank he looked over the land before him. There was nothing to be seen but gentle slopes of snow and the snow-spray blown from their tops by the cutting wind. The loss of Lady made him sick at heart, but he did not intend to risk his life for a horse. The matched team was ruined without her. In a lifetime he would not find another perfect match for Prince. He thought what a fool he had been to lend a horse to a stranger.

Prince went on smoothly, head up to the wind, galloping up the slopes and cantering down them. Almanzo did not intend to go far from the town, but the sky remained clear in the north-west and there was always another slope ahead of him, from which he might see farther north.

Lady, he thought, might have grown tired and dropped behind the antelope herd. She might be wandering, lost and bewildered. She might be in sight from the top of the next prairie swell.

When he reached it, there was only the white land beyond. Prince went smoothly down the slope and another one rose before him.

He looked back to see the town and there was no town. The huddle of tall false fronts and the thin smoke blowing from their stovepipes had vanished. Under the whole sky there was nothing but the white land, the snow blowing, and the wind and the cold.

He was not afraid. He knew where the town was and as long as the sun was in the sky or the moon or stars he could not be lost. But he had a feeling colder than the wind. He felt that he was the only life on the cold earth, under the cold sky; he and his horse alone in an enormous coldness.

'Hi-yup, Prince!' he said, but the wind carried away the sound in the ceaseless rush of its blowing. Then he was afraid of being afraid. He said to himself, 'There's nothing to be afraid of.' He thought, 'I won't turn back now. I'll turn back from the top of that next slope,' and he tightened the reins ever so little to hold the rhythm of Prince's galloping.

From the top of that slope he saw a low edge of cloud on the north-western sky line. Then suddenly the whole great prairie seemed to be a trap that knew it had caught him. But he also saw Lady.

Far away and small, on a ridge of the rolling snow fields, the brown horse stood looking eastward. Almanzo tore off his glove and putting two fingers into his mouth he blew the piercing whistle used to call Lady across his father's pastures in Minnesota when she was a colt. But this prairie wind caught the shrill note at his lips and carried it soundlessly away. It carried away the long, whickering call from Prince's stretched throat. Lady still stood, looking away from them.

Then she turned to look southward and saw them. The wind brought her far, faint whinny. Her neck arched, her tail curved up, and she came galloping.

Almanzo waited until she topped a nearer rise and again her call came down the wind. He turned then and rode towards the town. The low cloud fell below the sky line as he rode, but again and again Lady appeared behind him.

In the stable behind the feed store he put Prince in his stall and rubbed him down. He filled the manger and held the water pail to let Prince drink a little.

There was a rattling at the stable door and he opened it to let Lady in. She was white with lather. A foam of sweat dripped from her and her sides were heaving.

Almanzo shut the stable door against the cold while Lady went into her stall. Then with the currycomb he scraped the foam from her panting sides and her flanks and covered her warmly with a blanket. He squeezed a wet cloth into her mouth to moisten her tongue. He rubbed her slender legs and dried them where the sweat still ran down.

'Well, Lady, so you can outrun an antelope! Made a fool of yourself, didn't you?' Almanzo talked to her while he worked. 'It's the last time I'll let a fool ride you, anyway. Now you rest warm and quiet. I'll water and feed you after a while.'

Pa had come quietly into the kitchen and without a word he laid his shotgun on its hooks. No one said anything; there was no need to. Carrie sighed. There would be no venison, no gravy on the brown bread. Pa sat down by the stove and spread his hands to the warmth.

After a little, he said, 'Foster lost his head from excitement. He jumped off his horse and fired before he was anywhere near within gunshot. None of the rest of us had a chance. The whole herd's high-tailed it north.'

Ma put a stick of hay in the stove. 'They would have been poor eating anyway, this time of year,' she said.

Laura knew that antelope had to paw away the deep snow to reach the dry grass that was their food. In a blizzard they couldn't do that, and now the snow was so deep that they must be starving. It was true that their meat would have been thin and tough. But it would have been meat. They were all so tired of nothing but potatoes and brown bread.

'The younger Wilder boy's horse got away, too,' Pa said, and he told them how it had run with the antelope. He made a story for Carrie and Grace of the beautiful horse running free and far with the wild herd.

'And didn't it ever, ever come back, Pa?' Grace asked him, wide-eyed.

'I don't know,' said Pa. 'Almanzo Wilder rode off that way and I don't know whether he's come back or not.

While you're getting dinner ready, Caroline, I'll step up to the feed store and find out.'

The feed store was bare and empty, but Royal looked from the back room and said heartily, 'Come on in, Mr Ingalls! You're just in time to sample the pancakes and bacon!'

'I didn't know this was your dinnertime,' Pa said. He looked at the platter of bacon keeping hot on the stove hearth. Three stacks of pancakes were tall on a plate, too, and Royal was frying more. There was molasses on the table and the coffeepot was boiling.

'We eat when we get hungry,' said Royal. 'That's the advantage of baching it. Where there's no women-folks, there's no regular mealtimes.'

'You boys are lucky to have brought in supplies,' Pa said.

'Well, I was bringing out a carload of feed anyway and thought I might as well bring the stuff along,' Royal replied. 'I wish I'd brought a couple of carloads, now. I guess I could sell another carload before they get the train through.'

'I guess you could,' Pa agreed. He looked around the snug room, ran his eyes along the walls hung with clothes and harness, and noticed the empty spaces on the end wall. 'Your brother not got back yet?'

'He just came into the stable,' Royal answered. Then he exclaimed, 'Jiminy crickets, look there!' They saw Lady, dripping with lather and empty-saddled, streaking past the window to the stable.

While they were talking about the hunt and Mr Foster's crazy shot, Almanzo came in. He dumped the saddles in a corner to be cleaned before he hung them up and he warmed himself by the stove. Then he and Royal urged Pa to sit up to the table and eat with them.

'Royal don't make as good pancakes as I do,' Almanzo said. 'But nobody can beat this bacon. It's home-cured and hickory smoked from corn-fattened young hogs raised on clover, back on the farm in Minnesota.'

'Sit right up, Mr Ingalls, and help yourself. There's plenty more down cellar in a teacup!' said Royal. So Pa did.

21

The Hard Winter

The sun shone again next morning and the winds were still. The day seemed warmer than it was, because the sunshine was so bright.

'This is a beautiful day,' Ma said at breakfast, but Pa shook his head.

'The sun is too bright,' he said. 'I'll get a load of hay as soon as I can for we'll need plenty on hand if another storm comes.' And he hurried away.

Anxiously from time to time Ma or Laura or Carrie peeped out through the frosty window to see the north-western sky. The sun still was shining when Pa came safely back, and after the day's second meal of brown bread and potatoes he went across the street to hear the news.

In a little while he came gaily whistling through the front room and burst into the kitchen, singing out, 'Guess what I got!'

Grace and Carrie ran to feel the package he carried. 'It feels like . . . it feels like . . .' Carrie said, but she did not quite dare to say what it felt like for fear she was mistaken.

'It's beef!' Pa said. 'Four pounds of beef! To go with

our bread and potatoes.' He handed the package to Ma.

'Charles! However did you get beef?' Ma asked, as if she could not believe it.

'Foster butchered his oxen,' Pa answered. 'I got there just in time. Every last bit, to bones and gristle, sold twenty-five cents a pound. But I got four pounds and here it is! Now we'll live like kings!'

Ma quickly took the paper off the meat. 'I'll sear it all over well and pot-roast it,' she said.

Looking at it made Laura's mouth water. She swallowed and asked, 'Can you make a gravy, Ma, with water and brown flour?'

'Indeed I can,' Ma smiled. 'We can make this last a week, for flavouring at least, and by that time the train will surely come, won't it?'

She looked smiling at Pa. Then she stopped smiling and quietly asked, 'What is it, Charles?'

'Well,' Pa answered reluctantly, 'I hate to tell you.' He cleared his throat. 'The train isn't coming.'

They all stood looking at him. He went on, 'The railroad has stopped running trains, till spring.'

Ma threw up her hands and dropped into a chair. 'How can it, Charles? It can't. It can't do that. Till spring? This is only the first of January.'

'They can't get the trains through,' said Pa. 'They no sooner get a train through a cut than a blizzard comes and snows it in again. They've got two trains between here and Tracy, snowed under between cuts. Every time they cleared a cut they threw up the snow on both sides, and now all the cuts are packed full of snow to the top of the snowbanks. And at Tracy the superintendent ran out of patience.'

'Patience?' Ma exclaimed. 'Patience! What's *his* patience got to do with it I'd like to know! He knows we are out here without supplies. How does he think we are going to live till spring? It isn't his business to be patient. It's his business to run the trains.'

'Now, Caroline,' Pa said. He put his hand on her shoulder and she stopped rocking and rolling her hands in her apron. 'We haven't had a train for more than a month, and we are getting along all right,' he told her.

'Yes,' Ma said.

'There's only this month, then February is a short month, and March will be spring,' Pa encouraged her.

Laura looked at the four pounds of beef. She thought of the few potatoes left and she saw the partly filled sack of wheat standing in the corner.

'Is there any more wheat, Pa?' she asked in a low voice.

'I don't know, Laura,' Pa said strangely. 'But don't worry. I bought a full bushel and it's by no means gone.'

Laura could not help asking, 'Pa, you couldn't shoot a rabbit?'

Pa sat down before the open oven and settled Grace on his knee. 'Come here, Half-Pint,' he said, 'and you, too, Carrie. I'm going to tell you a story.'

He did not answer Laura's question. She knew what the answer was. There was not a rabbit left in all that country. They must have gone south when the birds went. Pa never took his gun with him when he was hauling hay, and he would have taken it if he had ever seen so much as one rabbit's track.

He put his arm around her as she stood close against Carrie on his knee. Grace cuddled in his other arm and laughed when his brown beard tickled her face as it used to tickle Laura's when she was little. They were all cosy in Pa's arms, with the warmth from the oven coming out pleasantly.

'Now listen, Grace and Carrie and Laura,' said Pa. 'And you, too, Mary and Ma. This is a funny story.' And he told them the story of the superintendent.

The superintendent was an Eastern man. He sat in his offices in the East and ordered the train dispatchers to keep the trains running. But the engineers reported that storms and snow stopped the trains.

'Snow storms don't stop us from running trains in the East,' the superintendent said. 'Keep the trains running in the Western end of the division. That's orders.'

But in the West the trains kept stopping. He had reports that the cuts were full of snow.

'Clear the cuts,' he ordered. 'Put on extra men. Keep the trains running. Hang the costs!'

They put on extra men. The costs were enormous. But still the trains did not run.

Then the superintendent said, 'I'll go out there and clear those tracks myself. What those men need is someone to show them how we do things in the East.'

So he came out to Tracy, in his special car, and he got off there in his city clothes and his gloves and his fur-lined coat and this is what he said. 'I've come out to take charge myself,' he said. 'I'll show you how to keep these trains running.'

In spite of that, he was not a bad fellow when you knew him. He rode out in the work train to the big cut west of Tracy, and he piled out in the snow with the work crew and gave his orders like any good foreman. He moved that snow up out of the cut in double-quick time and in a couple of days the track was clear.

'That shows you how to do it,' he said. 'Now run the train through tomorrow and keep it running.' But that night a blizzard hit Tracy. His special train couldn't run in that blizzard, and when it stopped blowing the cut was packed full of snow to the top of the snowbanks he'd had thrown up on both sides.

He got right out there with the men again, and again they cleared the cut. It took longer that time because they had to move more snow. But he got the work train through, just in time to be snowed under by the next blizzard.

You had to admit that the superintendent had stick-to-it-iveness. He tackled the cut again and got it cleared again, and then he sat in Tracy through another blizzard. This time he ordered out two fresh work crews and two locomotives with a snowplough.

He rode out to the Tracy cut on the first locomotive. The cut rose up like a hill now. Between the snowbanks that he'd had thrown up on both sides of them, the blizzard had packed earth and snow, frozen solid, one hundred feet deep and tapering off for a quarter of a mile.

'All right, boys!' he said. 'We'll clear her out with picks and shovels till we can run the snowploughs through.'

He kept them at it, double-quick and double pay, for two days. There was still about twelve feet of snow on the tracks, but he had learned something. He knew he would be lucky to get three clear days between blizzards. So on the third morning, he was going to run the snowploughs through.

He gave his orders to the two locomotive engineers. They coupled the locomotives together with the snowplough in front and ran the work train out to the cut. The two work crews piled out and in a couple of hours of fast work they had moved another couple of feet of snow. Then the superintendent stopped the work.

'Now,' he ordered the engineers, 'you boys back down the track a full two miles, and come ahead from there with all the steam pressure you've got. With two miles to get up speed you ought to hit this cut at forty miles an hour and go through her clean as a whistle.'

The engineers climbed into their locomotives. Then the man on the front engine got down again. The men of the work crews were standing around in the snow, stamping their feet and beating their hands to keep warm. They crowded in to hear what the engineer was going to say, but he walked up to the superintendent and said it just the same.

'I quit,' he said. 'I've been driving a locomotive for fifteen years and no man can call me a coward. But I'm not taking any orders to commit suicide. You want to send a locomotive up against ten foot of frozen snow at forty miles an hour, Mr Superintendent; you can get some other man to drive it. I quit, right here and now.'

Pa paused, and Carrie said, 'I don't blame him.'

'I do,' said Laura. 'He oughtn't to quit. He ought to figure out some other way to get through, if he thinks that way won't work. I think he was scared.'

'Even if he was scared,' Mary said, 'he ought to do as he was told. The superintendent must know best what to do or how would he be the superintendent?'

'He doesn't know best,' Laura contradicted. 'Or he'd be keeping the train running.'

'Go on, Pa, go on!' Grace begged.

'"Please," Grace,' Ma said.

'Please,' said Grace. 'Go on, Pa! What happened next?'

'Yes, Pa, what did the superintendent do then?' Mary asked.

'He fired him,' said Laura. 'Didn't he, Pa?'

Pa went on.

'The superintendent looked at that engineer, and he looked at the men standing around listening, and he said, "I've driven a locomotive in my time. And I don't order any man to do anything I won't do myself. I'll take that throttle."

'He climbed up into the locomotive, and he set her in reverse, and the two locomotives backed off down the track.

'The superintendent kept them backing for a good long two miles, till they looked smaller than your thumb, far off down the track. Then he signalled with the whistle to the engineer behind and they both put on the steam-power.

'Those locomotives came charging down that two miles of straight track with wide-open throttles, full speed ahead and coming faster every second. Black plumes of coal smoke rolling away far behind them, headlights glaring bigger in the sunshine, wheels blurring faster, faster, roaring up to fifty miles an hour they hit that frozen snow.'

'What . . . what happened . . . then, Pa?' Carrie asked, breathless.

'Then up rose a fountain of flying snow that fell in

chunks for forty yards around. For a minute or two no one saw anything clear, nobody knew what had happened. But when the men came running to find out, there was the second locomotive buried halfway in the snow and the engineer crawling out of its hind end. He was considerably shaken up, but not hurt badly enough to mention.

' "Where's the superintendent? What happened to him?" they asked the engineer. All he said was, "How the dickens do I know? All I know is I'm not killed. I wouldn't do that again," he said. "Not for a million dollars in gold."

'The foremen were shouting to the men to come on with their picks and shovels. They dug the snow loose from around the second engine and shovelled it away. The engineer backed it out and down the track out of the way, while the men dug furiously into the snow ahead, to come at the first engine and the superintendent. In hardly any time at all they struck solid ice.

'That first locomotive had run full speed, head on into that snow, its full length. It was hot with speed and steam. It melted the snow all around it and the snow-water froze solid in the frozen snow. There sat the superintendent, madder than a hornet, inside the locomotive frozen solid in a cake of ice!'

Grace and Carrie and Laura laughed out loud. Even Ma smiled.

'The poor man,' Mary said. 'I don't think it's funny.'

'I do,' said Laura. 'I guess now he doesn't think he knows so much.'

' "Pride goes before a fall," ' said Ma.

'Go on, Pa, please!' Carrie begged. 'Did they dig him out?'

'Yes, they dug down and cracked the ice and broke a hole through it to the engine and they hauled him out He was not hurt and neither was the locomotive. The snowplough had taken the brunt. The superintendent climbed out of the cut and walked back to the second engineer and said, "Can you back her out?"'

'The engineer said he thought so.

' "All right, do it," the superintendent said. He stood watching till they got the engine out. Then he said to the men, "Pile in, we're going back to Tracy. Work's shut down till spring."'

'You see, girls,' said Pa, 'the trouble is, he didn't have enough patience.'

'Nor perseverance,' said Ma.

'Nor perseverance,' Pa agreed. 'Just because he couldn't get through with shovels or snowploughs, he figured he couldn't get through at all and he quit trying. Well, he's an Easterner. It takes patience and perseverance to contend with things out here in the West.'

'When did he quit, Pa?' Laura asked.

'This morning. The news came on the electric telegraph, and the operator at Tracy told Woodworth how it happened,' Pa answered. 'And now I must hustle to do the chores before it's too dark.'

His arm tightened and gave Laura a little hugging shake, before he set Carrie and Grace down from his knees. Laura knew what he meant. She was old enough now to stand by him and Ma in hard times. She must not worry; she must be cheerful and help to keep up all their spirits.

So when Ma began to sing softly to Grace while she undressed her for bed, Laura joined in the song:

'Oh Canaan, bright Canaan,
I am bound for the . . .'

'Sing, Carrie!' Laura said hurriedly. So Carrie began to sing, then Mary's sweet soprano came in.

'On Jordan's stormy banks I stand
And cast a wishful eye
On Canaan's bright and shining strand
Where my possessions lie.
Oh Canaan, bright Canaan,
I am bound for the happy land of
    Canaan . . .'

The sun was setting so red that it coloured the frosted windowpanes. It gave a faintly rosy light to the kitchen where they all sat undressing and singing by the warm stove. But Laura thought there was a change in the sound of the wind, a wild and frightening note.

After Ma had seen them all tucked in bed and had gone downstairs, they heard and felt the blizzard strike the house. Huddled close together and shivering under the covers they listened to it. Laura thought of the lost and lonely houses, each one alone and blind and cowering in the fury of the storm. There were houses in town, but not even a light from one of them could reach another. And the town was all alone on the frozen, endless prairie, where snow drifted and winds howled and the whirling blizzard put out the stars and the sun.

Laura tried to think of the good brown smell and taste of the beef for dinner tomorrow, but she could not forget that now the houses and the town would be all alone till spring. There was half a bushel of wheat that they could grind to make flour, and there were the few potatoes, but nothing more to eat until the train came. The wheat and the potatoes were not enough.

22

Cold and Dark

T hat blizzard seemed never to end. It paused sometimes, only to roar again quickly and more furiously out of the north-west. Three days and nights of yelling shrill winds and roaring fury beat at the dark, cold house and ceaselessly scoured it with ice-sand. Then the sun shone out, from morning till noon perhaps, and the dark anger of winds and icy snow came again.

Sometimes in the night, half-awake and cold, Laura half-dreamed that the roof was scoured thin. Horribly the great blizzard, large as the sky, bent over it and scoured with an enormous invisible cloth, round and round on the paper-thin roof, till a hole wore through and squealing, chuckling, laughing a deep Ha! Ha! the blizzard whirled in. Barely in time to save herself, Laura jumped awake.

Then she did not dare to sleep again. She lay still and small in the dark, and all around her the black darkness of night, that had always been restful and kind to her, was

216

now a horror. She had never been afraid of the dark. 'I am not afraid of the dark,' she said to herself over and over, but she felt that the dark would catch her with claws and teeth if it could hear her move or breathe. Inside the walls, under the roof where the nails were clumps of frost, even under the covers where she huddled, the dark was crouched and listening.

Daytimes were not so bad as the nights. The dark was thinner then and ordinary things were in it. A dark twilight filled the kitchen and the lean-to. Mary and Carrie took turns at the coffee mill that must never stop grinding. Ma made the bread and swept and cleaned and fed the fire. In the lean-to Laura and Pa twisted hay till their cold hands could not hold the hay to twist it and must be warmed at the stove.

The hay-fire could not keep the cold out of the kitchen, but close to the stove the air was warm. Mary's place was in front of the oven with Grace in her lap. Carrie stood behind the stovepipe and Ma's chair was on the other side of the stove. Pa and Laura leaned over the stove hearth into the warmth that rose upward.

Their hands were red and swollen, the skin was cold, and covered with cuts made by the sharp slough hay. The hay was cutting away the cloth of their coats on the left side and along the underneath of their left coat sleeves. Ma patched the worn places, but the hay cut away the patches.

For breakfast there was brown bread. Ma toasted it crisp and hot in the oven and she let them dip it in their tea.

'It was thoughtful of you, Charles, to lay in such a supply of tea,' she said. There was still plenty of tea and there was still sugar for it.

For the second meal of the day she boiled twelve potatoes in their jackets. Little Grace needed only one, the others had two apiece, and Ma insisted that Pa take the extra one. 'They're not big potatoes, Charles,' she argued, 'and you must keep up your strength. Anyway, eat it to save it. We don't want it, do we, girls?'

'No, Ma,' they all said. 'No, thank you, Pa, truly I don't want it.' This was true. They were not really hungry. Pa was hungry. His eyes looked eagerly at the brown bread and the steaming potatoes when he came from struggling along the clothesline in the storm. But the others were only tired, tired of the winds and the cold and the dark, tired of brown bread and potatoes, tired and listless and dull.

Every day Laura found time to study a little. When enough hay was twisted to last for an hour, she sat down by Mary, between the stove and the table, and opened the schoolbooks. But she felt dull and stupid. She could not remember history and she leaned her head on her hand and looked at a problem on her slate without seeing how to solve it or wanting to.

'Come, come, girls! We must not mope,' Ma said. 'Straighten up, Laura and Carrie! Do your lessons briskly and then we'll have an entertainment.'

'How, Ma?' Carrie asked.

'Get your lessons first,' said Ma.

When study time was over, Ma took the Independent Fifth Reader. 'Now,' she said, 'let's see how much you can repeat from memory. You first, Mary. What shall it be?'

'The Speech of Regulus,' said Mary. Ma turned the leaves until she found it and Mary began.

' "Ye doubtless thought – for ye judge of Roman virtue by your own – that I would break my plighted oath rather than, returning, brook your vengeance!" ' Mary could repeat the whole of that splendid defiance. ' "Here in your capital do I defy you! Have I not conquered your armies, fired your towns, and dragged your generals at my chariot wheels, since first my youthful arms could wield a spear?" '

The kitchen seemed to grow larger and warmer. The blizzard winds were not as strong as those words.

'You did that perfectly, Mary,' Ma praised her. 'Now, Laura?'

'Old Tubal Cain,' Laura began, and the verses lifted her to her feet. You had to stand up and let your voice ring out with the hammer strokes of old Tubal Cain:

'Old Tubal Cain was a man of might,
  In the days when the earth was young.

By the fierce red light of his furnace bright,
The strokes of his hammer rung . . .'

Pa came in before Laura reached the end. 'Go on, go on,' he said, 'That warms me as much as the fire.' So Laura went on, while Pa got out of his coat that was white and stiff with snow driven into it, and leaned over the fire to melt the snow frozen in his eyebrows.

'And sang, "Hurrah for Tubal Cain!
Our staunch good friend is he;
And for the ploughshare and the plough
To him our praise shall be.
But while oppression lifts its head
Or a tyrant would be lord,
Though we may thank him for the plough,
We will not forget the sword."'

'You remembered every word correctly, Laura,' Ma said, shutting the book. 'Carrie and Grace shall have their turns tomorrow.'

It was time then to twist more hay but while Laura shivered and twisted the sharp stuff in the cold she thought of more verses. Tomorrow afternoon was something to look forward to. The Fifth Reader was full of beautiful speeches and poems and she wanted to remember perfectly as many of them as Mary remembered.

The blizzard stopped sometimes. The whirling winds straightened out and steadied, the air cleared above blowing snow, and Pa set out to haul hay.

Then Laura and Ma worked quickly to do the washing and hang it out in the cold to freeze dry. No one knew how soon the blizzard would come again. At any moment the cloud might rise and come faster than any horses could run. Pa was not safe out on the prairie away from the town.

Sometimes the blizzard stopped for half a day. Sometimes the sun shone from morning to sunset and the blizzard came back with the dark. On such days, Pa hauled three loads of hay. Until he came back and put David in the stable Laura and Ma worked hard and silently, looking often at the sky and listening to the wind, and Carrie silently watched the north-west through the peephole that she made on the window.

Pa often said that he could not have managed without David. 'He is such a good horse,' Pa said. 'I did not know a horse could be so good and patient.' When David fell through the snow, he always stood still until Pa shovelled him out. Then quietly and patiently he hauled the sled around the hole and went on until he fell through the snow crust again. 'I wish I had some oats or corn to give him,' Pa said.

When the roaring and shrieking winds came back and the scouring snow whirled again, Pa said, 'Well, there's hay enough to last awhile, thanks to David.'

The clothesline was there to guide him to the stable and back. There was hay and still some wheat and potatoes, and while the stormwinds blew Pa was safe at home. And in the afternoons Mary and Laura and Carrie recited. Even Grace knew 'Mary's Little Lamb', and 'Bo-peep Has Lost Her Sheep'.

Laura liked to see Grace's blue eyes and Carrie's shine with excitement when she told them:

> 'Listen, my children, and you shall hear
> Of the midnight ride of Paul Revere.
> The eighteenth of April in Seventy-five,
> Hardly a man is now alive
> Who remembers that famous day and
> year . . .'

She and Carrie both loved to repeat, in concert, 'The Swan's Nest':

> 'Little Ellie sits alone
> 'Mid the beeches of a meadow,
> By a stream side, on the grass,
> And the trees are showering down
> Doubles of their leaves in shadow
> On her shining hair and face . . .'

The air was warm and quiet there, the grass was warm in the sunshine, the clear water sang its song to itself, and the leaves softly murmured. The meadow's insects drowsily hummed. While they were there with little Ellie, Laura and Carrie almost forgot the cold. They hardly heard the winds and the whirling hard snow scouring the walls.

One still morning, Laura came downstairs to find Ma looking surprised and Pa laughing. 'Look out of the back door!' he told Laura.

She ran through the lean-to and opened the back door. There was a rough, low tunnel going into shadows in grey-white snow. Its walls and its floor were snow and its snow roof solidly filled the top of the doorway.

'I had to gopher my way to the stable this morning,' Pa explained.

'But what did you do with the snow?' Laura asked.

'Oh, I made the tunnel as low as I could get through. I dug the snow out and pushed it back of me and up through a hole that I blocked with the last of it. There's nothing like snow for keeping out wind!' Pa rejoined 'As long as that snowbank stands, I can do my chores in comfort.'

'How deep is the snow?' Ma wanted to know.

'I can't say. It's piled up considerably deeper than the lean-to roof,' Pa answered.

'You don't mean to say this house is buried in snow!' Ma exclaimed.

'A good thing if it is,' Pa replied. 'You notice the kitchen is warmer than it has been this winter?'

Laura ran upstairs. She scratched a peephole on the window and put her eyes to it. She could hardly believe them. Main Street was level with her eyes. Across the glittering snow she could see the blank, square top of Harthorn's false front sticking up like a short piece of solid board fence.

She heard a gay shout and then she saw horses' hoofs trotting rapidly before her eyes. Eight grey hoofs, with slender brown ankles swiftly bending and straightening, passed quickly by, and then a long sled with two pairs of boots standing on it. She crouched down, to look upward through the peephole, but the sled was gone. She saw only the sky sharp with sunlight that stabbed her eyes. She ran down to the warm kitchen to tell what she had seen.

'The Wilder boys,' Pa said. 'They're hauling hay.'

'How do you know, Pa?' Laura asked him. 'I only saw the horses' feet, and boots.'

'There's no one in town but those two, and me, that dares go out of town,' said Pa. 'Folks are afraid a blizzard'll come up. Those Wilder boys are hauling in all their slough hay from Big Slough and selling it for three dollars a load to burn.'

'Three dollars!' Ma exclaimed.

'Yes, and fair enough for the risk they take. They're making a good thing out of it. Wish I could. But they've got coal to burn. I'll be glad if we have enough hay to last us through. I wasn't counting on it for our winter's fuel.'

'They went by as high as the houses!' Laura exclaimed. She was still excited. It was strange to see horses' hoofs and a sled and boots in front of your eyes, as a little animal, a gopher, for instance, might see them.

'It's a wonder they don't sink in the drifts,' Ma said.

'Oh, no.' Pa was wolfing his toast and drinking his tea rapidly. 'They won't sink. These winds pack the snow as hard as rock. David's shoes don't even make tracks on it. The only trouble's where the grass is lodged and loose underneath.'

He got into his wraps in a hurry. 'Those boys have got the start of me this morning. I was digging the tunnel. Now I've got to dig David out of the stable. Got to haul hay while the sun shines!' he joked, as he shut the door behind him.

'He's feeling chipper because he's got that tunnel,' said Ma. 'It's a blessing he can do the chores in some comfort, out of the wind.'

That day they could not watch the sky from the kitchen window. So little cold came through the snow that Laura led Mary into the lean-to and taught her how to twist hay. Mary had wanted to learn but the lean-to had been too cold. It took her some time because she could not see how Laura twisted and held the strands and tucked in the ends, but at last she did it well. They stopped to warm themselves only a few times while they twisted the whole day's supply of hay sticks.

Then the kitchen was so warm that they need not crowd around the stove. The house was very still. The only sounds were the little sounds of Ma and Mary rocking, the slate pencil on the slate, the teakettle's pleasant hum, and their own low voices speaking.

'What a blessing this deep snowdrift is,' Ma said.

But they could not watch the sky. Watching it did no good. If the low grey cloud was swiftly rising, they could not stop it. They could not help Pa. He would see the cloud and reach shelter as quickly as he could. Laura thought this many times, but just the same she hurried upstairs through the cold to peep from the window.

Ma and Carrie looked at her quickly when she came down, and she always answered them out loud so that Mary would know. 'The sky's clear and not a thing is stirring but millions of glitters on the snow. I don't believe there's a breath of wind.'

That afternoon Pa dragged hay through the tunnel to cram the lean-to full. He had dug the tunnel past the stable door so that David could get out, and beyond the stable he had turned the tunnel at an angle, to check the winds that might blow into it.

'I never saw such weather,' he said. 'It must be all of forty degrees below zero and not a breath of air stirring. The whole world seems frozen solid. I hope this cold

226

holds. Going through that tunnel it's no chore at all to do the chores.'

Next day was exactly the same. The stillness and the dusk and the warmth seemed to be a changeless dream going on forever the same, like the clock's ticking. Laura jumped in her chair when the clock cleared its throat before it struck.

'Don't be so nervous, Laura,' Ma murmured as if she were half-asleep. They did not recite that day. They did not do anything. They just sat.

The night was still, too. But morning woke them with a howling fury. The winds had come again and the lashing whirl of snow.

'Well, the tunnel's going fast,' Pa said, when he came in to breakfast. His eyebrows were frozen white with snow again and his wraps were stiff with it. Cold was pressing the warmth back again to the stove. 'I did hope my tunnel would last through one of these onslaughts, anyway. Gosh dang this blizzard! It only lets go long enough to spit on its hands.'

'Don't swear, Charles!' Ma snapped at him. She clapped her hand to her mouth in horror. 'Oh, Charles, I'm sorry,' she apologized. 'I didn't mean to snap at you. But this wind, blowing and blowing . . .' Her voice died away and she stood listening.

'I know, Caroline,' Pa answered. 'I know just how it makes you feel. It tires you out. I'll tell you what, after breakfast we'll read for a while about Livingstone's Africa.'

'It's too bad I've burned so much hay this morning, Charles,' Ma said. 'I've had to burn more, trying to get the place warm.'

'Never mind, it's no trick to twist more,' Pa replied.

'I'll help, Pa,' Laura offered.

'We've got all day for it,' Pa said. 'Everything is snug at the stable till night. We'll twist hay first, then we'll read.'

Grace began to whimper. 'My feet's cold.'

'For shame, Grace! A big girl like you! Go warm your feet,' Laura told her.

'Come sit on my lap and warm them,' Mary said, feeling her way to her rocking chair before the oven.

After Laura and Pa had twisted a great pile of hay sticks and stacked them by the stove, Carrie brought Pa his big green book.

'Please read about the lions, Pa,' she asked him. 'We can play the wind is lions roaring.'

'I'm afraid I'll have to have a light, Caroline,' Pa said. 'This print is small.' Ma lighted the button lamp and set it by him. 'Now,' he said, 'this is a jungle night in Africa. The flickering light here is from our campfire. Wild animals are all around us, yowling and squealing and roaring, lions and tigers and hyenas and I guess a hippopotamus or two. They won't come anywhere near us because they are afraid of the fire. You hear big leaves rasping, too, and queer birds squawking. It's a thick, black, hot night with big stars overhead. Now I'm going to read what happens.' He began to read.

Laura tried to listen but she felt stupid and numb. Pa's voice slid away into the ceaseless noises of the storm. She felt that the blizzard must stop before she could do anything, before she could even listen or think, but it would never stop. It had been blowing forever.

She was tired. She was tired of the cold and the dark, tired of brown bread and potatoes, tired of twisting hay and grinding wheat, filling the stove and washing dishes and making beds and going to sleep and waking up. She was tired of the blizzard winds. There was no tune in them any more, only a confusion of sound beating on her ears.

'Pa,' she spoke suddenly, interrupting his reading, 'won't you play the fiddle?'

Pa looked at her in surprise. Then he laid down the book. 'Why yes, Laura,' he said. 'If you want to hear the fiddle, I'll play it.'

He opened and shut his hands and rubbed the fingers while Laura brought the fiddle-box from its warm shelter on the floor behind the stove.

Pa rosined the bow, tucked the fiddle under his chin, and touched the strings. He looked at Laura.

'Play "Bonnie Doon",' Laura said, and Pa played and sang:

'Ye banks and braes of bonnie Doon,
How can ye bloom sae fresh and fair?'

But every note from the fiddle was a very little wrong. Pa's fingers were clumsy. The music dragged and a fiddle string snapped.

'My fingers are too stiff and thick from being out in the cold so much, I can't play,' Pa spoke as if he were ashamed. He laid the fiddle in its box. 'Put it away, Laura, until some other time,' he said.

'I wish you'd help me, anyway, Charles,' Ma said. She took the coffee mill from Mary and emptied the ground wheat from its little drawer. She filled the small hopper with kernels and handed the mill to Pa. 'I'll need another grinding to make the bread for dinner,' she told him.

Ma took the covered dish of souring from its warm place under the stove. She stirred it briskly, then measured two cupfuls into a pan, added salt and saleratus, and the flour that Mary and Carrie had ground. Then she took the mill from Pa and added the flour he had made.

'That's just enough,' she said. 'Thank you, Charles.'

'I'd better be doing the chores now before it gets too dark,' Pa said.

'I'll have a hot meal ready and waiting by the time you come in,' Ma reminded him. He put on his wraps and went out into the storm.

Laura listened to the winds while she stared at the blank window without see it. The worst thing that had happened was that Pa could not play the fiddle. If she had not asked him to play it, he might not have known that he could not do it.

Ma, with Carrie crowded in beside her, sat in her rocking chair by the stove, opposite Mary. She held Grace in her arms and rocked slowly, softly singing to her:

> 'I will sing you a song of that beautiful land,
> The far away home of the soul
> Where no storms ever beat on that glittering
> strand
> While the years of eternity roll.'

THE LONG WINTER

The wailing hymn blended with the wail of the winds while night settled down, deepening the dusk of whirling snow.

23
The Wheat in the Wall

In the morning the snowdrift was gone. When Laura made a peephole on the upstairs window and looked through it she saw bare ground. Blown snow was driving over it in low clouds, but the street was hard, brown earth.

'Ma! Ma!' she cried. 'I can see the ground!'

'I know,' Ma answered. 'The winds blew all the snow away last night.'

'What time is it? I mean, what month is it?' Laura asked stupidly.

'It is the middle of February,' Ma answered.

Then spring was nearer than Laura had thought. February was a short month and March would be spring. The train would come again and they would have white bread and meat.

'I am so tired of brown bread with nothing on it,' Laura said.

'Don't complain, Laura!' Ma told her quickly. 'Never

complain of what you have. Always remember you are fortunate to have it.'

Laura had not meant to complain but she did not know how to explain what she had meant. She answered meekly, 'Yes, Ma.' Then, startled, she looked at the wheat sack in the corner. There was so little wheat left in it that it lay folded like an empty sack.

'Ma!' she exclaimed, 'Did you mean . . .' Pa had always said she must never be afraid. She must never be afraid of anything. She asked, 'How much more wheat is there?'

'I think enough for today's grinding,' Ma answered.

'Pa can't buy any more, can he?' Laura said.

'No, Laura. There's no more in town.' Ma laid the slices of brown bread carefully on the oven grate to toast for breakfast.

Then Laura braced herself, she steadied herself, and she said, 'Ma. Will we starve?'

'We won't starve, no,' Ma replied. 'If Pa must, he will kill Ellen and the heifer calf.'

'Oh, no! No!' Laura cried.

'Be quiet, Laura,' Ma said. Carrie and Mary were coming downstairs to dress by the stove, and Ma went up to carry Grace down.

Pa hauled hay all day, and came into the house only to say that he was going to Fuller's store for a minute before supper. When he came back he brought news.

'There's a rumour in town that some settler, eighteen or twenty miles south or south-east of here, raised some wheat last summer,' he said. 'They say he's wintering in his claim shanty.'

'Who says so?' Ma asked.

'It's a rumour,' Pa said again. 'Nearly everybody says so. Nearest I can find out, Foster is the man that started it. He says he heard it from somebody working on the railroad. Some fellow that was passing through last fall, he says, was telling about the crop of wheat this settler raised, said he had a ten-acre patch that must run thirty or forty bushels to the acre. Say three hundred bushels of wheat, within about twenty miles of here.'

'I trust you aren't thinking of starting out on such a wild-goose chase, Charles,' Ma said gently.

'A fellow might do it,' Pa remarked. 'With a couple of days clear weather and a snowfall to hold up the sled, he ought to be able to make it all ri—'

'No!' said Ma.

Pa looked at her, startled. They all stared at her. They had never seen Ma look like that. She was quiet but she was terrible.

Quietly she told Pa, 'I say, No. You don't take such a chance.'

'Why . . . Caroline!' Pa said.

'Your hauling hay is bad enough,' Ma told him. '*You don't go hunting for that wheat.*'

235

Pa said mildly, 'Not as long as you feel that way about it, I won't. But . . .'

'I won't hear any buts,' Ma said, still terrible. 'This time I put my foot down.'

'All right, that settles it,' Pa agreed.

Laura and Carrie looked at each other. They felt as if thunder and lightning had come down on them suddenly, and suddenly gone. Ma poured the tea with a trembling hand.

'Oh, Charles, I'm sorry, I spilled it,' she said

'Never mind,' said Pa. He poured the spilled tea from his saucer into the cup. 'A long time since I had to pour my tea into the saucer to cool it,' he mentioned.

'I'm afraid the fire's going down,' said Ma.

'It isn't the fire. The weather's turning colder,' said Pa.

'You couldn't go, anyway,' Ma said. 'There'd be nobody to do the chores and nobody to haul hay.'

'You're right, Caroline, you always are,' Pa assured her. 'We'll make out with what we have.' Then he glanced at the corner where the wheat sack had been. But he said nothing about it until he had done the chores and twisted some hay. He laid down the armful of hay sticks by the stove and spread his hands to warm.

'Out of wheat, Caroline?' he asked.

'Yes, Charles,' Ma said. 'There's bread for breakfast.'

'Running out of potatoes?'

'It seems as though everything is giving out at once,'

Ma answered. 'But I have six potatoes for tomorrow.'

'Where is the milk pail?' Pa asked.

'The milk pail?' Ma repeated.

'I'm going up the street a few minutes and I want the milk pail,' Pa said.

Laura brought him the milk pail. She could not help asking, 'Is there a milch cow in town, Pa?'

'No, Laura,' he said. He went through the front room and they heard the front door shut.

Almanzo and Royal were eating supper. Almanzo had stacked the pancakes with brown sugar and he had made plenty of them. Royal had eaten half-way down his stack, Almanzo was nearing the bottom of his, and one tall stack of two dozen pancakes, dripping melted brown sugar, was standing untouched when Pa knocked at the door. Royal opened it.

'Come in, Mr Ingalls! Sit up and have some pancakes with us!' Royal invited him.

'Thank you just the same. Could you be persuaded to sell me some wheat?' Pa asked, stepping in.

'Sorry,' Royal said. 'We have no more to sell.'

'Clean sold out, uh?' said Pa.

'Clean sold out!' said Royal.

'I'd be willing to pay pretty high for some wheat,' Pa said.

'I wish I'd brought out another carload,' Royal replied. 'Sit up and have some supper with us anyway. Manzo brags on his pancakes.'

Pa did not answer. He walked to the end wall and lifted one of the saddles from its peg. Almanzo exclaimed, 'Hey, what are you doing?'

Pa held the milk pail's rim firmly against the wall. He pulled the plug out of the knothole. A round stream of wheat, as large as the hole, poured rattling into the pail.

'I'm buying some wheat from you boys,' Pa answered Almanzo.

'Say, that's my seed wheat; and I'm not selling it!' Almanzo declared.

'We're out of wheat at my house and I am buying some,' Pa replied. The wheat kept on pouring into the pail, sliding down the climbing pile and tinkling a little against the tin. Almanzo stood watching him, but after a minute Royal sat down. He tipped his chair back against the wall, put his hands in his pockets, and grinned at Almanzo.

When the pail was full, Pa thrust the plug into the hole. He tapped it firm with his fist and then tapped lightly up the wall and across it.

'You've got plenty of wheat there,' he said. 'Now we'll talk price. What do you figure this pailful's worth?'

'How did you know it was there?' Almanzo wanted to know.

'The inside of this room doesn't fit the outside,' said Pa. 'It's a good foot short, allowing for two by four studding besides. Gives you a sixteen-inch space there. Any man with an eye can see it.'

'I'll be darned,' said Almanzo.

'I noticed that plug in the knothole, the day you had the saddles off on that antelope hunt,' Pa nodded. 'So I figured you had grain there. It's the only thing likely to run out of a knothole.'

'Anybody else in town know it?' Almanzo asked.

'Not that I know of,' Pa said.

'See here,' Royal put in, 'We didn't know you were out of wheat. That's Almanzo's wheat, it's not mine, but he wouldn't hang on to it and see anybody starve.'

'It's my seed wheat,' Almanzo explained. 'Extra good seed, too. And no telling either if seed will be shipped in here in time for spring planting. Of course I won't see

239

anybody starve, but somebody can go after that wheat that was raised south of town.'

'South-east, I heard,' Pa said. 'I did think of going myself, but . . .'

'You can't go,' Royal interrupted. 'Who'd take care of your folks if you got caught in a storm and . . . got delayed or anything?'

'This isn't settling what I'm to pay for this wheat,' Pa reminded them.

Almanzo waved that away, 'What's a little wheat between neighbours? You're welcome to it, Mr Ingalls. Draw up a chair and sample these pancakes before they get cold.'

But Pa insisted on paying for the wheat. After some talk about it, Almanzo charged a quarter and Pa paid it. Then he did sit down, as they urged him, and lifting the blanket cake on the untouched pile, he slipped from under it a section of the stack of hot, syrupy pancakes. Royal forked a brown slice of ham from the frying pan on to Pa's plate and Almanzo filled his coffee cup.

'You boys certainly live in the lap of luxury,' Pa remarked. The pancakes were no ordinary buckwheat pancakes. Almanzo followed his mother's pancake rule and the cakes were light as foam, soaked through with melted brown sugar. The ham was sugar-cured and hickory-smoked, from the Wilder farm in Minnesota. 'I don't know when I've eaten a tastier meal,' said Pa.

They talked about weather and hunting and politics, railroads and farming, and when Pa left both Royal and Almanzo urged him to drop in often. Neither of them played checkers, so they did not spend much time in the stores. Their own place was warmer.

'Now you've found the way, Mr Ingalls, come back!' Royal said heartily. 'Be glad to see you any time; Manzo and I get tired of each other's company. Drop in any time, the latchstring is always out!'

'I'll be glad to!' Pa was answering; he broke off and listened. Almanzo stepped out with him into the freezing wind. Stars glittered overhead, but in the north-west sky they were going out rapidly as solid darkness swept up over them. 'Here she comes!' said Pa. 'I guess nobody'll do any visiting for a spell. I'll just about make it home if I hurry.'

The blizzard struck the house when he was at the door so no one heard him come in. But they had little time to worry, for almost at once he came into the kitchen where they were all sitting in the dark. They were close to the stove and warm enough, but Laura was shivering, hearing the blizzard again and thinking that Pa was out in it.

'Here's some wheat to go on with, Caroline,' Pa said, setting the pail down beside her. She reached down to it and felt the kernels.

'Oh, Charles. Oh, Charles,' she said, rocking, 'I might have known you'd provide for us, but wherever did you

241

get it? I thought there was no wheat left in town.'

'I wasn't sure there was or I'd have told you. But I didn't want to raise hopes to be disappointed,' Pa explained. 'I agreed not to tell where I got it, but don't worry, Caroline. There's more where that came from.'

'Come, Carrie, I'm going to put you and Grace to bed now,' Ma said with new energy. When she came downstairs she lighted the button lamp and filled the coffee mill. The sound of the grinding began again, and it followed Laura and Mary up the cold stairs until it was lost in the blizzard's howling.

24

Not Really Hungry

'It's remarkable how the potatoes came out exactly even,' said Pa.

Slowly they ate the last potatoes, skins and all. The blizzard was beating and scouring at the house, the winds were roaring and shrieking. The window was pale in the twilight and the stove pressed out its feeble heat against the cold.

'I'm not hungry, honest, Pa,' Laura said. 'I wish you'd finish mine.'

'Eat it, Laura,' Pa told her, kindly but firmly. Laura had to choke down mouthfuls of the potato that had grown cold on the cold plate. She broke a little piece from her slice of brown bread and left the rest. Only the hot, sweet tea was good. She felt numb and half-asleep.

Pa put on his overcoat and cap again and went into the lean-to to twist hay. Ma roused herself. 'Come, girls!

243

Wash up the dishes and wipe the stove and sweep while I make the beds, and then settle down to your studies. When they're done I'll hear your recitations, and then I have a surprise for supper!'

No one really cared but Laura tried to answer Ma.

'Have you, Ma? That's nice,' she said. She washed the dishes and swept the floor, and getting into her patched coat she went into the lean-to to help Pa twist hay. Nothing seemed real but the blizzard that never stopped.

That afternoon she began:

'Old Tubal Cain was a mighty man, a mighty man was he,
He called for his pipe and he called for his bowl
And he called for his fiddlers three . . .'

'Oh, Ma, I don't know what's the matter with me! I can't think!' she almost wailed.

'It's this storm. I believe we are all half-asleep,' Ma said. After some time she went on, 'We must stop listening to it.'

Everything was very slow. Mary asked after a while, 'How can we stop listening to it?'

Ma slowly let the book close. At last she got up. 'I will get the surprise,' she said.

She brought it from the front room. It was a part of a salt codfish, frozen solidly, that she had been keeping there. 'We'll have codfish gravy on our bread, for dinner!' she told them.

'By George, Caroline, nothing can beat the Scotch!' Pa exclaimed.

Ma put the codfish in the open oven to thaw, and took the coffee mill from him. 'The girls and I will finish the grinding. I'm sorry, Charles, but I'll need more hay, and you must have time to warm before you do the chores.'

Laura went to help him. When they brought in the armfuls of hay sticks, Carrie was wearily grinding at the coffee mill and Ma was flaking the codfish.

'Just the smell of it chirks a fellow up,' Pa said. 'Caroline, you are a wonder.'

'I think it will be tasty for a change,' Ma admitted. 'But the bread's what we have to be thankful for, Charles.' She saw him looking at the wheat in the milk pail and she told him, 'There's enough to outlast this storm, if it's no longer than usual.'

Laura took the coffee mill from Carrie. It worried her to see how thin and white Carrie was, and so exhausted from grinding. But even worry was dull and farther away than the hateful ceaseless pounding of the storm. The coffee mill's handle ground round and round, it must not stop. It seemed to make her part of the whirling winds driving the snow round and round over the earth in the air, whirling and beating at Pa on his way to the stable, whirling and shrieking at the lonely houses, whirling the snow between them and up to the sky and far away, whirling forever over the endless prairie.

25

Free and Independent

All the days of that storm Almanzo was thinking. He did not crack jokes as usual, and when doing the chores he curried and brushed his horses mechanically. He even sat thoughtfully whittling and let Royal make the supper pancakes.

'You know what I think, Roy?' he asked at last.

'It ought to be something worth while, the time you've been spending on it,' Royal replied.

'I think there's folks in this town that are starving,' Almanzo stated.

'Some are getting pretty hungry, maybe,' Royal admitted, turning the pancakes.

'I said starving,' Almanzo repeated. 'Take Ingalls, there's six in his family. You notice his eyes and how thin he was? He said he was out of wheat. Well, take a peck, say a peck and a quarter, of wheat, how long will it last a family of six? Figure it out for yourself.'

'He must have other provisions,' said Royal.

'They came out here summer before last and they didn't go west with the railroad jobs. He took a

247

homestead. You know yourself how much a man can raise the first summer on sod. And there's been no work around here for wages.'

'What are you getting at?' Royal asked. 'Going to sell your seed wheat?'

'Not on your tintype! Not if there's any way to save it,' Almanzo declared.

'Well, then what?' Royal demanded.

Almanzo paid no attention to the question. 'I figure Ingalls isn't the only man in about the same fix,' he continued. Slowly and methodically he reckoned up the supply of provisions in town when the train stopped running, and named the families that he had reason to believe were already running short. He estimated the time it would take to clear the railroad cuts of snow, after the blizzard stopped.

'Say they stop in March,' he concluded, 'I've proved that folks will have to eat up my wheat or starve before provisions can be shipped in, haven't I?'

'I guess you have, for a fact,' Royal admitted soberly.

'On the other hand, suppose this weather keeps up till April. That old Indian predicted seven months of it, don't forget. If trains aren't running before April, or if they don't bring in seed wheat before then, I've got to save my seed wheat, or lose a year's crop.'

'Looks that way,' Royal agreed.

'And to top that, if trains don't run early in April folks will starve anyway. Even if they have eaten up my wheat.'

'Well, come to the point,' said Royal.

'This is the point. Somebody's got to go get that wheat that was raised south of town.'

Royal slowly shook his head. 'Nobody'll do it. It's as much as a man's life is worth.'

All at once, Almanzo was cheerful again. He pulled up to the table, lifted a stack of pancakes on to his plate. 'Oh well, why not take a chance?' he asked gaily, pouring molasses over the steaming pile. 'You can't sometimes 'most always tell!'

'Forty miles?' Royal said. 'Go out on these prairies looking for a needle in a haystack – twenty miles and back? Man alive, you know yourself nobody can tell when a blizzard will hit you. We haven't had more than one clear day at a time since this thing started. More often, half a day. It can't be done, Manzo. A fellow wouldn't have the chance of a snowball in hades.'

'Somebody's got to do it,' Almanzo replied reasonably. 'I proved that.'

'Yes, but, gee whillikins!' said Royal.

'"Be sure you're right, then go ahead,"' Almanzo quoted their father.

'"Better be safe than sorry,"' Royal retorted with their mother's saying.

'Oh well, you're a storekeeper, Roy,' Almanzo returned. 'A farmer takes chances. He has to.'

'Almanzo,' Royal said solemnly, 'if I let you lose your fool self out on these prairies, what'll I say to Father and Mother?'

'You tell 'em you had nothing to say about it, Roy,' Almanzo answered. 'I'm free, white, and twenty-one . . . or as good as. Anyway, this is a free country and I'm free and independent. I do as I please.'

'Don't go off half-cocked, Manzo,' Royal urged him. 'Think it over.'

'I been thinking it over,' said Almanzo.

Royal was silent. They sat quietly eating in the steady warmth of the coal fire and the strong light shining from the lamp and its bright tin reflector. The walls trembled a little and the shadows on them slightly quivered under the blows of winds that squealed along the eaves, split shrieking at the corners, and always roared like a waterfall.

Almanzo took another stack of pancakes.

Suddenly Royal laid down his knife and pushed back his plate.

'One thing's sure,' he said. 'You're not going to tackle any such foolhardy trip alone. If you're bound and determined to do it, I'm going along with you.'

'See here!' Almanzo exclaimed. 'We *can't* both of us go!'

26
Breathing Spell

Next morning was still. The sun shone bright and cold and only the round-and-round growl of the coffee grinder, the rush of a steady wind, and the crackling of the hay sounded in the lean-to where Laura and Mary worked. They were very cold. Neither could twist more than two or three sticks of hay without going to thaw their hands over the stove.

They could barely keep the fire alive; they could not pile up a store of sticks and get time to help with the washing. So Ma put the washing by till later. 'Perhaps it will be warmer tomorrow,' she said, and she helped twist hay. She spelled Mary and Laura in turns so that they could spell Carrie at the coffee grinder.

Pa did not come home until late afternoon. The afternoon meal of bread and tea was waiting when he came at last.

'Gee whillikins, it's a cold day,' he said.

He had been able to haul only one load of hay that

day. The haystacks were buried in snow. He had to dig the hay out of enormous drifts. Fresh snow had covered the sled's old tracks and changed the look of the slough. David had continually fallen deep into hidden pockets of slough grass.

'Did your nose freeze, Pa?' Grace asked him anxiously. Of course in this weather Pa's ears and his nose froze so that he had to rub them with snow to thaw them. He pretended to Grace that his nose grew longer every time it froze, and Grace pretended to believe that it did. This was their own special joke.

'Froze it five or six times today,' Pa answered her, tenderly feeling his red, swollen nose.

'If spring doesn't come soon, I'm going to have a nose as long as an elephant's. Ears like an elephant's, too.' That made Grace laugh.

After they had eaten the daily bread, Pa twisted hay enough to last till bedtime. He had done the chores when he put David in the stable. There was still a little daylight left, and he said, 'I believe I'll go over to Bradley's drugstore and watch the checker game awhile.'

'Do, Charles,' Ma said. 'Why don't you play some checkers yourself?'

'Well, you see, those bachelors spend all their time this winter at checkers and cards,' Pa answered. 'They are good checker players, having nothing else to do. Too good for me. So I'll just look on but I don't know's there's anything more enjoyable than watching a good game of checkers.'

He was not gone long. The drugstore was so cold, he said, that there was no game of checkers that day. But there was news.

'Almanzo Wilder and Cap Garland are going after that wheat south of town.'

Ma's face went still and her eyes opened as if she saw something frightening. 'How far did you say it was?'

'No one knows exactly,' Pa said. 'Nor exactly where it is. There's only a rumour that a settler around there somewhere raised wheat last year. Nobody around here sold wheat to anybody in town, so it must be there, if he is, and if he raised wheat. Foster says somebody told him the settler was wintering on his claim. The boys are going to try to find it. Loftus has put up the money for them to buy all that they can haul.'

Grace began to clamour at his knee, trying to climb up to measure his nose with her finger. He lifted her absently. Even Grace, little as she was, saw that this was no time for a joke. She looked anxiously up at him and then at Ma, and sat still on Pa's knee.

'When are they starting?' Ma asked.

'First thing tomorrow morning. They built a sled for Cap Garland today. Both Wilders were going but they decided that one of them ought to stay in case the one who goes gets caught in a blizzard.'

No one said anything for a moment.

'They may make it all right,' Pa said. 'So long as this clear weather holds, they'll be able to travel. It may hold for two or three days. You can't tell.'

'That's the trouble,' said Ma. 'You can't tell.'

'If they do make it,' Pa pointed out, 'we'll have wheat enough to last us till spring. If the wheat's there and they find it.'

In the night Laura felt the shock and heard the howls of the blizzard winds. There had been only one short day of rest. The blizzard would let nobody start out tomorrow to look for wheat.

27
For Daily Bread

In the third night of that storm a stillness woke Almanzo. The blizzard had stopped. He reached out through the cold to his waistcoat hanging on a chair, got out his watch and a match, and saw that the time was nearly three o'clock.

In winter's dark, cold mornings he still missed his father's routing him out of bed. Now he had to rout himself out of warm blankets into the cold. He must light the lantern, stir up the fire, and break the ice in the water pail himself, and he could choose between getting his own breakfast and going hungry. Three o'clock on winter mornings was the only time that he was not glad to be free and independent.

Once out of bed and into his clothes, though, he liked early morning better than any other part of the day. The air was fresher then than at any other time. Low in the eastern sky hung the morning star. The temperature was ten below zero, the wind blew steadily. The day promised to be fair.

When he rode down Main Street on the hay-sled, the sun had not yet risen but the morning star had melted in an upward rush of light. The Ingalls' building stood solid black against the endless eastern prairie covered with snow. Down Second Street, beyond it, the two stables with their haystacks looked small, and beyond them Garland's little house had a speck of light in its kitchen. Cap Garland came riding up on his sled, driving his buckskin gelding.

He waved to Almanzo and Almanzo lifted his own arms, stiff in the weight of woollen sleeves. Their faces were wrapped in mufflers and there was no need to say anything. Three days ago, before the last blizzard struck, they had made their plan. Almanzo drove on without stopping and Cap Garland swung the buckskin into Main Street behind him.

At the end of the short street Almanzo turned south-east to cross the neck of Big Slough at its narrowest place. The sun was rising. The sky was a thin, cold blue and the earth to its far horizon was covered with snowdrifts, flushed pink and faintly shadowed with blue. The horse's breath made a white cloud about his head.

The only sounds were the clumping of Prince's hoofs on the hard snow and the rasp of the sled's runners. There was not a track on the waves of snow, not a print of rabbit's paw or bird's claws. There was no trace of a road, no sign that any living thing had ever been on the frozen snow fields where every curve was changed and unknown. Only the wind had furrowed them in tiny wavelets, each holding its own faint line of blue shadow, and the wind was blowing a spray of snow from every smooth, hard crest.

There was something mocking in the glitter of that trackless sea where every shadow moved a little and the blown snow spray confused the eyes searching for lost landmarks. Almanzo judged directions and distance as well as he could, where everything was changed and uncertain, and he thought, 'Well, we'll have to make it by guess and by golly!'

He guessed that he had struck the neck of the buried Big Slough somewhere near the place where he crossed to haul hay. If he was right, the snow underneath the sled would be packed hard and in five minutes or less he would be safe on upland again. He glanced back. Cap had slowed the buck-skin and was following at a cautious distance. With no warning, Prince went down.

'Whoa-oa, steady!' Almanzo shouted through his muffler but he shouted calmly and soothingly. Only the horse's snorting head stuck up from the grassy air-pocket in front of the sled. The sled ran on, sliding forward; there is no way to put brakes on a sled, but it stopped in time.

'Whoa, Prince. Steady now,' Almanzo said, drawing the reins firmly. 'Steady, steady.' Buried deep in snow, Prince stood still.

Almanzo jumped off the sled. He unhitched the whiffletree from the chain fastened to the sled's runners. Cap Garland drove around him and stopped. Almanzo went to Prince's head and wallowing down into the broken snow and tangling dead grass he took hold of the reins under the bits. 'Steady, Prince old fellow, steady, steady,' he said, for his own flounderings were frightening Prince again.

Then he trampled down the snow until he could persuade Prince that it was firm enough to step on. Holding Prince by the bits again he urged him forward till with a mighty heave he burst up out of the hole and Almanzo led him rapidly climbing up out of the hole to the solid snow again. He led him on to Cap Garland's sled and handed over the reins to Cap.

Cap's light eyes showed that he was cheerfully grinning under the muffler. 'So that's the way you do it!' he said.

'Nothing much to it,' Almanzo replied.

'Fine day for a trip,' Cap remarked.

'Yep, it's a fine, large morning!' Almanzo agreed.

Almanzo went to pull his empty sled sidewise behind the large hole that Prince and he had made in the snow. He liked Cap Garland. Cap was lighthearted and merry but he would fight his weight in wildcats. When Cap Garland had reason to lose his temper his eyes narrowed and glittered with a look that no man cared to stand up to. Almanzo had seen him make the toughest railroader back down.

259

Taking a coiled rope from his sled Almanzo tied one end of the sled's chain. The other end he tied to Prince's whiffle-tree, and with Prince helping him pull he guided the sled round the hole. Then he hitched Prince to the sled, coiled the long rope again, and drove on.

Cap Garland fell in behind him once more. He was really only a month younger than Almanzo. They were both nineteen. But because Almanzo had a homestead claim, Cap supposed that he was older than twenty-one. Partly for that reason, Cap treated Almanzo with respect. Almanzo made no objection to that.

Leading the way, he drove towards the sun until he was sure he had crossed Big Slough. Then he headed southwards towards the twin lakes, Henry and Thompson.

The only colour now on the endless snow-fields was a pale reflection of the blue sky. Everywhere tiny glints sparkled sharply. The glitter stabbed Almanzo's eyes, screwed almost shut in the slot between his cap and muffler. The icy wool blew out and sucked back against his nose and mouth with every breath.

His hands grew too cold to feel the reins, so he shifted the reins from hand to hand, beating the free arm against his chest to make the blood flow warm in it.

When his feet grew numb he stepped off the sled and ran beside it. His heart, pumping fast, forced warmth to his feet until they tingled and itched and burned, and he jumped on to the sled again.

'Nothing like exercise to warm you up!' he shouted back to Cap.

'Let me in by the stove!' Cap shouted, and he jumped off his sled and ran beside it.

So they went on, running, riding, and thumping their chests, then running again, while the horses briskly trotted. 'Say, how long do we keep this up?' Cap shouted once, joking. 'Till we find wheat, or hell freezes!' Almanzo answered.

'You can skate on it now!' Cap shouted back.

They went on. The rising sun poured down sunshine that seemed colder than the wind. There was no cloud in the sky, but the cold steadily grew more intense.

Prince went down again in some unknown little slough. Cap drove up and stopped. Almanzo unhitched Prince, got him up on the firm snow, hauled the sled around the hole, hitched up again.

'See the Lone Cottonwood anywhere ahead?' he asked Cap.

'Nope. But I can't depend on my eyes,' Cap answered. The sun-glare made them see black spots everywhere.

They rewound their mufflers, shifting the ice-patches away from their raw faces. To the far horizon all around them, there was nothing but glittering snow and the cruel wind blowing.

'Lucky so far,' Almanzo said. 'Gone down only twice.'

He stepped on to his sled and started and heard Cap

shout. Swinging in to follow, the buckskin had gone down.

Cap dug him out, hauled the sled around the hole, and hitched up again.

'Nothing like exercise to keep a fellow warm!' he reminded Almanzo.

From the top of the next low swell they saw the Lone Cottonwood, bare and gaunt. Snow covered the twin lakes and the low bushes that grew between them. Only the lonely tree's bare top rose up from the endless whiteness.

As soon as he saw it, Almanzo turned westward quickly to keep well away from the sloughs around the lakes. On the upland grass the snow was solid.

The Lone Tree was the last landmark. It was soon lost again in the trackless waves of snow. There was no road, no trace nor track of any kind to be seen anywhere. No one knew where the settler lived who had raised wheat. No one was even sure that he was still in that country. It might be that he had gone out for the winter. It might be that there had never been such a man. There was only a rumour that someone had told somebody that a man living somewhere in that region had raised wheat.

One wave of the endless frozen snow-sea was like another. Beneath the snow-spray blown from their crests, the low prairie swells seemed to come on forever, all the same. The sun slowly rose higher and the cold increased.

There was no sound but the horses' hoofs and the rasp of the sled runners that made no tracks on the ice-hard snow, and the rushing sound of the wind that faintly whistled against the sled.

From time to time Almanzo looked back and Cap shook his head. Neither of them saw any wisp of smoke against the cold sky. The small, cold sun seemed to hang motionless but it was climbing. The shadows narrowed, the waves of snow and the prairie's curves seemed to flatten. The white wilderness levelled out, bleak and empty.

'How far we going?' Cap shouted.

'Till we find that wheat!' Almanzo called back. But he, too, was wondering whether there was any wheat in that endless emptiness. The sun was in the zenith now, the day half gone. There was still no threat in the north-western sky, but it would be unusual to have more than this one clear day between blizzards.

Almanzo knew they should turn back towards town. Numb from cold, he stumbled off the sled and ran on beside it. He did not want to go back to the hungry town and say that he had turned back with an empty sled.

'How far you figure we've come?' Cap asked.

'About twenty miles,' Almanzo guessed. 'Think we better go back?'

'Never give up till you're licked!' Cap said cheerfully.

They looked around. They were on an upland. If the lower air had not been a little hazy with a glitter of blowing snow, they could have seen perhaps twenty miles. But the prairie swells, that seemed level under the high

263

sun, hid the town to the north-west. The north-west sky was still clear.

Stamping their feet and beating their arms on their chests they searched the white land from west to east, as far south as they could see. There was not a wisp of smoke anywhere.

'Which way'll we go?' Cap asked.

'Any way's as good as any other,' Almanzo said. They rewound their mufflers again. Their breath had filled the mufflers with ice. They could hardly find a spot of wool to relieve the pain of ice on skin that it had chafed raw. 'How are your feet?' he asked Cap.

'They don't say,' Cap replied. 'They'll be all right, I guess. I'm going on running.'

'So am I,' Almanzo said. 'If they don't warm up pretty soon, we better stop and rub them with snow. Let's follow this swell west a ways. If we don't find anything that way we can circle back, farther south.'

'Suits me,' Cap agreed. Their good horses went willingly into a trot again and they ran on beside the sleds.

The upland ended sooner than they had expected. The snow-field sloped downward and spread into a flat hollow that the upland had hidden. It looked like a slough. Almanzo pulled Prince to a walk and got on to the sled to look the land over. The flat hollow ran on towards the west; he saw no way to get around it without turning back along the upland. Then he saw, ahead and across the slough, a smear of grey-brown in the snow blowing from a drift. He stopped Prince and yelled, 'Hi, Cap! That look like smoke ahead there?'

Cap was looking at it. 'Looks like it comes out of a snowbank!' he shouted.

Almanzo drove on down the slope. After a few minutes he called back, 'It's smoke all right! There's some kind of house there!'

They had to cross the slough to reach it. In their hurry, Cap drove alongside Almanzo and the buckskin went down. This was the deepest hole they had got a horse out of yet, and all around it the snow broke down into air-pockets under the surface till there seemed no end to their floundering. Shadows were beginning to creep eastward before they got the buckskin to solid footing and began cautiously to go on.

The thin smoke did rise from a long snowbank, and there was not a track on the snow. But when they circled and came back on the southern side, they saw that the snow had been shovelled away from before a door in the snowbank. They pulled up their sleds and shouted.

The door opened and a man stood there, astonished. His hair was long and his unshaven beard grew up to his cheekbones.

'Hello! Hello!' he cried. 'Come in! Come in! Where did you come from? Where are you going? Come in! How long can you stay? Come right in!' He was so excited that he did not wait for answers.

'We've got to take care of our horses first,' Almanzo answered.

The man snatched on a coat and came out, saying, 'Come along, right over this way, follow me. Where did you fellows come from?'

'We just drove out from town,' Cap said. The man led the way to a door in another snowbank. They told him their names while they unhitched, and he said his name was Anderson. They led the horses into a warm, sod stable, snug under the snowbank.

The end of the stable was partitioned off with poles and a rough door, and grains of wheat had trickled through a crack. Almanzo and Cap looked at it and grinned to each other.

They watered Prince and the buckskin from the well at the door, fed them on oats, and left them tied to a mangerful of hay beside Anderson's team of black horses. Then they followed Anderson to the house under the snowbank.

The one room's low ceiling was made of poles covered with hay and sagging under the weight of snow. The walls were sods. Anderson left the door ajar to let in a little light.

'I haven't got my window shovelled out since the last blow,' he said. 'The snow piles over that little rise to the north-west and covers me up. Keeps the place so warm I don't need much fuel. Sod houses are the warmest there are, anyway.'

The room was warm, and steamy from a kettle boiling on the stove. Anderson's dinner was on a rough table built against the wall. He urged them to draw up and eat with him. He had not seen a soul since last October, when he had gone to town and brought home his winter's supplies.

Almanzo and Cap sat down with him and ate heartily of the boiled beans, sourdough biscuit and dried-apple sauce. The hot food and coffee warmed them, and their thawing feet burned so painfully that they knew they were not frozen. Almanzo mentioned to Mr Anderson that he and Cap might buy some wheat.

'I'm not selling any,' Mr Anderson said flatly. 'All I raised, I'm keeping for seed. What are you buying wheat for, this time of year?' he wanted to know.

They had to tell him that the trains had stopped running, and the people in town were hungry.

'There's women and children that haven't had a square meal since before Christmas,' Almanzo put it to him. 'They've got to get something to eat or they'll starve to death before spring.'

'That's not my lookout,' said Mr Anderson. 'Nobody's responsible for other folks that haven't got enough forethought to take care of themselves.'

'Nobody thinks you are,' Almanzo retorted. 'And

nobody's asking you to give them anything. We'll pay you the full elevator price of eighty-two cents a bushel, and save you hauling it to town into the bargain.'

'I've got no wheat to sell,' Mr Anderson answered, and Almanzo knew he meant what he said.

Cap came in then, his smile flashing in his raw-red face chapped by the icy wind. 'We're open and above-board with you, Mr Anderson. We've put our cards on the table. The folks in town have got to have some of your wheat or starve. All right, they've got to pay for it. What'll you take?'

'I'm not trying to take advantage of you boys,' Mr Anderson said. 'I don't want to sell. That's my seed wheat. It's my next year's crop. I could have sold it last fall if I was going to sell it.'

Almanzo quickly decided. 'We'll make it a dollar a bushel,' he said. 'Eighteen cents a bushel above market price. And don't forget we do the hauling to boot.'

'I'm not selling my seed,' said Mr Anderson. 'I got to make a crop next summer.'

Almanzo said meditatively, 'A man can always buy seed. Most folks out here are going to. You're throwing away a clear profit of eighteen cents a bushel above market price, Mr Anderson.'

'How do I know they'll ship in seed wheat in time for sowing?' Mr Anderson demanded.

Cap asked him reasonably, 'Well, for that matter, how

do you know you'll make a crop? Say you turn down this cash offer and sow your wheat. Hailstorm's liable to hit it, or grasshoppers.'

'That's true enough,' Mr Anderson admitted.

'The one thing you're sure of is cash in your pocket,' said Almanzo.

Mr Anderson slowly shook his head. 'No, I'm not selling. I like to killed myself breaking forty acres last summer. I got to keep the seed to sow it.'

Almanzo and Cap looked at each other. Almanzo took out his wallet. 'We'll give you a dollar and twenty-five cents a bushel. Cash.' He laid the stack of bills on the table.

Mr Anderson hesitated. Then he took his gaze away from the money.

'"A bird in the hand is worth two in the bush,"' Cap said.

Mr Anderson glanced again at the bills in spite of himself. Then he leaned back and considered. He scratched his head. 'Well,' he said finally, 'I might sow some oats.'

Neither Almanzo nor Cap said anything. They knew his mind was quivering in the balance and if he decided now against selling, he would not change. At last he decided, 'I guess I could let you have around sixty bushels at that price.'

Almanzo and Cap rose quickly from the table.

'Come on, let's get it loaded!' said Cap. 'We're a long way from home.'

Mr Anderson urged them to stay all night but Almanzo agreed with Cap. 'Thanks just the same,' he said hurriedly, 'but one day is all we have between blizzards lately, and it's past noon now. We're already late getting back.'

'The wheat's not sacked,' Mr Anderson pointed out, but Almanzo said, 'We brought sacks.'

They hurried to the stable. Mr Anderson helped them shovel the wheat from the bin into the two-bushel sacks, and they loaded the sleds. While they hitched up they asked Mr Anderson how best to get across the slough, but he had not crossed it that winter, and for lack of landmarks he could not show them exactly where he had driven through the grass last summer.

'You boys better spend the night here,' he urged them again, but they told him good-bye and started home.

They drove from the shelter of the big snowbanks into the piercing cold wind, and they had hardly begun to cross the flat valley when Prince broke down into an airpocket. Swinging out to circle the dangerous place, Cap's buckskin felt the snow give way under him so suddenly that he screamed as he went plunging down.

The horse's scream was horrible. For a moment Almanzo had all he could do to keep Prince quiet. Then he saw Cap down in the snow, hanging on to the frantic buckskin by the bits. Plunging and rearing, the buckskin almost jerked Cap's sled into the hole. It tipped on the very edge and the load of wheat slid partly off it.

'All right?' Almanzo asked when the buckskin seemed quiet.

'Yep!' Cap answered. Then for some time they worked, each unhitching his own horse down in the broken snow and wiry grass, and floundering about in it, trampling and stamping to make a solid footing for the horse. They came up chilled to the bone and covered with snow.

They tied both horses to Almanzo's sled, then unloaded

Cap's sled, dragged it back from the hole, and piled the snowy, hundred and twenty-five pound sacks on to it again. They hitched up again. It was hard to make their numb fingers buckle the stiff, cold straps. And gingerly once more Almanzo drove on across the treacherous slough.

Prince went down again but fortunately the buckskin did not. With Cap to help, it did not take so long to get Prince out once more. And with no further trouble they reached the upland.

Almanzo stopped there and called to Cap, 'Think we better try to pick up our trail back?'

'Nope!' Cap answered. 'Better hit out for town. We've got no time to lose.' The horses' hoofs and the sleds had made no tracks on the hard snowcrust. The only marks were the scattered holes where they had floundered in the sloughs and these lay east of the way home.

Almanzo headed towards the north-west, across the wide prairie white in its covering of snow. His shadow was his only guide. One prairie swell was like another, one snow-covered slough differed from the next only in size. To cross the lowland meant taking the risk of breaking down and losing time. To follow the ridges of higher ground meant more miles to travel. The horses were growing tired. They were afraid of falling into hidden holes in the snow and this fear added to their tiredness.

Time after time they did fall through a thin snow crust.

Cap and Almanzo had to unhitch them, get them out, hitch up again.

They plodded on, into the sharp cold of the wind. Too tired now to trot with their heavy loads, the horses did not go fast enough so that Almanzo and Cap could run by the sleds. They could only stamp their feet hard as they walked to keep them from freezing, and beat their arms against their chests.

They grew colder. Almanzo's feet no longer felt the shock when he stamped them. The hand that held the lines was so stiff that the fingers would not unclasp. He put the lines around his shoulders to leave both hands free, and with every step he whipped his hands across his chest to keep the blood moving in them.

'Hey, Wilder!' Cap called. 'Aren't we heading too straight north?'

'How do I know?' Almanzo called back.

They plodded on. Prince went down again and stood with drooping head while Almanzo unhitched him and trampled the snow, led him out and hitched him again. They climbed to an upland, followed it around a slough, went down to cross another slough. Prince went down.

'You want me to take the lead awhile?' Cap asked, when Almanzo had hitched up again. 'Save you and Prince the brunt of it.'

'Suits me,' said Almanzo. 'We'll take turns.'

After that, when a horse went down, the other took the

lead until he went down. The sun was low and a haze was thickening in the north-west.

'We ought to see the Lone Cottonwood from that rise ahead,' Almanzo said to Cap.

After a moment Cap answered, 'Yes, I think we will.'

But when they topped the rise there was nothing but the same endless, empty waves of snow beyond it and the thick haze low in the north-west. Almanzo and Cap looked at it, then spoke to their horses and went on. But they kept the sleds closer together.

The sun was setting red in the cold sky when they saw the bare top of the Lone Cottonwood away to the north-east. And in the north-west the blizzard cloud was plain to be seen, low along the horizon.

'It seems to be hanging off,' Almanzo said. 'I've been watching it from away back.'

'So have I,' said Cap. 'But we better forget about being cold and *drive*. Let's ride awhile.'

'You bet you,' Almanzo agreed. 'I could do with a few minutes' rest.'

They said nothing more except to urge the tired horses to a faster walk. Cap led the way straight over the rises and straight across the hollows, into the teeth of the wind. Heads bent against it, they kept going till the buckskin broke through a snowcrust.

Almanzo was so close behind that he could not avoid the hidden airhole. He turned quickly aside but Prince went down near the buckskin. Between them the whole snow crust gave way and Almanzo's sled tipped, load and all, into the broken snow and grass.

Darkness slowly settled down while Cap helped Almanzo drag back the sled and dig out and carry the heavy sacks of wheat. The snow was palely luminous. The wind had died, not a breath of air moved in the darkening stillness. Stars shone in the sky overhead and to the south and the east, but low in the north and the west the sky was black. And the blackness rose, blotting out the stars above it one by one.

'We're in for it, I guess,' Cap said.

'We must be nearly there,' Almanzo answered. He spoke to Prince and moved on ahead. Cap followed, he and the sled a bulky shadow moving over the dim whiteness of snow.

Before them in the sky, star after star went out as the black cloud rose.

Quietly Almanzo and Cap spoke to the tired horses, urging them on. There was still the neck of Big Slough to cross. They could not see the swells or the hollows now. They could see only a little way by the paleness of the snow and the faint starshine.

28

Four Days' Blizzard

All day, while Laura turned the coffee mill or twisted hay, she remembered that Cap Garland and the younger Wilder brother were driving across the trackless snowfields, going in search of wheat to bring to town.

That afternoon she and Mary went out in the backyard for a breath of air and Laura looked fearfully to the north-west dreading to see the low-lying rim of darkness that was the sure sign of a coming blizzard. There was no cloud, but still she distrusted the bright sunshine. It was too bright and the snow-covered prairie, glittering as far as eye could see, seemed menacing. She shivered.

'Let's go in, Laura,' Mary said. 'The sunshine is too cold. Do you see the cloud?'

'There is no cloud,' Laura assured her. 'But I don't like the weather. The air feels savage, somehow.'

'The air is only air,' Mary replied. 'You mean it is cold.'

'I don't either mean it's cold. I mean it's savage!' Laura snapped.

They went back into the kitchen through the lean-to entryway.

Ma looked up from Pa's sock that she was darning. 'You didn't stay out long, girls,' she said. 'You should get what fresh air you can, before the next storm.'

Pa came into the entry. Ma put away her work and took from the oven the loaf of sourdough brown bread, while Laura poured the thin codfish gravy into a bowl.

'Gravy again. Good!' Pa said, sitting down to eat. The cold and the hard work of hauling hay had made him hungry. His eyes glittered at sight of the food. Nobody, he said, could beat Ma at making good bread, and nothing was better on bread than codfish gravy. He made the coarse bread and the gruel of groundwheat flour with a bit of salt fish in it seem almost a treat.

'The boys have a fine day for their trip,' he said. 'I saw where one of the horses went down in Big Slough, but they got him out with no trouble.'

'Do you think they will get back all right, Pa?' Carrie asked timidly, and Pa said, 'No reason why not, if this clear weather holds.'

He went out to do the chores. The sun had set and the light was growing dim when he came back. He came through the front room so they knew that he had gone across the street to get the news. They knew when they saw him that it was not good news.

'We're in for it again,' he said, as he hung his coat

and cap on the nail behind the door. 'There's a cloud coming fast.'

'They didn't get back?' Ma asked him.

'No,' Pa said.

Ma silently rocked and they all sat silent while the dusk deepened. Grace was asleep in Mary's lap. The others drew their chairs closer to the stove, but they were still silent, just waiting, when the jar of the house came and the roar and howl of the wind.

Pa rose with a deep breath. 'Well, here it is again.'

Then suddenly he shook his clenched fist at the north-west. 'Howl! blast you! howl!' he shouted. 'We're all here safe! You can't get at us! You've tried all winter but we'll beat you yet! We'll be right here when spring comes!'

'Charles, Charles,' Ma said soothingly. 'It is only a blizzard. We're used to them.'

Pa dropped back in his chair. After a minute he said, 'That was foolish, Caroline. Seemed for a minute like that wind was something alive, trying to get at us.'

'It does seem so, sometimes,' Ma went on soothing him.

'I wouldn't mind so much if I could only play the fiddle,' Pa muttered, looking down at his cracked and stiffened hands that could be seen in the glow of fire from the cracks of the stove.

In all the hard times before, Pa had made music for them all. Now no one could make music for him. Laura tried to cheer herself by remembering what Pa had said;

they were all there, safe. But she wanted to do something for Pa. Then suddenly she remembered. 'We're all here!' It was the chorus of the 'Song of the Freed Men'.

'We can sing!' she exclaimed, and she began to hum the tune.

Pa looked up quickly. 'You've got it, Laura, but you are a little high. Try it in B flat,' he said.

Laura started the tune again. First Pa, then the others, joined in, and they sang:

'When Paul and Silas were bound in jail,
Do thy-self-a no harm,
One did sing and the other did pray,
Do thy-self-a no harm.

We're all here, we're all here,
Do thy-self-a no harm,
We're all here, we're all here,
Do thy-self-a no harm.

If religion was a thing that money could buy,
Do thy-self-a no harm,
The rich would live and the poor would die,
Do thy-self-a no harm.'

Laura was standing up now and so was Carrie, and Grace was awake and singing with all her might:

'We're all here, we're all here!
Do thy-self-a no harm.
We're all here, we're all here!
Do thy-self-a no harm!'

'That was fine!' Pa said. Then he sounded a low note and began:

'De old Jim riber, I float down,
I ran my boat upon de groun'
De drif' log come with a rushin' din,
An' stove both ends of my ol' boat in.'

'Now, all together on the chorus!' And they all sang:

'It will neber do to gib it up so,
It will neber do to gib it up so,
It will neber do to gib it up so, Mr Brown!
It will neber do to gib it up so!'

When they stopped singing, the storm seemed louder than ever. It was truly like a great beast worrying the house, shaking it, growling and snarling and whining and roaring at the trembling walls that stood against it.

After a moment Pa sang again, and the stately measures were suited to the thankfulness they were all feeling:

'Great is the Lord
And greatly to be prais-ed
In the city of our God,
In the mountain of His holiness.'

Then Ma began:

'When I can read my title clear
To mansions in the skies,
I'll bid farewell to every fear
And wipe my weeping eyes.'

The storm raged outside, screaming and hammering at walls and window, but they were safely sheltered, and huddled in the warmth of the hay fire they went on singing.

281

It was past bedtime when the warmth died from the stove, and because they could not waste hay they crept from the dark, cold kitchen through the colder darkness upstairs and to the beds.

Under the quilts, Laura and Mary silently said their prayers and Mary whispered, 'Laura.'

'What?' Laura whispered.

'Did you pray for them?'

'Yes,' Laura answered. 'Do you think we ought to?'

'It isn't like asking for anything for ourselves,' Mary replied. 'I didn't say anything about the wheat. I only said please to save their lives if it's God's will.'

'I think it ought to be,' Laura said. 'They were doing their best. And Pa lived three days in that Christmas blizzard when we lived on Plum Creek.'

All the days of that blizzard nothing more was said about Cap Garland and the young Wilder brother. If they had found shelter they might live through the storm. If not, nothing could be done for them. It would do no good to talk.

The constant beating of the winds against the house, the roaring, shrieking, howling of the storm, made it hard even to think. It was possible only to wait for the storm to stop. All the time, while they ground wheat, twisted hay, kept the fire burning in the stove, and huddled over it to thaw their chapped, numb hands and their itching, burning, chilblained feet, and while they chewed and swallowed the coarse bread, they were all waiting until the storm stopped.

It did not stop during the third day or the third night. In the fourth morning it was still blowing fiercely.

'No sign of a letup,' Pa said when he came in from the stable. 'This is the worst yet.'

After a while, when they were all eating their morning bread, Ma roused herself and answered, 'I hope everyone is all right in town.'

There was no way to find out. Laura thought of the other houses, only across the street, that they could not even see. For some reason she remembered Mrs Boast. They had not seen her since last summer, nor Mr Boast since the long-ago time when he brought the last butter.

'But we might as well be out on a claim too,' she said. Ma looked at her, wondering what she meant, but did not ask. All of them were only waiting for the blizzard noises to stop.

That morning Ma carefully poured the last kernels of wheat into the coffee mill.

There was enough to make one last small loaf of bread. Ma scraped the bowl with the spoon and then with her finger to get every bit of dough into the baking pan.

'This is the last, Charles,' she said.

'I can get more,' Pa told her. 'Almanzo Wilder was saving some seed wheat. I can get to it through the blizzard if I have to.'

Late that day, when the bread was on the table, the walls stopped shaking. The howling shrillness went away and only a rushing wind whistled under the eaves. Pa got up quickly, saying, 'I believe it's stopping!'

He put on his coat and cap and muffler and told Ma that he was going across the street to Fuller's store. Looking through peepholes that they scratched in the frost, Laura and Carrie saw snow blowing by on the straight wind.

Ma relaxed in her chair and sighed, 'What a merciful quiet.'

The snow was settling. After a while Carrie saw the sky and called Laura to see it. They looked at the cold, thin blue overhead and at the warm light of sunset on the low-blowing snow. The blizzard really was ended. And the north-west sky was empty.

'I hope Cap Garland and young Mr Wilder are somewhere safe,' Carrie said. So did Laura, but she knew that saying so would not make any difference.

29
The Last Mile

Almanzo thought that perhaps they had crossed the neck of Big Slough. He could not be sure where they were. He could see Prince and the slowly moving bulk of the loaded sled. Beyond them the darkness was like a mist thickening over a flat, white world. Stars twinkled far away around part of its rim. Before him, the black storm climbed rapidly up the sky and in silence destroyed the stars.

He shouted to Cap, 'Think we've crossed Big Slough?'

He had forgotten that they need not shout since the wind had stopped. Cap said, 'Don't know. You think so?'

'We haven't broken down,' Almanzo said.

'She's coming fast,' Cap said. He meant the rising black storm.

There was nothing to say to that. Almanzo spoke encouragingly to Prince again and trudged on. He stamped his feet as he walked but he could hardly feel the shock; his legs were like wood from the knees down. Every muscle in his body was drawn tight against the cold.

He could not relax the tightness and it hurt his jaws and ached in his middle. He beat his numb hands together.

Prince was pulling harder. Though the snow underfoot looked level, it was an upward slope. They had not seen the hole where Prince had broken down in Big Slough that morning, but they must somehow have crossed the slough.

Yet everything seemed unfamiliar. The darkness mixed with faint starshine coming up from the snow made the way strange. In the blackness ahead there was no star to steer by.

'Guess we've crossed it!' Almanzo called back. Cap's sled came on behind him and after a while Cap answered, 'Looks that way.'

But Prince still pulled hesitatingly, trembling not only from cold and tiredness but from fear that his footing would give way.

'Yep! We're across!' Almanzo sang out. He was sure of it now. 'We're on the upland, all right!'

'Where's town?' Cap called.

'We must be pretty near there,' Almanzo answered.

'It'll take fast driving,' Cap said.

Almanzo knew that. He slapped Prince's flank. 'Get up, Prince! Get up!' But Prince quickened only one step, then plodded again. The horse was tired out and he did not want to go towards the storm. It was rising fast now; almost half the sky was blotted out and the dark air was stirring.

'Get on and drive or we won't make it!' Cap said. Almanzo hated to do it, but he stepped on to the sled and taking the stiff lines from his shoulders he beat Prince with the knotted ends.

'Get up there, Prince! Get up!' Prince was startled and frightened; Almanzo had never beaten him before. He lunged against the neckyoke and jerked the sled forward, then on a downward slope he trotted. Cap was beating the buckskin, too. But they were not sure where the town was.

Almanzo headed for it as well as he could. It was somewhere in the thick darkness ahead.

'See anything?' Almanzo called.

'Nope. We're in for it, I guess,' Cap answered.

'Town can't be far ahead,' Almanzo told him.

The corner of his eye caught a gleam of light. He looked towards it and saw nothing in the storm-dark. Then he saw it again – a glow that shone bright, then abruptly went out. He knew what it was; light was shining out from a door opened and shut. Near where it had been, he thought he saw now the faint glow of a frost-covered window, and he yelled to Cap.

'See that light? Come on!'

They had been going a little too far to the west. Now, headed straight north, Almanzo felt that he knew the way. Prince, too, went more eagerly and the buckskin came trotting behind. Once more Almanzo saw the glow flash

287

out across the street, and now the dim blur of the window was steady. It was the window of Loftus' store.

As they pulled up in front of it, the winds struck them with a whirl of snow.

'Unhitch and run for it!' Almanzo told Cap. 'I'll take care of the wheat.'

Cap unfastened the tugs and swung on to the buckskin.

'Think you can make it?' Almanzo asked him through the storm.

'Can I? I got to,' Cap shouted as he started the buckskin on a run across the vacant lots towards his stable.

Almanzo clumped into the warm store. Mr Loftus got up from his chair by the stove. No one else was there. Mr Loftus said, 'So you boys made it. We figured you hadn't.'

'Cap and I figure we'll do what we set out to do,' Almanzo said.

'Find that fellow that raised wheat?' Mr Loftus asked.

'And bought sixty bushels. Want to help bring it in?' Almanzo answered.

They lugged in the sacks of wheat and stacked them by the wall. The storm was blowing fiercely. When the last sack was on the pile, Almanzo gave Mr Loftus the receipt that Mr Anderson had signed and handed over the balance in change.

'You gave me eighty dollars to buy wheat with, and here's what's left, just five dollars even.'

'A dollar and twenty-five cents a bushel. That's the best

you could do?' Mr Loftus said, looking at the receipt.

'Any time you say, I'll take it off your hands at that price,' Almanzo retorted.

'I don't go back on a bargain,' the storekeeper hastily replied. 'How much do I owe you for hauling?'

'Not a red cent,' Almanzo told him, leaving.

'Hey, aren't you going to stay and thaw out?' Mr Loftus called after him.

'And let my horse stand in this storm?' Almanzo slammed the door.

He took Prince by the bridle bits and led him up the straight street, along the row of hitching posts and the porch edges in front of the stores. By the long side wall of the feed store they plodded to the stable. Almanzo unhitched and led Prince into the stable's quiet where Lady whinnied a welcome. He barred the door against the storm, then pulled off a mitten and warmed his right hand in his armpit until the fingers were supple enough to light the lantern.

He put Prince in his stall, watered him, and fed him, then curried and brushed him well. That done, he spread for the tired horse a soft, deep bed of clean hay.

'You saved the seed wheat, old boy,' he told Prince, giving him a gentle slap.

He took the water pail on his arm and struggled through the blizzard. Just outside the door of the back room he filled the pail with snow. When he stumbled in,

Royal was coming from the empty feed store in front.

'Well. Here you are,' Royal said. 'I was trying to see down the street, looking for you, but you can't see a foot into this blizzard. Listen to it howl! Lucky you got in when you did.'

'We brought sixty bushels of wheat,' Almanzo told him.

'You don't say! And I thought it was a wild-goose chase.' Royal put coal on the fire. 'How much did you pay for it?'

'A dollar and a quarter.' Almanzo had got his boots off.

'Whew!' Royal whistled. 'That the best you could do?'

'Yes,' Almanzo said shortly, peeling down layers of socks.

Then Royal noticed what he was doing and saw the pail full of snow. He exclaimed, 'What's that snow for?'

'What do you suppose?' Almanzo snorted. 'To thaw my feet.'

His feet were bloodless-white and dead to the touch. Royal helped him rub them with snow, in the coldest corner of the room, until they began to tingle with a pain that made his stomach sick. Tired as he was, he could not sleep that night with the feverish pain of his feet and he was glad because the pain meant that they were not dangerously frozen.

All the days and nights of that blizzard his feet were so swollen and painful that he had to borrow Royal's

boots when it was his turn to do the chores. But when
the blizzard stopped, in the late afternoon of the fourth
day, he was able to get into his own boots and go down
the street.

It was good to be out in the fresh, clean cold, to see
sunshine and hear only the straight wind after hearing the
storm so long. But the strength of that wind would wear
a man out, and before he had gone a block he was so
chilled that he was glad enough to blow into Fuller's
Hardware store.

The place was crowded. Nearly every man in town

was there and they were talking angrily in growing excitement.

'Hello, what's up?' Almanzo asked.

Mr Harthorn turned round to him. 'Say, you charge Loftus anything for hauling that wheat? Cap Garland, here, says he didn't.'

Cap's grin lighted up his face. 'Hello, Wilder! You soak it to that skinflint, why don't you? I was fool enough to tell him we made that trip for the fun of it. I wish now I'd charged him all he's got.'

'What's all this about?' Almanzo demanded. 'No, I'm not charging a red cent. Who says we took that trip for pay?'

Gerald Fuller told him, 'Loftus is charging three dollars a bushel for that wheat.'

They all began to talk again, but Mr Ingalls rose up thin and tall from the box by the stove. His face had shrunken to hollows and jutting cheekbones above his brown beard, and his blue eyes glittered bright.

'We aren't getting anywhere with all this talk,' he said. 'I say, let's all go reason with Loftus.'

'Now you're talking!' another man sang out. 'Come on, boys! We'll help ourselves to that wheat!'

'Reason with him, I said,' Mr Ingalls objected to that. 'I'm talking about reason and justice.'

'Maybe *you* are,' someone shouted. 'I'm talking about something to eat, and by the Almighty! I'm not going back to my youngsters without it! Are the rest of you fellows?'

'No! No!' several agreed with him. Then Cap spoke up.

'Wilder and I have something to say about this. We brought in the wheat. We didn't haul it in to make trouble.'

'That's so,' Gerald Fuller said. 'See here, boys, we don't want any trouble in town.'

'I don't see any sense in flying off the handle,' said Almanzo. He was going on, but one of the men interrupted him.

'Yes, and you've got plenty to eat! Both you and Fuller. I'm not going home without –'

'How much you got to eat at your house, Mr Ingalls?' Cap interrupted him.

'Not a thing,' Mr Ingalls answered. 'We ground up the last wheat we had, yesterday. Ate it this morning.'

'There you are!' said Almanzo. 'Let Mr Ingalls engineer this.'

'All right, I'll take the lead,' Mr Ingalls agreed. 'The rest of you boys come along and we'll see what Loftus has to say.'

They all tramped along after him single file over the snowdrifts. They crowded into the store where Loftus, when they began coming in, went behind his counter. There was no wheat in sight. Loftus had moved the sacks into his back room.

Mr Ingalls told him that they thought he was charging too much for the wheat.

'That's my business,' said Loftus. 'It's my wheat, isn't it? I paid good hard money for it.'

'A dollar and a quarter a bushel, we understand,' Mr Ingalls said.

'That's my business,' Mr Loftus repeated.

'We'll show you whose business it is!' the angry man shouted.

'You fellows so much as touch my property and I'll have the law on you!' Mr Loftus answered. Some of them laughed snarlingly. But Loftus was not going to back down. He banged his fist on the counter and told them, 'That wheat's mine and I've got a right to charge any price I want to for it.'

'That's so, Loftus, you have,' Mr Ingalls agreed with him. 'This is a free country and every man's got a right to do as he pleases with his own property.' He said to the crowd, 'You know that's a fact, boys,' and he went on, 'Don't forget every one of us is free and independent, Loftus. This winter won't last forever and maybe you want to go on doing business after it's over.'

'Threatening me, are you?' Mr Loftus demanded.

'We don't need to,' Mr Ingalls replied. 'It's a plain fact. If you've got a right to do as you please, we've got a right to do as we please. It works both ways. You've got us down now. That's your business, as you say. But your business depends on our good will. You maybe don't notice that now, but along next summer you'll likely notice it.'

'That's so, Loftus,' Gerald Fuller said. 'You got to treat folks right or you don't last long in business, not in this country.'

The angry man said, 'We're not here to palaver. Where's that wheat?'

'Don't be a fool, Loftus,' Mr Harthorn said.

'The money wasn't out of your till more than a day,' Mr Ingalls said. 'And the boys didn't charge you a cent for hauling it. Charge a fair profit and you'll have the cash back inside of an hour.'

'What do you call a fair profit?' Mr Loftus asked. 'I buy as low as I can and sell as high as I can; that's good business.'

'That's not my idea,' said Gerald Fuller. 'I say it's good business to treat people right.'

'We wouldn't object to your price, if Wilder and Garland here had charged you what it was worth to go after that wheat,' Mr Ingalls told Loftus.

'Well, why didn't you?' Mr Loftus asked them. 'I stood ready to pay any reasonable charge for hauling.'

Cap Garland spoke up. He was not grinning. He had the look that had made the railroader back down. 'Don't offer us any of your filthy cash. Wilder and I didn't make that trip to skin a profit off folks that are hungry.'

Almanzo was angry, too. 'Get it through your head if

you can, there's not money enough in the mint to pay for that trip. We didn't make it for you and you can't pay us for it.'

Mr Loftus looked from Cap to Almanzo and then around at the other faces. They all despised him. He opened his mouth and shut it. He looked beaten. Then he said, 'I'll tell you what I'll do, boys. You can buy the wheat for just what it cost me, a dollar twenty-five cents a bushel.'

'We don't object to your making a fair profit, Loftus,' Mr Ingalls said, but Loftus shook his head.

'No, I'll let it go for what it cost me.'

This was so unexpected that for a moment no one knew exactly how to take it. Then Mr Ingalls suggested, 'What do you say we all get together and kind of ration it out, on a basis of how much our families need to last through till spring?'

They did this. It seemed that there was wheat enough to keep every family going for eight to ten weeks. Some had a few potatoes left and some even had crackers. One man had molasses. They bought less wheat. Almanzo bought none. Cap Garland bought half a bushel and Mr Ingalls paid for a two-bushel sack.

Almanzo noticed that he did not swing it on to his shoulder as a man naturally would. 'That's quite a load to handle,' Almanzo said, and helped him lift and balance it. He would have carried it across the street for him, but a man does not like to admit that he cannot carry a hundred and twenty-five pounds.

'Bet you a cigar I can beat you at a game of checkers,' Almanzo then said to Cap, and they went up the street to the drugstore. Mr Ingalls was going into his store building as they passed by in the blowing snow.

Laura heard the front door open and shut. They all sat still in the dark and, as if in a dream, they heard Pa's steps coming heavily the length of the front room, and the kitchen door opening. Pa let a heavy weight come down on the floor with a thud that painfully shook it. Then he shut the door against the solid cold coming in with him.

'The boys got back!' he said, breathing hard. 'Here's some of the wheat they brought, Caroline!'

30
It Can't Beat Us

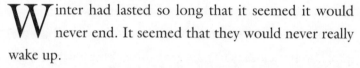

Winter had lasted so long that it seemed it would never end. It seemed that they would never really wake up.

In the morning Laura got out of bed into the cold. She dressed downstairs by the fire that Pa had kindled before he went to the stable. They ate their coarse brown bread. Then all day long she and Ma and Mary ground wheat and twisted hay as fast as they could. The fire must not go out; it was very cold. They ate some coarse brown bread. Then Laura crawled into the cold bed and shivered until she grew warm enough to sleep.

Next morning she got out of bed into the cold. She dressed in the chilly kitchen by the fire. She ate her coarse brown bread. She took her turns at grinding wheat and twisting hay. But she did not ever feel awake. She felt beaten by the cold and the storms. She knew she was dull and stupid but she could not wake up.

There were no more lessons. There was nothing in the world but cold and dark and work and coarse brown bread and winds blowing. The storm was always there, outside the walls, waiting sometimes, then pouncing, shaking the house, roaring, snarling, and screaming in rage.

Out of bed in the morning to hurry down and dress by the fire. Then work all day to crawl into a cold bed at night and fall asleep as soon as she grew warm. The winter had lasted so long. It would never end.

Pa did not sing his trouble song in the mornings any more.

On clear days he hauled hay. Sometimes a blizzard lasted only two days. There might be three days of clear cold, or even four days, before the blizzard struck again. 'We're outwearing it,' Pa said. 'It hasn't got much more time. March is nearly gone. We can last longer than it can.'

'The wheat is holding out,' Ma said. 'I'm thankful for that.'

The end of March came. April began. Still the storm was there, waiting a little longer now perhaps but striking even more furiously. There was the bitter cold still, and the dark storm days, the wheat to be ground, the hay to be twisted. Laura seemed to have forgotten summer; she could not believe it would ever come again. April was going by.

'Is the hay holding out, Charles?' Ma asked.

'Yes, thanks to Laura,' Pa said. 'If you hadn't helped

me in the haying, little Half-Pint, I'd not have put up enough hay. We would have run short before this.'

Those hot days of haying were very far away and long ago. Laura's gladness because Pa said that seemed far away too. Only the blizzard and the coffee mill's grinding, the cold and the dusk darkening to night again, were real. Laura and Pa were holding their stiff, swollen red hands over the stove, Ma was cutting the coarse brown bread for supper. The blizzard was loud and furious.

'It can't beat us!' Pa said.

'Can't it, Pa?' Laura asked stupidly.

'No,' said Pa. 'It's got to quit sometime and we don't. It can't lick us. We won't give up.'

Then Laura felt a warmth inside her. It was very small but it was strong. It was steady, like a tiny light in the dark, and it burned very low but no winds could make it flicker because it would not give up.

They ate the coarse brown bread and went through the dark and cold upstairs to bed. Shivering in the cold bed Laura and Mary silently said their prayers and slowly grew warm enough to sleep.

Sometime in the night Laura heard the wind. It was still blowing furiously but there were no voices, no howls or shrieks in it. And with it there was another sound, a tiny, uncertain, liquid sound that she could not understand.

She listened as hard as she could. She uncovered her ear to listen and the cold did not bite her cheek. The dark was warmer. She put out her hand and felt only a coolness. The little sound that she heard was a trickling of waterdrops. The eaves were dripping. Then she knew.

She sprang up in bed and called aloud, 'Pa! Pa! The Chinook is blowing!'

'I hear it, Laura,' Pa answered from the other room. 'Spring has come. Go back to sleep.'

The Chinook was blowing. Spring had come. The blizzard had given up; it was driven back to the north. Blissfully Laura stretched out in bed; she put both arms on top of the quilts and they were not very cold. She listened to the blowing wind and dripping eaves and she knew that in the other room Pa was lying awake, too, listening and glad. The Chinook, the wind of spring, was blowing. Winter was ended.

In the morning the snow was nearly gone. The frost was melted from the windows, and outdoors the air was soft and warm.

Pa was whistling as he came from doing the chores.

'Well, girls,' he said gaily. 'We beat old Winter at last! Here it is spring, and none of us lost or starved or frozen! Anyway, not *much* frozen,' and he felt his nose tenderly. 'I do believe it is longer,' he said anxiously to Grace, and his eyes twinkled. He looked in the glass. 'It is longer, and red, too.'

'Stop worrying about your looks, Charles,' Ma told him. ' "Beauty is only skin deep." Come eat your breakfast.'

She was smiling and Pa chucked her under the chin as he went to the table. Grace scampered to her chair and climbed into it laughing.

Mary pushed her chair back from the stove. 'It is really too warm, so close to the fire,' she said.

How marvellous that anyone could be too warm.

Carrie would hardly leave the window. 'I like to see the water run,' she explained.

Laura said nothing; she was too happy. She could hardly believe that the winter was gone, that spring had come. When Pa asked her why she was so silent, she answered soberly, 'I said it all in the night.'

'I should say you did! Waking us all from a sound sleep to tell us the wind was blowing!' Pa teased her. 'As if the wind hadn't blown for months!'

'I said the Chinook,' Laura reminded him. 'That makes all the difference.'

31
Waiting for the Train

'We've got to wait for the train,' Pa said. 'We can't move to the claim till it comes.'

Tightly as he had nailed and battened the tar-paper to the shanty, blizzard winds had torn it loose and whipped it to shreds, letting in the snow at sides and roof. And now the spring rains were beating in through the cracks. The shanty must be repaired before anyone could live in it and Pa could not repair it until the train came, for there was no tar-paper at the lumberyard.

The snow had all disappeared from the prairie. In its place was the soft green of new grass. All the sloughs brimmed with water that had run into them when the deep snow melted. Big Slough had spread until it was a part of Silver Lake and Pa must drive miles around it to reach the homestead from the south.

One day Mr Boast came walking into town. He explained that he could not drive in, because much of the road was under water. He had walked the railroad track on the long fill that crossed the slough.

Mrs Boast was well, he told them. She had not come with him because of the slough-lakes spreading everywhere. He had not known whether he could reach town by the railroad track. He promised that Mrs Boast would walk in with him some day soon.

One afternoon Mary Power came, and she and Laura took Mary walking on the high prairie west of town. It was so long since Laura had seen Mary Power that they felt like strangers again, beginning to get acquainted.

All over the softly green prairie the sloughs were a broken network of water, reflecting the warm, blue sky. Wild geese and ducks were flying high overhead, their clamouring calls coming faintly down. None of them stopped at Silver Lake. They were hurrying, late, to their nesting grounds in the North.

Soft spring rains fell all day long from harmless grey skies and swelled still wider the brimming sloughs. Days of sunshine came and then again rain. The feed store was locked and vacant. The Wilder brothers had hauled the seed wheat around the slough north of town to their claims. Pa said that they were sowing the wheat on their big fields.

And still the train did not come. Still, day after day, Laura and Mary and Carrie took turns at the endless grind of the coffee mill, and morning and evening they ate the coarse brown bread. The wheat was low in the sack. And the train did not come.

The blizzard winds had blown earth from the fields where the sod was broken, and had mixed it with snow packed so tightly in the railroad cuts that snowploughs could not move it. The icy snow could not melt because of the earth mixed with it, and men with picks were digging it out inch by inch. It was slow work because in many big cuts they must dig down twenty feet to the steel rails.

April went slowly by. There was no food in the town except the little wheat left from the sixty bushels that young Mr Wilder and Cap had brought in the last week of February. Every day Ma made a smaller loaf and still the train did not come.

'Could something be hauled in, Charles?' Ma asked.

'We've talked that over, Caroline. None of us see how,' Pa answered. He was tired from working all day with a pick. The men from town were digging away at the cut to the west, for the stranded work train must go on to Huron before a freight train could come on the single track.

'There's no way to get a team and wagon out to the east,' Pa said. 'All the roads are under water, the sloughs are lakes in every direction, and even on the uplands a wagon would mire down in the mud. If worst comes to worst, a man can walk out on the railroad ties, but it's more than a hundred miles to Brookings and back. He couldn't carry much and he'd have to eat some of that while he was getting here.'

'I've thought of greens,' Ma said. 'But I can't find any weeds in the yard that are big enough to pick yet.'

'Could we eat grass?' Carrie asked.

'No, Nebuchadnezzar,' Pa laughed. 'You don't have to eat grass! The work crews at Tracy are more than half-way through the big cut already. They ought to get the train here inside of a week.'

'We can make the wheat last that long,' said Ma. 'But I wish you wouldn't work so hard, Charles.'

Pa's hands were shaking. He was very tired from working all day with pick and shovel. But he said that a good night's sleep was all he needed. 'The main thing is to get the cut clear,' he said.

On the last day of April the work train went through to Huron. It seemed to wake the whole town up to hear the train whistle again and see the smoke on the sky. Puffing and steaming and clanging its bell, it stopped at the depot, then pulled out, whistling loud and clear again. It was only a passing train that brought nothing, but a freight train was coming tomorrow.

In the morning Laura woke thinking, 'The train is coming!' The sun was shining brightly; she had overslept, and Ma had not called her. She jumped out of bed and hurried to dress.

'Wait for me, Laura!' Mary begged. 'Don't be in such a hurry, I can't find my stockings.'

Laura looked for them. 'Here they are. I'm sorry, I pushed them out of the way when I jumped out of bed. Now hurry! Come on, Grace!'

'When will it get here?' Carrie asked breathless.

'Any minute. Nobody knows when,' Laura answered, and she ran downstairs singing:

> 'If you're waking call me early,
> Call me early, mother dear.'

Pa was at the table. He looked up and laughed at her. 'Well, Flutterbudget! you're to be Queen of the May, are you? And late to breakfast!'

'Ma didn't call me,' Laura made excuse.

'I didn't need help to cook this little bit of breakfast,' Ma said. 'Only one biscuit apiece, and small ones at that. It took the last bit of the wheat to make them.'

'I don't want even one,' Laura said. 'The rest of you can divide mine. I won't be hungry till the train comes in.'

'You will eat your share,' Pa told her. 'Then we'll all wait till the train brings more.'

They were all merry over the biscuits. Ma said that Pa must have the biggest one. When Pa agreed to that, he insisted that Ma take the next size. Mary's of course came next. Then there was some doubt about Laura and

Carrie; they had to have the two most nearly alike. And the smallest one was for Grace.

'I thought I made them all the same size,' Ma protested.

'Trust a Scotchwoman to manage,' Pa teased her. 'You not only make the wheat come out even with the very last meal before the train comes, but you make the biscuits in sizes to fit the six of us.'

'It is a wonder, how evenly it comes out,' Ma admitted.

'You are the wonder, Caroline,' Pa smiled at her. He got up and put on his hat. 'I feel good!' he declared. 'We really got winter licked now! with the last of the blizzards thrown out of the cuts and the train coming in!'

Ma left the doors open that morning to let in the spring air, moist from the sloughs. The house was fresh and fragrant, the sun was shining, and the town astir with men going towards the depot. Clear and long across the prairie, the train whistle sounded and Laura and Carrie ran to the kitchen window. Ma and Grace came, too.

They saw the smoke from the smokestack rolling up black against the sky. Then puffing and chuffing the engine came hauling the line of freight cars towards the depot. A little crowd of men on the depot platform stood watching the engine go by. White steam puffed up through its smoke and its clear whistle came after every puff. Brakemen along the top of the train were jumping from car to car and setting the brakes.

The train stopped. It was really there, a train at last.

'Oh, I do hope that Harthorn and Wilmarth both get all the groceries they ordered last fall,' said Ma.

After a few moments the engine whistled, the brakemen ran along the tops of the cars loosening the brakes. Clanging its bell, the engine went ahead, then backed, then went ahead again and rushed on away to the west, trailing its smoke and its last long whistle. It left behind it three freight cars standing on the sidetrack.

Ma drew a deep breath. 'It will be so good to have enough of everything to cook with again.'

'I hope I never seen another bite of brown bread,' Laura declared.

'When is Pa coming? I want Pa to come!' Grace insisted. 'I want Pa to come now!'

'Grace,' Ma reproved her, gently but firmly, and Mary took Grace into her lap while Ma added, 'Come, girls, we must finish airing the bedding.'

It was almost an hour before Pa came. At last even Ma wondered aloud what could be keeping him. They were all impatiently waiting before he came. His arms were filled with a large package and two smaller ones. He laid them on the table before he spoke.

'We forgot the train that was snowed in all winter,' he said. 'It came through, and what do you suppose it left for De Smet?' He answered his own question, 'One carload of telegraph poles, one carload of farm machinery, and one emigrant car.'

'No groceries?' Ma almost wailed.

'No. Nothing,' Pa said.

'Then what is this?' Ma touched the large package.

'That is potatoes. The small one is flour and the smallest is fat salt pork. Woodworth broke into the emigrant car and shared out what eatables he could find,' said Pa.

'Charles! He ought not to do that,' Ma said in dismay.

'I'm past caring what he ought to do!' Pa said savagely. 'Let the railroad stand some damages! This isn't the only family in town that's got nothing to eat. We told Woodworth to open up that car or we'd do it. He tried to argue that there'll be another train tomorrow, but we didn't feel like waiting. Now if you'll boil some potatoes and fry some meat, we'll have us a dinner.'

Ma began to untie the packages. 'Put some hay in the stove, Carrie, to make the oven hot. I'll mix up some white-flour biscuits, too,' she said.

32

The Christmas Barrel

Next day the second train came. After its departing whistle had died away, Pa and Mr Boast came down the street carrying a barrel between them. They upended it through the doorway and stood it in the middle of the front room.

'Here's that Christmas barrel!' Pa called to Ma.

He brought his hammer and began pulling nails out of the barrel-head, while they all stood around it waiting to see what was in it. Pa took off the barrel-head. Then he lifted away some thick brown paper that covered everything beneath.

Clothes were on top. First Pa drew out a dress of beautifully fine, dark-blue flannel. The skirt was full pleated and the neat, whaleboned basque was buttoned down the front with cut-steel buttons.

'This is about your size, Caroline,' Pa beamed. 'Here, take it!' and he reached again into the barrel.

He took out a fluffy, light-blue fascinator for Mary, and

some warm flannel underthings. He took out a pair of black leather shoes that exactly fitted Laura. He took out five pairs of white woollen stockings, machine-knit. They were much finer and thinner than home-knit ones.

Then he took out a warm, brown coat, a little large for Carrie, but it would fit her next winter. And he took out a red hood and mittens to go with it.

Next came a silk shawl!

'Oh, Mary!' Laura said. 'The most beautiful thing – a shawl made of silk! It is dove-coloured, with fine stripes of green and rose and black and the richest, deep fringe with all those colours shimmering in it. Feel how soft and rich and heavy the silk is,' and she put a corner of the shawl in Mary's hand.

'Oh, lovely!' Mary breathed.

'Who gets this shawl?' Pa asked, and they all said, 'Ma!' Such a beautiful shawl was for Ma, of course. Pa laid it on her arm, and it was like her, so soft and yet firm and well-wearing, with the fine, bright colours in it.

'We will all take turns wearing it,' Ma said. 'And Mary shall take it with her when she goes to college.'

'What is there for you, Pa?' Laura asked jealously. For Pa there were two fine, white shirts, and a dark brown plush cap.

'That isn't all,' said Pa, and he lifted out of the barrel one, two little dresses. One was blue flannel, one was green-and-rose plaid. They were too small for Carrie and too big for Grace, but Grace would grow to fit them. Then there was an A-B-C book printed on cloth, and a small, shiny Mother Goose book of the smoothest paper, with a coloured picture on the cover.

There was a pasteboard box full of bright-coloured yarns and another box filled with embroidery silks and sheets of perforated thin cardboard, silver-coloured and gold-coloured. Ma gave both boxes to Laura, saying, 'You gave away the pretty things you had made. Now here are some lovely things for you to work with.'

Laura was so happy that she couldn't say a word. The delicate silks caught on the roughness of her fingers, scarred from twisting hay, but the beautiful colours sang together like music, and her fingers would grow smooth again so that she could embroider on the fine, thin silver and gold.

'Now I wonder what this can be?' Pa said, as he lifted from the very bottom of the barrel something bulky and lumpy that was wrapped around and around with thick brown paper.

'Je-ru-salem crickets!' he exclaimed. 'If it isn't our Christmas turkey, still frozen solid!'

He held the great turkey up where all could see. 'And fat! Fifteen pounds or I miss my guess.' And as he let the mass of brown paper fall, it thumped on the floor and out of it rolled several cranberries.

'And if here isn't a package of cranberries to go with it!' said Pa.

Carrie shrieked with delight. Mary clasped her hands and said, 'Oh my!' But Ma asked, 'Did the groceries come for the stores, Charles?'

'Yes, sugar and flour and dried fruit and meat – Oh, everything anybody needs,' Pa answered.

'Well, then, Mr Boast, you bring Mrs Boast day after tomorrow,' Ma said. 'Come as early as you can and we will celebrate the springtime with a Christmas dinner.'

'That's the ticket!' Pa shouted, while Mr Boast threw back his head and the room filled with his ringing laugh. They all joined in, for no one could help laughing when Mr Boast did.

'We'll come! You bet we'll come!' Mr Boast chortled. 'Christmas dinner in May! That will be great, to feast after a winter of darn near fasting! I'll hurry home and tell Ellie.'

33
Christmas in May

Pa bought groceries that afternoon. It was wonderful to see him coming in with armfuls of packages, wonderful to see a whole sack of white flour, sugar, dried apples, soda crackers, and cheese. The kerosene can was full. How happy Laura was to fill the lamp, polish the chimney, and trim the wick. At suppertime the light shone through the clear glass on to the red-checked tablecloth and the white biscuits, the warmed-up potatoes, and the platter of fried salt pork.

With yeast cakes, Ma set the sponge for light bread that night, and she put the dried apples to soak for pies.

Laura did not need to be called next morning. She was up at dawn, and all day she helped Ma bake and stew and boil the good things for next day's Christmas dinner.

Early that morning Ma added water and flour to the bread sponge and set it to rise again. Laura and Carrie picked over the cranberries and washed them. Ma stewed them with sugar until they were a mass of crimson jelly.

Laura and Carrie carefully picked dried raisins from their long stems and carefully took the seeds out of each one. Ma stewed the dried apples, mixed the raisins with them, and made pies.

'It seems strange to have everything one could want to work with,' said Ma. 'Now I have cream of tartar and plenty of saleratus, I shall make a cake.'

All day long the kitchen smelled of good things, and when night came the cupboard held large brown-crusted loaves of white bread, a sugar-frosted loaf of cake, three crisp-crusted pies, and the jellied cranberries.

'I wish we could eat them now,' Mary said. 'Seems like I can't wait till tomorrow.'

'I'm waiting for the turkey first,' said Laura, 'and you may have sage in the stuffing, Mary.'

She sounded generous but Mary laughed at her. 'That's only because there aren't any onions for you to use!'

'Now, girls, don't get impatient,' Ma begged them. 'We will have a loaf of light bread and some of the cranberry sauce for supper.'

So the Christmas feasting was begun the night before.

It seemed too bad to lose any of that happy time in sleep. Still, sleeping was the quickest way to tomorrow morning. It was no time at all, after Laura's eyes closed, till Ma was calling her and tomorrow was today.

What a hurrying there was! Breakfast was soon over,

then while Laura and Carrie cleared the table and washed the dishes, Ma prepared the big turkey for roasting and mixed the bread-stuffing for it.

The May morning was warm and the wind from the prairie smelled of springtime. Doors were open and both rooms could be used once more. Going in and out of the large front room whenever she wanted to gave Laura a spacious and rested feeling, as if she could never be cross again.

Ma had already put the rocking chairs by the front windows to get them out of her way in the kitchen. Now the turkey was in the oven, and Mary helped Laura draw the table into the middle of the front room. Mary raised its drop-leaves and spread smoothly over it the white tablecloth that Laura brought her. Then Laura brought the dishes from the cupboard and Mary placed them around the table.

Carrie was peeling potatoes and Grace was running races with herself the length of both rooms.

Ma brought the glass bowl filled with glowing cranberry jelly. She set it in the middle of the white tablecloth and they all admired the effect.

'We do need some butter to go with the light bread, though,' Ma said.

'Never mind, Caroline,' said Pa. 'There's tar-paper at the lumberyard now. I'll soon fix up the shanty and we'll move out to the homestead in a few days.'

The roasting turkey was filling the house with scents that made their mouths water. The potatoes were boiling and Ma was putting the coffee on when Mr and Mrs Boast came walking in.

'For the last mile, I've been following my nose to that turkey!' Mr Boast declared.

'I was thinking more of seeing the folks, Robert, than of anything to eat,' Mrs Boast chided him. She was thin and the lovely rosy colour was gone from her cheeks, but she was the same darling Mrs Boast, with the same laughing black-fringed blue eyes and the same dark hair curling under the same brown hood. She shook hands warmly with Ma and Mary and Laura and stooped down to draw Carrie and Grace close in her arms while she spoke to them.

'Come into the front room and take off your things, Mrs Boast,' Ma urged her. 'It is good to see you again after so long. Now you rest in the rocking chair and talk to Mary while I finish up dinner.'

'Let me help you,' Mrs Boast asked, but Ma said she must be tired after her long walk and everything was nearly ready.

'Laura and I will soon have dinner on the table,' said Ma, turning quickly back to the kitchen. She ran against Pa in her haste.

'We better make ourselves scarce, Boast,' said Pa. 'Come along, and I'll show you the *Pioneer Press* I got this morning.'

'It will be good to see a newspaper again,' Mr Boast agreed eagerly. So the kitchen was left to the cooks.

'Get the big platter to put the turkey on,' Ma said, as she lifted the heavy dripping-pan out of the oven.

Laura turned to the cupboard and saw on the shelf a package that had not been there before.

'What's that, Ma?' she asked.

'I don't know. Look and see,' Ma told her, and Laura undid the paper. There on a small plate was a ball of butter.

'Butter! It's butter!' she almost shouted.

They heard Mrs Boast laugh. 'Just a little Christmas present!' she called.

Pa and Mary and Carrie exclaimed aloud in delight and Grace squealed long and shrill while Laura carried the butter to the table. Then she hurried back to slide the big platter carefully beneath the turkey as Ma raised it from the dripping-pan.

While Ma made the gravy Laura mashed the potatoes. There was no milk, but Ma said, 'Leave a very little of the boiling water in, and after you mash them beat them extra hard with the big spoon.'

The potatoes turned out white and fluffy, though not with the flavour that plenty of hot milk and butter would have given them.

When all the chairs were drawn up to the well-filled table, Ma looked at Pa and every head bowed.

'Lord, we thank Thee for all Thy bounty.' That was

all Pa said, but it seemed to say everything.

'The table looks some different from what it did a few days ago,' Pa said as he heaped Mrs Boast's plate with turkey and stuffing and potatoes and a large spoonful of cranberries. And as he went on filling the plates he added, 'It has been a long winter.'

'And a hard one,' said Mr Boast.

'It is a wonder how we all kept well and came through it,' Mrs Boast said.

While Mr and Mrs Boast told how they had worked and contrived through that long winter, all alone in the blizzard-bound shanty on their claim, Ma poured the coffee and Pa's tea. She passed the bread and the butter and the gravy and reminded Pa to refill the plates.

When every plate had been emptied a second time Ma refilled the cups and Laura brought on the pies and the cake.

They sat a long time at the table, talking of the winter that was past and the summer to come. Ma said she could hardly wait to get back to the homestead. The wet, muddy roads were the difficulty now, but Pa and Mr Boast agreed that they would dry out before long. The Boasts were glad that they had wintered on their claim and didn't have to move back to it now.

At last they all left the table. Laura brought the red-bordered table cover and Carrie helped her to spread it to cover neatly out of sight the food and the empty dishes.

Then they joined the others by the sunny window.

Pa stretched his arms above his head. He opened and closed his hands and stretched his fingers wide then ran them through his hair till it all stood on end.

'I believe this warm weather has taken the stiffness out of my fingers,' he said. 'If you will bring me the fiddle, Laura, I'll see what I can do.'

Laura brought the fiddle-box and stood close by while Pa lifted the fiddle out of its nest. He thumbed the strings and tightened the keys as he listened. Then he rosined the bow and drew it across the strings.

A few clear, true notes softly sounded. The lump in Laura's throat almost choked her.

Pa played a few bars and said, 'This is a new song I learned last fall, the time we went to Volga to clear the tracks. You hum the tenor along with the fiddle, Boast, while I sing it through the first time. A few times over, and you'll all pick up the words.'

They all gathered around him to listen while he played again the opening bars. Then Mr Boast's tenor joined the fiddle's voice and Pa's voice singing:

> 'This life is a difficult riddle,
> For how many people we see
> With faces as long as a fiddle
> That ought to be shining with glee.
> I am sure in this world there are plenty

Of good things enough for us all,
And yet there's not one out of twenty
But thinks that his share is too small.

Then what is the use of repining,
For where there's a will, there's a way,
And tomorrow the sun may be shining,
Although it is cloudy today.

Do you think that by sitting and sighing
You'll ever obtain all you want?
It's cowards alone that are crying
And foolishly saying, 'I can't!'
It is only by plodding and striving
And labouring up the steep hill
Of life, that you'll ever be thriving,
Which you'll do if you've only the will.'

They were all humming the melody now and when the
chorus came again, Mrs Boast's alto, Ma's contralto, and
Mary's sweet soprano joined Mr Boast's tenor and Pa's
rich bass, singing the words, and Laura sang, too, soprano:

'Then what is the use of repining,
For where there's a will, there's a way,
And tomorrow the sun may be shining,
Although it is cloudy today.'

And as they sang, the fear and the suffering of the long winter seemed to rise like a dark cloud and float away on the music. Spring had come. The sun was shining warm, the winds were soft, and the green grass growing.

Inside the cosy little house in the
Big Woods lives the Ingalls family:
Ma, Pa, Mary, Laura and baby Carrie.
Outside the little house, in the snow
and the cold, are the wild animals.

This is the classic tale of how they live together,
mostly in harmony, but sometimes in fear . . .

The sun-kissed prairie stretches out around
the Ingalls family, smiling its welcome after
their long, hard journey across America.

But looks can be deceiving, and they soon
find that they must share the land with
wild bears and Indians.

Will there be enough land for all of them?

The Ingalls family have left the
prairie and found a new place to settle
at Plum Creek. There's a town close by
and new people to meet. For the first time,
Mary and Laura can go to school.

But how will they settle in such a busy place
after the wild lands in which they've grown up?

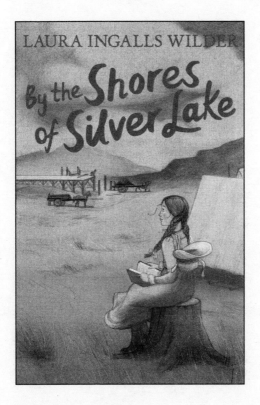

Pa Ingalls has found a new job on a railroad out
West and Laura and her family set out once
again across the prairie.

Silver Lake is bustling with people arriving to work
on the land. Pa finds the perfect place to build a home
and it seems as though the Ingalls' travelling
days might be over.

But will Pa get to the homestead before
someone else arrives to claim it?

Read all the books in

Little House on the Prairie series:

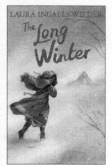